C000103763

JANET JACKSON
SUPERHOST

By the same author

Janet Jackson's Yorkshire B&B

JANET JACKSON SUPERHOST

Becky Papworth

First published in Great Britain in 2024 by Cancan Press
Copyright © Becky Papworth, 2024
Print Edition

The right of Becky Papworth to be identified as the Author of the Work has been asserted by her in accordance with the Copyright, Designs and Patents Act, 1988.

All rights reserved. No part of this publication may be reproduced, stored in a retrieval system, or transmitted, in any form or by any means without the prior written permission of the publisher, nor be otherwise circulated in any form of binding or cover other than that in which it is published and without a similar condition being imposed on the subsequent purchaser.

All characters in this publication other than those clearly in the public domain are fictitious, or used fictitiously, and any resemblance to real persons, living or dead is purely coincidental.

A CIP catalogue record for this title is available from the British Library

ISBN: 978-1-7385691-2-0

Cover design by © Design by Sim

For Margaret, a lover of books

'I'm sure I don't know half the people
who come to my house.
Indeed, from all I hear, I shouldn't like to.'

Oscar Wilde

THE 'HERE WE GO AGAIN' BIT

Do you ever get a strange feeling on New Year's Day? *I don't mean the hangover.* I mean the 'anything can happen' feeling. The 'here we go again for another crazy spin round the sun' feeling. I think it's something to do with getting a teeny bit older. Of course, a New Year can be exciting and full of possibility, as in 'This is gonna be my year, Janet, I can feel it.' Mind you, after a bottle of Baileys, my older sister Mitzi (the poet formerly known as Maureen*) reckons she could conquer Everest in her flip-flops.

I don't say this out loud, but secretly I'm thinking, Will I cope? Will everyone get out alive? What have you got in store for me, universe?

Mitzi approaches it in a different way. For instance, New Year's Day requires her to wear a turban to protect her head from negative influences, and an ancient Tibetan blanket for inspiration, the smell of which inspires me to reach for the Febreze. Then she settles down for the day and binges on all the annual horoscopes in print and online. By 6 p.m. on New Year's Day, Aquarian Mitzi knows *exactly* what's coming up this year. She even reads mine for me, so I get the highlights. Lots of romance, a new job, and don't buy anything electrical when Mercury is retrograde. Right. It's the same every year. And that's OK

1

with me.

I always try to get out on a walk, New Year's Day, to savour the things that stay the same. Like the big tree on the rec, or the walk-up Daisy Bank that's always guaranteed to be a bugger. Today, once at the top, I take a big breath and let my eyes do some lingering on the wide spread of fields that haven't changed in centuries. Fill myself up with a big lung of the wonderful Yorkshire air and rejoice. My heart's still pumping, my eyes with a bit of squinting can still read the small print, and my knees are still in one piece, just about. I made it, another turn of the wheel.

*See *Janet Jackson's Yorkshire B&B*

If I really concentrate and peer like a lunatic, I can see the chimney of our house and the outline of Lavander Cottage, where our paying guests stay. I can scarcely believe it: I've been a B&B owner for *one whole year*. I've loved it, I've hated it, I've cleaned a lot of toilets and changed a lot of beds and could put 'laundrywoman' as a secondary occupation. I've struggled like mad to pay the bills to make it happen, and even earned a little bit of *nudge nudge* cash.

My New Year's resolution is to make it as a B&B Superhost. Why not? *Janet Jackson, Superhost* – it's got a definite ring to it. Here is what it says online: 'A Superhost is a Host who goes above and beyond to provide excellent hospitality. Guests can easily identify a Superhost from the badge that appears on their listing and profile'.

I want to be *so* busy and *so* blooming good at this thing that I can finally pay off all the credit cards I used to build it, and at last be able to take my daughter Chloe on holiday somewhere warm. She deserves it, *I* bloody deserve it. So that's my plan.

Here we go: another year of Janet Jackson's Yorkshire B&B. I'll send you details. Remember, we are open for bookings ☺

CHAPTER 1

Miles the Dentist

Miles is my boss at the dental practice called Valley Dental, where I work as a receptionist. He's mid-divorce and this is his first Christmas and New Year away from the family. Poor Miles. He was looking really depressed in the run-up to the holiday period, mooching around reception in between patients, dropping hints about how he was going to be all alone at Christmas for the first time in his life. After he welled up, talking about when his girls were little and begging a tissue off me, followed by a 'Is the cottage available, Janet?' I fell soft and agreed to let him stay there for Christmas week. I'd no one else booked in – and what could possibly go wrong?

Here's the answer.

We're three weeks into January and he's *still* here! The baubles are all wrapped up and back in the old biscuit tin gathering spider webs up in the attic along with the wonky pine-cone wreath. Oh, and the four-foot cardboard Grinch that Mitzi turned up with on Christmas Eve, declaring tipsily, 'Christmas is a commercial capitalist invention and so on principle I've decided not to partake in the exchange of Christmas presents this year.'

'Tight arse,' is how my seventeen-year-old daughter Chloe responded to that. She then crawled under the Christmas tree to retrieve and unwrap the bottle of expensive perfume she'd purchased for her aunt, replacing it with a crumbly lime-coloured bath bomb that she'd bought months ago.

'She can have the giant bogey instead.'

Eurgh. Sometimes my sister is her own worst enemy. She's so clever too, with a degree and everything, but it doesn't translate to thinking things through. I suppose on reflection there's always a bit too much booze involved. She's rarely without a tipple, and any destructive self-centredness is beefed up with the stuff. My own weakness is food: cake, bread, pies, puddings, biscuits and pastry – although I do have a theory that baking only increases your judgement, thanks to all that stirring and relaxing and planning and taking one's time to savour things.

I think my enjoyment of food might also have caused this issue with Miles: I've turned him with my dedication to cooking. He *loves* my onion and rosemary gravy. Take last Sunday. I was desperately trying not to notice that Miles (who, let's not forget, is a well-brought-up, frankly quite posh bloke with dental qualifications and his own practice) had his face on the dinner plate and was licking up the last dregs of gravy from it. Even Mitzi's current beau Carl, tattooed to the max, a rough-as-they-come builder with hands like shovels, was looking on agog.

Chloe pulled a disgusted face at me and stood up from the table deliberately slowly, scraping her chair for maximum drama, saying, 'Er . . . try and leave some pattern on the plate, Miles.'

This did seem to stir my boss out of his hypnotic slurp.

'Ha, yes. I will. Sorry. Blame your mother, Chloe,

for her gravy of the gods. I could die happy, drowning in a bowl of that.'

'Well, hurry up and get on with the drowning bit as we need the cottage next week. Carl's family are coming.'

Mitzi delivers this lie completely deadpan, with one leg inside the room, one leg outside the patio door. She flicks a cigarette end into the garden, and it lands somewhere close to where my sweet peas came up last year. She then closes the door and sashays back to the table to play with her one carrot and potato Sunday dinner. My sister isn't a fan of food.

Miles has no idea how to take Mitzi and looks at me for reassurance.

'Don't worry,' I tell him. 'We'll sort something out.'

Oh, why did I say that? It's like I have a pleasing disease. I can't stop saying yes. So much for using my better judgement. This is now week four of a stay, which is pretty much three weeks longer than we originally agreed. I mean, on the upside, he's paying – so why would I say no? Lavander Cottage is full. Great. I'm only cleaning it once a week. Great. He's very tidy so he doesn't make much of a mess. Great. Only it's not so great. My boss is living *next door*. Imagine, your boss! The lack of privacy!

Take today, a perfect Saturday January morning, and here I am, shuffling round the garden getting dazzled by a brilliant white sun whilst the frost nips at my exposed bits. No bra, giant green wader wellies – the only shoes I could rustle up from the mountain in the hall cupboard. I'm drowning in an enormous Pudsey Bear dressing gown that has seen better days, tied with a random scarf 'cos I couldn't find the belt. I'm sipping my first cup of tea without a hint of mascara. I've not even cleaned my teeth and I'm chewing on the crust of Chloe's last night take-out pizza crust. Sorry, I know it's not a pretty picture.

So there I am, happy as Larry, bent double in the flowerbeds searching for evidence of bulb leaves poking up, everything roaming free, when the cottage door flies opens and out pops Miles. Dashing dentist Miles. Literally dashing. I mean it, he never stops. If he's not going on twenty-mile cycle rides, he's fell-running: rain, hail or snow – he doesn't care. He arrived back at the cottage yesterday drenched to the bones, looking as if he'd just stepped out of the shower. These days, he's so skinny, I reckon I could fell him like timber with one misjudged trip. Honestly, I'm tired just watching him – and here he is, freshly showered and shaved, his racing bicycle at his side, immaculate in body-hugging silver and black Lycra, leaving my eyes with absolutely *NOWHERE* to go. I reckon that I, on the other hand, look like I'm auditioning for the part of abandoned half-sister of Jabba the Hutt.

'Morning, Janet, it's a glorious one.'

'Morning, Miles. You're up bright and early.'

'Yes, on the road for seven-thirty. I'll be able to get a good sixty miles in today, all being well.'

'Wow.'

'Isn't it. You should come out with me.'

'Yes, I should.' (Never going to happen.) 'I don't know if my rusty wheels could do six miles, never mind sixty.'

'I'll take a look at it, if you like. Probably just needs a service. You around later?'

'Probably.'

'Smith and Kline are playing at the White King this evening if you fancy going for a drink.'

'Smith and Kline?'

'Excellent, hard folk, bit of Northumbrian pipe. They were long-listed for the Mercury a few years ago.'

'Amazing.' (Mercury? Must have been retrograde at the time.)

'Excellent. See you there, say, around seven?'

'Great.'

He leans on his razor blade of a bike and then with an energetic stride his leg is over and he pedals off with a jolly salute.

I think about my pleasing disease. I wonder what medics would call it – 'Yes Pox'? Anyway, I've got a strong case of it. Hard folk? I'm a fan of Abba and Billy Joel, given half a chance. These days, I never even get to choose the music in my house or my car. Someone else is always deciding what's playing, Chloe with her Dua Lipa and Mitzi with her 80s' Goth medleys. So, do I like hard folk? I've absolutely no idea. Well, there go my plans for a repeat binge of *The Crown*.

Mind you, it will do me good to get out. Mitzi and Carl are always staying in these days, since they're saving for *the wedding*. Really? Who has a big wedding when they're over forty? They are three weddings in, for goodness sake, and those are just the ones Mitzi can remember. I'm being mean but I end up feeling like a third wheel in the living room once they start cuddling and giggling after a second bottle of wine.

It'll be good to go out. At least he's friendly, Miles, and he does things. He looks after himself. Maybe I should stop moaning and leave him in the cottage? It could work. It WOULD NOT work. I don't want to have to worry about what my boss does or doesn't know about my private life; it's all way too close for comfort. *Hold on, Janet*. Did Miles just ask me out on a date? And did I just say yes? What was I thinking?

Right – that's it. I'm unblocking the calendar. Miles is getting his notice. I am officially re-opening the cottage for general business. Whatever I do, I can't mix up my personal life and my work life and my home-work life – you know what I mean. Now that really *would* be a disaster.

I arrive at the gig determined to establish that this date isn't officially a date. I've deliberately not gone too dressed up. Too much and it would look like I've assumed it was a date and I can't have that. My outfit needs to be relaxed enough for a gig, nice enough to not be too unattractive. I opt for a fluffy jumper – I always think fluffy is good, it's got a sensuality about it that's not 'in your face'. Burgundy, to go with the jeggings and ankle boots with a heel. I've nailed it. I hope.

I walk into Hebden. It's a crispy night, with a bright tiny crescent of a moon, and the ground's not too slippery underfoot. I don't really like going into a bar by myself. It's as if people are staring and judging, and though I tell myself that no one cares, that everyone is too involved in their own life, and what's more that it's twenty-first-century Britain for heaven's sake and a woman can be out on her own, none of that makes any difference.

Putting an 'I don't give a monkey's' expression on my face, I open the pub door and am instantly hit by a waft of chatter and warmth. It's so busy that no one even turns to look. I head to the bar and I'm only there a moment before Miles slips in beside me.

'Hello, Janet, you look very nice,' he greets me. 'Have you walked here? You feel cold.'

'Hi, yes, it's a lovely night, and wow, it's packed in here.'

'Yes, it's obviously got out that Smith and Kline are playing. Come and take a seat, I've bagged us a table. What's your tipple?'

'Half . . .' I ponder.

'. . . a bottle of Rioja?'

I laugh, Miles is funny. By the time he returns with a half of lager and a bottle of red the band are starting to hit their groove and it's impossible not to enjoy the atmosphere. The White King is a lovely new bar, one of so many bars in Hebden, with dark walls and loads of greenery, and a tiny stage the musicians struggle to fit on. The sound is a strange mix of cello and tub-thumping, some noisy drums and a weird bit of pipe. But the singers' voices are gorgeous, with brilliant harmonies and uplifting cheery lyrics, and our bottle of wine goes down a treat. It is followed by another and then a Jamaican Mule cocktail drink of some kind.

We're in the taxi home and before we know it there's lots of laughter and some hand-holding and a kiss. I can feel the waves of chastisement from here, but hey ho, I end up spending the night with Miles in the cottage. No regrets. It was lively, to say the least. He's certainly got some energy, let's put it that way. I make sure I disappear early morning and now we have reverted pretty much to business as usual. No big discussion, no heart-to-heart, just a grown-up mutual understanding and that is fine by me.

Janet Jackson, wild woman.

And the next morning, all fired up and confident, I tell him he has to go. Get me! Boundaries – I knew I had some tucked away somewhere. He's a bit shocked. It was after the second cup of tea. I had made some buttermilk blueberry pancakes with maple syrup, just so you know I'm not without heart.

'Oh. Really? You're getting rid of me already? When I'm enjoying these pancakes *sooo* much.' He looks downcast. 'What a shame. When do I need to go?'

'This week? You have been here three weeks longer than we agreed, Miles. And I need to get my business up and running again.'

'Would raising the rent change your mind?' (*Argh*, stay strong, Janet, stay strong.)

'I think things have got a bit . . . blurry.'

'OK. Yes. Blurry. Of course. I'll get myself organised. Go this week.'

'Thank you.'

Three weeks, two days and a bonk later, Miles moves out. It takes a whole day. Strapping the bikes to the roof-rack of his car is the most time-consuming part. Carl gives him a hand after one falls off and the scream of anguish from Miles brings us all out to check he's OK. Everything else fits into two holdalls. As he gets into the car, I ask him to leave a review.

'I don't usually leave reviews, Janet.'

'I bet you don't usually stay three weeks longer than originally agreed and take home a six-pack of home-made frozen gravy and a chicken-and-mushroom pie, either?' I hand him over a freezer bag with some Tupperware containers of gravy and a fabulous, if I say so myself, puff-pastry pie. He couldn't look happier if he'd pipped the Yellow Jersey winner from the Tour de France at the last leg finish line.

'Oh Janet, you absolute star.'

'Oh Janet, you absolute Five Stars, please. I'm going for Superhost.'

He laughs. 'Once I'm settled and on the laptop, I promise I'll do a glowing review.'

'Thank you.'

We hug. It's nice. It's friendly. It's grown-up and I'm feeling absolutely in control.

Until today.

One week later, I'm in work. At Valley Dental, it's

been a busy morning and I'm in the kitchen making a peppermint tea for Mrs Fashanu and a water for Thomas Driver, who felt a bit dizzy after a root canal. When Miles wanders into the tiny kitchen I don't want to be presumptuous, but I think he's looking for me.

'Janet! You look very nice today,' he says, followed by, 'I love the colour of your skirt.' It's dark green, I've worn it a hundred times.

'Thank you,' I reply. 'I'm making some drinks, would you like one?'

'Yes, please, will you bring me one up? A tea, please, if it's not too much trouble.'

It's a pain to take one up to him as he's right at the top of the building, but it's not very often he asks, and as always, he's very polite.

'No bother. You don't like a lot of milk, is that right?'

'Sturdy, Janet, that's the way I like it: strong enough for the spoon to stand up.'

I totter up the stairs with a tray of drinks, drop them off with everyone and arrive at Miles's room last as Judy, his dental nurse, is coming out.

'He wants me to go and buy him some jelly babies for the young ones,' she says, vexed. 'I thought we were trying to wean kids *off* sweets. I'll take my drink back down, thanks, and warm it up in the kitchen when I get back from the shop.'

As I enter the room and put his mug of tea down on the side, Miles immediately removes his mask and smiles.

'Janet, what a treat. Thank you.'

He comes round the chair, and before I know it, he's got his arm around my waist and we are kissing. KISSING! IN WORK! I'm leaning back then somehow I'm lying on his chair and Miles is pretty much climbing on top of me. *What if Judy comes back early?* In my panic I hit the electric switch and we are both slowly elevated upright.

'Janet,' he pants, 'I have a huge crush on you.'

'Miles, you *are* crushing me.'

'Sorry, sorry.'

He leaps off me and I pull down my ruffled skirt, adjust my tights and rearrange my blouse. As I clamber off the chair, I accidentally press the water jet, which launches a spear of water onto my skirt, creating a dodgy-looking patch. I'm feeling flustered and a tad annoyed.

'We cannot carry on like this in work,' I snap. 'It's not professional, Miles.'

'Of course. I'm so sorry. You just look *sooo* nice.' And his arm is curling round my waist.

'*Miles*. Enough! I've got Mr Driver in reception.'

'Sorry. Sorry. So sorry.' Miles steps back and scurries behind the chair. 'Can I take you out for dinner tonight, Janet? A thank-you for letting me stay at your lovely cottage and for all the wonderful meals I've eaten at yours.'

I'm floundering a bit. He's so intense, charming, and direct. I want to say simply, 'Yes,' but after what happened last time, us ending up in bed, it could develop into something. He, this . . . it makes me nervous. What is this all about – and do I really want any of it?

I gulp. 'I er . . .'

He smiles and takes my hand and kisses it. Oh crikey. I might melt. 'We had such a nice time last week.'

Why did I go to that bloody gig? How old am I? Old enough to know much better.

'Yes,' I say, 'but that was just after Christmas, Miles. Special circumstances.'

He laughs. 'A dentist isn't just for Christmas, Janet.'

'Ha. You know that's not what I mean. Are you sure? You're not even divorced yet, Miles.'

'I'm sure, all right. I'd love to see you again and again.'

'Well, I've guests to sort out in the cottage.' I'm lying now, but I'm trying to buy myself time. Something is bothering me, but I'm not sure what it is.

'Well, we can eat later if you prefer?'

'No, I prefer to eat earlier, otherwise I get indigestion and won't sleep.'

I am saying this just as Judy returns with the sweets. I collect his mug, which is still full but thank goodness she doesn't notice – and make my escape.

The text comes later in the afternoon.

Thai Rose. Booked for 6 p.m. Hope early enough for you. Looking forward to it. Mx

Oh gosh. Am I really doing this? I decide to drive so I don't get tempted to drink. I need to chat to Miles sober. What is this guy after? What does he want? What do *I* want? What will it feel like when work know we're a thing? What if we fall out? What do I do for a job then? And do I need a man at the moment? I have my motorbike man, Malky, but that's a casual every-now-and-again do, and being available every time he can be bothered – well, it makes me feel a teeny bit cheap. And let's be honest, winter isn't bike-riding weather.

The thing is, it's nice having a bit of fun, and I do like having something to look forward to. Something that doesn't involve cottage cleaning, dental reception work, laundry or emptying the dishwasher. Maybe that's all I want, some fun. Who am I kidding? I want to fall in love and find a wonderful man who'll worship the ground I walk on and we'll live happily ever after, The End. Oh gosh. What a deluded romantic I am. Do I honestly think that's Miles? Aren't I simply the rebound divorce stocking-filler? There is no point starting things and complicating my life if I'm not really sure.

Bloody hell, Janet Jackson, *lighten up*. You're going out for an average Chow Mein with a work colleague. That's all.

It's great to park in Hebden after five, there are plenty of spaces. I've got the parking app, so I spend five minutes having my face recognised, and the bloody two-type verification carry-on, which means I have to have a code sent to me by the bank, which I then approve, all for a twenty-pence ticket. *The world is ridiculous.*

I open the door of the Thai and, like at the pub, am greeted by a wave of warmth, accompanied by the heady scent of hot oil and jasmine. There's Miles. He looks good – I think he's even ironed a shirt. I wonder who he has hovering in the background to do his ironing? Must be a woman. I shall be disciplined and try to find out. I make a mental note: Don't eat too much, ask lots of questions, and definitely *don't drink*.

Three glasses of sake later I'm in Miles's apartment in Hebden. You're right – it's pathetic, though the question that keeps popping up in my head is, Why not? No one even notices I'm not at home, unless they're hungry or the washing pile threatens to crawl out of the house and take over the neighbourhood. My daughter is currently at a sixth-form college studying for A-levels, and she has no interest in housework at all.

Miles apologises because his new rented flat is so cold. I'm just grateful that the peri-menopause seems to have turned my core temperature up a degree. Whilst he fiddles with the handset that is supposed to get the heating going, I take in the room. Huge TV, enormous rowing machine, with the best spot in the house located beside the floor-to-ceiling windows. Here, in the daytime you could sit and stare out onto the canal. There are weights of every shape and size spread across the floor. I peer into the kitchen. No evidence of cooking or food. Back in the sitting room, there's not much comfort. No cushions or blankets. It's all a bit grim. However, I spot a photo of his grown-up girls. Sweet. And a basil plant that seems to have found its way here by mistake. As Miles curses and bashes his handset on the sofa arm, I grab a cup and give the plant some water.

'I think that's on.' Miles flings away the handset and marches up to me. 'Looking at you, Janet, let me tell you that *I'm* very turned on.'

'That's so cheesy, Miles.'

'I know.' We both laugh, he pulls me to the brink of the sofa and over we go.

It might be something to do with being a farmer's daughter, but I can manage on not a lot of sleep. I leave at 4.30 a.m. Pick up the car and toodle home, shower, have a big breakfast of porridge, berries and toast, sort some washing, do a bit of cleaning and am in Valley Dental and on reception fifteen minutes early. I am determined to keep things professional at work, so I ignore Miles completely. Every time he wanders into the kitchen, which he does a lot today, and even when he gestures at me to join him as he heads out of the main door for lunch, I refuse. At no point do I compromise myself professionally. I convince myself that

I'll stay strong.

He sends me a song on Spotify that I attempt to listen to but turn it off mid-way as it comes across like men shouting at each other in a tin factory. I'm packing up, last in the building as it's my job to lock up, and anxious to get out on time, when Miles appears. He gives me a huge smile and I can't help flushing up, though I do my very best to disguise it. He sidles round the reception desk and cosies up to me.

'Where have you been hiding?' he asks. 'Fancy a drink?'

'Not tonight, Miles, I've promised Chloe I'll watch something with her.' Lies, lies, lies.

'OK, well, let me give you a lift home. It's dreadful out there.'

'I'm all right, thanks, I need the fresh air.' True, true, true.

As I tramp along the cycle path getting wet through from the mist, I try to clear my head. What is it about this guy that has me feeling so nervous? Is it that it feels only about the sex? And if so, why does that matter? What 1950s moral universe do I come from? It's as if there's something else bothering me that I can't put my finger on. I know I shouldn't, but I can't help myself, I send him a text.

Miles, I hope I'm not just your bit of rough?

What would be wrong with that?

A LOT would be wrong with that.

The answer comes immediately:

Can I not just like you very much? Plus you don't have any rough bits, you're all wonderful, soft and delicious ... can I come round tonight?

Yes, after 8.

I have the willpower of a gnat.

REVIEW

***** Five Stars

Fabulous location, wonderful warm host. Highly Recommend.

TIP FOR RUNNING A B&B

Don't book your boss into your accommodation. It's one of those rookie errors. Proves awkward when you want them to move out.

TIP ON LIFE

If you make good gravy, *be careful*. It can lead places.

CHAPTER 2

Mr Dark Skies & Sons

'How old are the sons?'
'I've no idea, Chloe. They don't need a travel cot and asked for the sofa-bed, so they're adults, I'm guessing.'

'Hmm, nice, hope they're good-looking. When are they arriving?'

'Tomorrow, sometime after two. These are not boyfriend material, Chloe, they're guests here just for the weekend, remember.'

'Who said anything about boyfriends?'

I'm racing around the kitchen attempting to tidy up so I can get to work and not return to a bombsite. I sweep crumbs into the bin, wipe the side, put the milk away and add a random sock into the wash-pile. Chloe then decides to tip the entire contents of her bag all over the freshly wiped worktop. Pencil shavings, coins, crushed sweet wrappers, Post-it notes, another random sock, pencils, grubby make-up – and a marble polar bear?

'Chloe, I've just wiped up there.'

'I NEED to find my bus-pass and I'm late. You'll have to give me a lift.'

'Then I'll be late.'

'Miles will let you off.'

'That's not the point.' I'm quite cross now. 'I'm never late and I don't want to start now just because you're not organised.'

'All right, keep your hair on, I've found it, bye.'

Out she goes in a waft of attitude, leaving the debris from her college bag where it has landed. I'm now up against it timewise, and I'm racing to the door when I accidentally tread on Harvey the cat's tail. He does an almighty yowl and flicks a claw that hurts like buggery and puts a ladder in my tights. I don't have time to change and I'm pulling the door to when Mitzi waves at me frantically through the window. My sister is never up before ten, so I don't want to know what's going on, and I especially don't want to know if I need to get involved.

Pretending I haven't seen her, I jump in the car and turn on the ignition. That's when the front door flies open. She is wrapped in what looks like a bedsheet, except it is cowled around her head so it's taken on a monkish quality, exacerbated by the fact that Mitzi drops to her knees and puts her hands up in prayer mode. I can't ignore her now.

'*What!*' I snap. 'I'm going to be late.'

'His mum is coming for tea.'

'So?'

'His *mum*, Janet.' She is looking panicked.

I sigh. 'Right. When?'

She's practically wringing her hands now. 'Tonight.'

Eurgh. 'All right.'

'It's not all right. I said TONIGHT, Janet.'

'Yes, I heard you.'

'Help me, please.' She's giving me eyes like the cat off *Shrek* as she shuffles on her knees towards me.

'What do you need? Do you want me to cook?'

'Oh, thank God. Yes. Please.'

She immediately leaps up from the ground and pulls out a fag and a lighter from somewhere inside the rolls of her outfit.

'Anything she doesn't like?' I shout as I put the car in a U-turn.

My sister looks blank, as if someone has pushed her on to a stage to deliver a speech without notes or trousers.

'Me,' she says mournfully.

'OK, well, text me.'

My heart is now racing as I mentally check off all the things I need to do today. Number one: I must go to work and be a good dental receptionist. This means I feed the fish, rearrange magazines, navigate the desperate phone calls from people in pain and try to get them emergency appointments. This is increasingly difficult as the Denplan regulars take up 70 per cent of the space as regular clients. Finding *them* dates and times they want or can manage with work and school is not easy. Miles doesn't do Mondays after 2 p.m., Fridays, or lunchtimes as he's cycling. Tony, the other partner, is approaching early retirement and he specialises in being miserable. He now only does Tuesdays to Fridays, no doubt in order to prep himself for the long days of being miserable at home, rather than miserable at work. The hygienist, Mrs Fashanu, is mad about her horses, so she only does Tuesdays and Wednesdays so as to be available for hacks. Wanda, the other hygienist, is Mondays only. The rest of the time she's dedicated to crochet: according to her and her mum, she pioneered the letter-box topper. You know, those lovely little knitted scenarios you find tucked over the top of a post-box round your way.

If any of the team at Valley Dental is off with a cold, the whole system grinds to a halt and is thrown into chaos.

Phew. On top of all that, there's the gentle phone manner I need to sustain, to re-direct the poor buggers who are ringing up looking for an NHS dentist. Above all, whatever I do, I have to avoid any intimate or meaningful looks, sighs, glances or accidental touches with Miles. I have no brain space for any of *that* at the moment.

Number two: today I must focus on becoming a Superhost as I prepare for the arrival of Mr Dark Skies – that's what he calls himself – & Sons. This means supplying a quality welcome basket that over time I have got down to a fine art. The basket contains: milk (semi-skimmed, sorry no oat), bread (50/50 sliced since anything else gets left), butter (never *ever* margarine), sugar, coffee (mid-price posh instant), dish-washer tablets and clean tea-towels. After preparing the basket I then do a quick spot-check of Lavander Cottage, spray some polish around and turn on the plug-in smelly thing. As a finishing touch, I put on the heating early to bring it up to temperature, since it's so cold at the moment.

Going for Superhost puts on quite the pressure, but I'm gunning for it. To succeed, I need back-to-back Five and Four Stars over a six-month period. Thank heavens I'm on a half-day today so I can be out for twelve-thirty, leaving me 1.5 hours precisely to pick up everything I need from the shops and get back and go through my checklist.

Number three: today I need to be a good sister and think about what I could cook for Mitzi's future mother-in-law. Blimey. Carl's mum. What's she going to be like? He's lovely, is Carl, but a bit rough around the edges. I bet she's hard as nails. Mitzi said the woman doesn't like her. Let's face it, *they never do*.

Most mums take one look at my sister and go straight into Code Red: girlfriend removal. Always the same, even way back when she got together with her first boyfriend, dozy Fred on next door's farm. I remember him well. Fred had a Led Zeppelin poster on his wall and a working Walkman in his tractor. He had stopped going to school at fourteen and got into trouble with the police for rolling a tractor tyre down Lakey Hill into the allotments – breaking three sheds and Sid's greenhouse on its way. It's not as if he was a catch or anything. But his mum, Mrs Sheila Murgatroyd, well, she made life difficult the first time Mitzi turned up holding hands with Fred. She insisted on feeding her tripe so she could be offended when Mitzi gagged at the second mouthful. Then asked her to go and 'make herself useful' and collect eggs from the pen, where a giant cockerel called Rambo was running round, attacked her and nearly had her eye out. When my poor sister returned with just three intact and two broken eggs, Mrs Murgatroyd accused her of being lazy and feckless. At that, Mitzi dropped the basket, breaking the other three eggs, and stomped out leaving Fred and two Collies howling.

I laugh, and my mind clears. Steak and mushroom pie . . . that's what I'll do. With mash. It rarely misses.

It's an uneventful morning on reception. I'm not sure if Miles knows I'm in today or not, but I'm not bothered anyway. I'm so busy being a receptionist with a Superhost side hustle that I don't have headroom to think about anything else for longer than thirty seconds. I'm grateful to hand over at lunchtime to Susan. Especially when I bump into Verity Stamp, full mouth of veneers, coming in as I leave. No one has raised more complaints than Verity, and that's a face set for combat. I race via the Co-op to pick up some shopping, and before I know it I'm in Lavander Cottage in Superhost mode. I'm wafting scent, plumping pillows and plugging in the extra heater because gosh, it's chilly. That's when a text arrives from Miles.

Sorry I missed you today, fancy a drink tonight? Mx

Do I? I certainly don't fancy being in to meet Carl's mum.

Yes. 7. Crown? JJx

That's that sorted. I'm feeling very happy and pleased with myself for being decisive, when within minutes of being in the cottage Mitzi appears.

'Hi love, need a hand?' she asks.

I'm in shock. Mitzi *never* offers to help.

'Who are you and where is Mitzi?' I say, peering around.

'Absolutely no need for that. I'm always available – you just need to ask.'

Yeah right. This is about his mum. 'OK,' I say. 'Go and peel me some potatoes and put them in water to soak.'

Mitzi wasn't expecting this. She looks mortified. 'Peel? How many?'

'Ten.'

'*Ten?* It'll take me all day.'

'It's either peel some spuds or hoover in here.'

Mitzi stares into the middle distance before deciding, 'I can't vacuum, it depresses me, like it's sucking the life from me.'

I laugh at that. 'Given I've only seen you touch one three times in ten years I think you'll be OK.'

'That's a bit bitchy.'

'Those are the facts.'

'Oh, all right. Where do you hide the potatoes?'

By 3.30 p.m. I've got some puff pastry on defrost and the pie filling made, with the mash whipped up and sitting on the counter in a bowl ready for a microwave blast. I am enjoying a well-deserved cup of Earl Grey and a lemon shortbread when Mr Dark Skies arrives. I've emailed him earlier to let him know the cottage door is ready and open for them, and they head straight to it.

Mr Dark Skies is in his late fifties, I'd guess, dressed in a head-to-toe khaki puffa coat, followed closely by two very tall young men, both equally wrapped up in those full-length duvet coats that look like they could double as an emergency sleeping bag in an Arctic blast. I watch as they walk down the drive, go into the cottage, and then come back out. They disappear back down the drive only to return moments later carrying between them a huge box. I mean a HUGE box.

I'm drying my hands to go and say hello when there's a tap on the patio door.

'Hello.' It's Khaki Puffa. He's got very intense grey eyes sunk back in his sockets that make him look very tired.

'Hello, I'm Janet,' I greet him. 'You're in and settled?'

'Yes, great, thank you.'

'OK, well, let me know if you need anything.' I don't want to invite too much in the way of cottage critique and, hoping this opening gambit might be enough to steer them on their way, I'm slowly closing the patio door when he speaks up.

'Do you have a size eighteen Allen key?'

I'm flummoxed. 'Er . . .'

'A seventeen, nineteen or twenty-two might do it.'

'Er . . .'

'It's quite important,' Mr Dark Skies says insistently. 'It's the only thing we need. Troika made a schoolboy error and left the toolkit at home.'

'Ah, I see.' He's not moving, I really am going to

have to do this now. 'Maybe I have one in amongst my bike stuff?'

'Yes. It's that kind of tool. Thank you.'

He is glued to me as I go round the back to the shed, dig out the toolkit and unpack it. I rummage around and *hallelujah* find a small plastic box of rusty Allen keys at the bottom. Before I can hold it up or say anything, he whips it off me.

'Mmm . . . twelve to seventeen. Right, let's see.' And he disappears with the box, leaving me to tidy up.

As I go back to the house, I can hear the sound of muffled music and spot Chloe turn up the drive. I notice she's got her EarPod things in.

'You'll hurt your ears with those, can't you turn them down a bit?' I know it's like a stock phrase mums say to kids, and sure enough, she pulls a stock phrase eyeroll in return.

'I've only got one in!'

I'm aware that Mr Dark Skies might be back at any moment looking for another set of spanners or something, and I need to get that pie in the oven to bake.

'Mum?' Chloe follows me into the kitchen, whilst I root through the drawer full of odds and sods, trying to find any more key things because I have a feeling those others won't do.

'*Mum.*'

'Yes, love, what?' I'm not really paying much attention: would a tiny electric screwdriver fit? 'Did you have a good day? Do you want a cup of tea?'

'I hate tea.'

'I know, I meant a drink. A hot chocolate? *I* need a tea.'

I put the kettle on, turn on the oven to get it warmed up and crack an egg, roughly stir it with the pastry brush and brush the egg across the crust of the pie. It looks nice with its crimped edge and a couple of pastry dots I put on for decoration. I return to rifling through the drawer, finding batteries, gift receipts, old birthday cards and candles, a half-empty book of stamps . . . and *yes!* Here is another set of the blooming things. I think these were for putting together an Ikea wardrobe. My timing is good because Mr Dark Skies is back at the patio door. He opens it without asking and steps into the kitchen, which I really *don't like.*

'These are no good,' he says, without a greeting or a nod to my daughter. 'Do you have any others?'

I walk over and pass him the new set, saying rather crisply, 'That's my last bet, I'm afraid. If those don't fit, you might need to try B&Q in Halifax. They stay open until eight, so you should be able to pick some up there. OK, thanks, must get on.'

I give a forced smile and physically edge him out the door and close it on him. I don't want to be rude, but I *do* want him out of my kitchen. I stick the pie in the oven, get milk out of the fridge for the tea and as I turn around, I realise my daughter is sitting at the table with big fat tears running down her face. My heart drops to my boots.

'Chloe sweetheart, what's wrong?' I pull up a chair next to her and wrap my arms around her. 'I'm sorry, sweetheart, I was distracted and didn't realise you were upset. What's up, darling?'

'Mum.' Then she weeps some more.

'Love, come on, tell me, you can tell me. Honestly. Whatever it is, I promise we can sort it out.' But this just makes her cry harder.

'Oh, Mum.'

I'm really worried now. It must be something serious, as Chloe is not a crier. In fact, I've only seen her well up very occasionally, and that's usually when an unexpected donkey adoption video pops up between adverts. I'm on absolute pins, what can be wrong? Seeing that she's building up to say something between sobs, I rush round, snatch up some tissues and hand them to her one by one.

'Come on, Chloe love, it can't be that bad.' What if it is? *What is it?*

She's at the point of spilling the beans when Mitzi swans in wearing a floral tea dress that sweeps the ground, her hair pinned up in a wonky updo, looking like Helena Bonham Carter disturbed mid-nap. My sister immediately seizes on the drama like a magnet and is all over Chloe, smothering her with kisses. I'm physically wriggled out of my seat, so Mitzi can get a better position in front of Chloe.

'Breathe it out, breathe it out, shake it out, come on, stand up with me, you too, Janet, let's all stand up, let everything hang, that's it, shimmy and shake, come on, let it all go.'

We are all now standing up, flopping our arms and heads about, arms up in the air, fingers wiggling, twisting our hips, twisting our feet, tongues out now.

'*Aaah*, repeat after me, *Aaah*,' my sister shrills.

Chloe smiles, then she giggles, which encourages Mitzi and me to get even sillier. We are leaping about making daft noises and shaking ourselves like loons when I turn around and notice that Mr Dark Skies & Sons are standing in the kitchen staring at us. I stop, Chloe stops, Mitzi is of course reluctant to stop but finally comes to a steady brake.

'Just letting you know that set fits,' Mr Dark Skies says.

'Great,' I answer breathlessly. 'Thank you.'

'We'll get set up now then. Thanks for everything, the bread et cetera. The cottage is champion.'

'Good, very pleased, you're welcome.'

They awkwardly back out of the patio door and

Chloe, Mitzi and I all turn to one another and laugh as soon as the door is closed. Eventually the giggles peter out and I take a hold of Chloe.

'Come on, tell us what's up, sweetheart?'

Her bottom lip wobbles. 'I hate my course, I want to drop out of college. Mum, I don't know what I want to do.'

My heart sinks but I mustn't let it show. 'That's nothing to worry about. We can sort it.'

'I just don't like it there, Mum.'

'I see.'

I ponder over all the things I've not enjoyed during my lifetime. The parade of awful bosses and crummy jobs is like *The Generation Games* conveyor belt: the pie-making one where I permanently hurt my wrist, the card-folding one with the train of bitter old women who gossiped mercilessly about you in front of you. The shoe-packing, the spiteful lechers, the pickled onion factory, the scary night-time office cleaning. The list goes on and on.

I pull myself together. 'Well, let's get out the prospectus and see if there's any other course you fancy. It's always possible to change course.'

'I don't want to do another course, Mum. I just want to leave.' Delivered in monotone, matter-of-fact, entirely deadpan.

Mitzi, of course, can't wait to put her oar in. 'Education is over-rated,' she says. 'Life is where the experiences are.'

I give her a hard stare and flick my eyes meaningfully towards the oven. She picks up the hint, and hastily follows her words with, 'Although it does generally mean higher wages and much better prospects.'

'I want a break from school,' my daughter tells us. 'I've had enough. I'm gonna look for a job.' Having got that off her chest, she then gets up, blows her nose, throws the tissue in the bin and looks in the oven. 'I'm starving, what's for tea?'

'Not the pie. Do NOT go near that pie.' Mitzi leaps in front of the oven, bodyguard-style.

'That's for Carl's mum,' I explain. 'Mitzi's cooking a pie.'

'*Mitzi's* cooking?' Chloe makes sly progress toward the oven, but Mitzi is on her.

'Yes,' she hisses, 'so you can just turn around and leave this general area, or I'll insist you stay at college.'

I rustle up a pizza for Chloe, then battle with a fast shower with the nozzle set low to avoid my hair. I select a rather crumpled gypsy-ish type of dress and dangly earrings for my date. I haven't time to iron the dress and am hoping the pattern is so busy that Miles's eyes will be preoccupied roaming around the Paisley pattern, which is dizzily pointing every which way.

I'm spraying a bit of perfume and hurrying down the stairs as Carl's mum Rowena arrives. She's not what I imagined. She's tall, with big blonde hair – in those waves that look as if a professional has been on it for hours, and those puffy lips you see on a lot of women these days. She's in quite a fancy outfit – a tight-fitting shirtdress thing and heels. *Heels.* I feel like we misjudged it with pie: this is much more of a Caesar salad woman. Too late now, I try and compensate for what's coming with a slightly OTT hello.

'*Hello*, so sorry I'm flying out, nice to meet you.'

'Rowena Bellingham, we have met. I had a crown fitted a couple of years ago now.'

'Oh right, yes of course.' (I don't remember.) 'How is it?'

'It's still there, put it that way, though it's a pain to get round with the brush.'

'Yes, we find that, they're a magnet for debris.'

'Right. You not stopping, avoiding the in-laws?' She

smiles with a hint of menace.

'I already had plans, sadly,' which is, after all, the truth. 'Hopefully we'll have a chance to catch up properly another time. Mitzi is very entertaining, she'll look after you.'

Carl has his arm draped around Mitzi in the kitchen doorway; he looks relaxed, smiling, but Mitzi has a rigid grin attached to her face that's not reaching her eyes. Carl guides his mum through to the kitchen. Mitzi maintains the grimace as I get my coat. She doesn't move.

'What's up?' I whisper.

'Carl's invited his kids round too, they're on their way.'

I gulp for her. 'Oh well, get it over with, I suppose. There are some chips in the freezer, so maybe throw some in? How old are they?'

'Ten, twelve and thirteen.'

'In that case, I'd definitely get some chips on. Well, good luck.'

'I'm gonna bloody need it. Hurry back?'

'Of course. I'll be as quick as I can.' (I am *so* lying.)

I get in the car and text Chloe with all the details about tonight's guests. She sends me lots of laughter emojis and promises to diss the goss on my return. I've no idea what she's on about but I reply with a smiley face.

My thoughts turn to Miles. Do I honestly think there's any mileage in a relationship with him? There's no point in starting things and complicating my life if I'm not really sure. Once you're older, like we both are, you have stuff going on. People have people who will judge and complain and get in the way. Look at poor Mitzi, entertaining a crowd of strangers and grumpy ones, I bet. She's useless with kids – unless they're rebellious ones – and she never understands mothers, since she never wanted to be one. She wants to hug Carl's bones off him and that's pretty much it. That engagement announcement Carl put on social media – that was a mistake. That is what's brought all these relatives to the door.

Then I relax and tell myself: 'You're going for a little drink, Janet. I don't think you need to be worrying about wedding favours *just* yet.'

Three hours later and Miles and I jump out of the taxi and stagger up the drive, both giggly as I scrabble in my bag for the keys. Miles is cupping my bottom in the most comical way whilst tickling my neck deliberately with his breath. I'm mightily distracted, trying very hard to keep the noise to a minimum when I drop the keys and suddenly find a torch beam illuminating them on the drive. I blink, look around and pick out a group of crouching figures that I realise must be Mr Dark Skies & Sons, all positioned on the lawn by a giant telescope that is pointed at the sky.

'Thank you,' I whisper, as I pick up the keys and simultaneously push Miles away and attempt to straighten up in order to open the front door.

'Mars retrograde, boys?' Miles casually throws out. I can tell he's being mischievous.

'No. Saturn shift.'

'Ah, I thought so.'

'Shut up, Miles.'

I nearly fall over, and the torchlight flickers up to reveal that Chloe is one of the shadowy figures. She too is crouching on the ground, her eyes on the stars.

'Chloe love.' I cringe and feel myself sobering up as the cold creeps in, and I instinctively create a gap between myself and Miles.

'I'm stargazing, Mum. It's good. Don't lock the door.'

I manage the key at last, and collapse into the hall, giggling away with Miles. I am returning a long leisurely kiss when the landing light powers on and Mitzi's head drops over the banister. FFS!

'Oh, hi, Miles. I just thought I'd tell you first, Janet. The wedding's off.'

I'm shocked. 'Oh gosh. Was the pie that bad?'

'It's for the best. I'll tell you tomorrow. Night.'

The light then goes off, plunging us back into darkness. I start to compute the myriad of scenarios that must have gone wrong for Mitzi or Carl to be calling the wedding off, but I don't have long to wonder as Miles pulls me into his arms and though I can feel his ribs, I worry my tummy is wobbling like a giant whoopee cushion. Chloe is outside rolling on the ground with strange men, Mitzi is up to her usual; nothing stands still long in this lifetime whirl of chaos. Miles's lips are planted on mine, I'm not worrying any more about anything, and reflect that that delicious second bottle of Sauvignon really did the trick.

REVIEW

***** Five Stars

Helpful hosts. Dark Sky friendly. Plenty of Allen Keys. We'll be back.

Thanks, Mr Dark Skies & Sons.

TIPS FOR RUNNING A B&B

Privacy. When you run a B&B you don't really get any. This can be hard to live with.

Strangers are sort of in your house. You've got to be able to live with this and also be strong enough to push them out of the door.

Guests are unpredictable. They bring things like telescopes and ask for stuff you haven't anticipated. Like Allen Keys. So be prepared for every eventuality. I know that's impossible. Get a big drawer.

TIPS ON LIFE

Kids too are unpredictable. They do things like drop out of perfectly good college courses for no reason. They leave mess everywhere. Be ready for constant change. I know that too is impossible. Get big drawers for all the big pants you're going to need to wear in order to cope with your kids.

CHAPTER 3

The Walkers

Chloe has decided to set up a family textappthing group. The notification came through today. She has used a truly awful photo of me with my eyes closed and grimacing at the camera whilst she, of course, looks absolutely beautiful and Mitzi is in profile in the background.

Chloe's first message was *hello losers you are now on a family WhatsApp*, to which Mitzi responded with a rude hand-gesture emoji. Chloe has way too much free time now, having stopped going to college. I spoke to her Admissions tutor, who was very sympathetic. I explained that I didn't know that my daughter had been intending to quit, nor the reason why she was doing it, and that I didn't agree with her leaving – in fact, I said, I was very concerned about what she was going to do instead. The tutor reassured me, saying it was not uncommon amongst this age group to change courses and drop out left, right and centre.

I told Miles over a cup of tea in the work kitchen and he too was sympathetic – up to a point. His own daughter had driven him and his ex-wife mad trying to decide between what I heard as Gerton College in Cambridge and Lady Marjorie Hall in Oxford, or somewhere else unbelievably grand. I'm not sure I got the names right but anyway, I quickly decided we weren't really talking about the same thing at all, not even in the same universe. What am I doing getting wrapped up with him? I walk home for some thinking time.

As I stroll past snooty neighbour Laura Watson's home, grandly named Larkspur House, I notice a lot of activity. An extension is being added to her property – part of her strategy to build a bigger, better B&B cottage than I could ever dream of. A ruddy cheek, when I remember all the mean things she did to try to get me to close down Lavander Cottage when I first set it up a year ago! She's out in the front garden, talking on the phone, and for once she's not looking her usual immaculate self. Her hair is sticking out at random points and her pastel linen trousers are caked in mud. It also looks like she's crying, in fact is almost hysterical, as builders rush about around her.

Just then, a flatbed truck pulls up outside her drive and wooden planks are thrown off it on to what was once her pristine front lawn but is now like a muddy rugby pitch, torn into with footprints and wheelbarrow tracks.

'Everything all right, Laura?' I call. A couple of other neighbours have come out now and are standing alongside me, as the noise and air of chaos is quite magnetic. Laura runs down the drive towards us, looking distraught.

'I can't get Oliver on the phone and it's collapsed, the whole thing.' She screams: 'It's collapsing into the sodding hole!'

'What do you mean? What's collapsing?'

'The bloody extension – the builder's got the footings wrong!' She returns to the phone and bursts out, 'Thank God you're there, Oliver. You've got to come home, right now! What's wrong? I'll tell you what's f***ing wrong – it's f***ing unbelievable, that's what. The f***ing builder has completely lost the plot and *the extension is falling into the f***ing hole!*'

Gosh. Well, this is not like the Laura I know. I am peering into her driveway when Mitzi's boyfriend Carl pulls up in his van behind the flatbed truck and leaps out. He immediately starts dragging planks off the crushed lawn at speed and running down the drive with them.

'Make some room!' he bawls. 'Right, Frank, clear off out of it and let me take a look. Bloody hell, man, what the f*** have you done now?'

Later, when Carl joins us for tea, we learn over shepherd's pie that Frank was once Carl's apprentice, but the lad was always determined to get out of Carl's shadow and set up on his own. So he did exactly that, two years ago.

'That Frank always was a cocky twat,' Carl says now, shovelling a huge fork-load into his mouth. Licking his lips, he goes on grimly, 'Well, he's in the shit now, 'cos that two-hundred-and fifty-thousand-pound extension has just taken a burton into the footings. He's made them too wide and too deep and hasn't propped them right.'

'Poor Laura.'

'I quoted her two-eighty,' Carl explains, wiping his plate with a slice of bread, 'reasonable price, but she went for Frank instead.'

'I hope the whole house sinks.'

'Mitzi, that's not very nice.' I'm a bit shocked.

'She's competition, Janet, she needs to go.'

'There's room for more than one B&B in Hebden,' I counter. 'Anyway, I'm sure she's done everything properly, and knowing Laura, she's bound to be insured.'

I do not like Laura but can't help but feel sorry for the woman in her predicament. I start planning a red velvet cake I've got the ingredients for and will take her one down tomorrow for a little bit of comfort.

'But will *he* be insured?' Chloe has been entirely silent throughout and these words feel very ominous, like the drum beats at the start of the theme for *EastEnders*. I notice she's now on a second portion of a pear and hazelnut cake I've made from a recipe in the paper at the weekend. It's absolutely delicious. Warm with ice cream it's more like a sponge dessert than your average cake. The batter mixture with lots of eggs and oil makes it very light.

'I doubt it.' Carl lets out a huge sigh. 'What a dick. This could ruin him. Give us a piece of that cake, Chloe.'

Mitzi takes hold of Carl's face in her hands. 'Do not get involved. I mean it. Not yet. Wait . . .' she does a big, dramatic, TV antiques dealer David Dickinson-style pause '. . . *until the price is right.*'

She's a ruthless one, our Mitzi. She's also very tight. It turns out the wedding plans were getting wildly out of control after Carl's mum and kids got involved. Balloon arches, pre-nups, favours, stag dos, converted decorated barn, bridesmaids . . . The suggestion that broke the camel's back was using a wedding planner Rowena knows.

'Anyway, I've got something to tell you all,' my sister announces, standing up at the table with a glass of red in her hand.

What now? I thought. She can't be pregnant, can she? Please God, no more announcements. I'm just not ready.

'As the wedding is permanently postponed, Carl and I have been talking, and I was wondering, Janet' (oh, here we go, I knew I'd have to get involved) 'if we could use the money we've saved to convert a bit of the attic into an ensuite?' She then sits back down, having given Carl a 'Cheers!' clink.

'Oh, right,' I say slowly. 'That sounds like a good idea. Is there room for an ensuite up there?' They have squatted in the attic, making it their home, for quite some time. I suppose they could fit an ensuite up there too, since it's a big space – the whole size of the house, in fact – with one old skylight window. You have to use a dodgy pull-down ladder to get up there – that definitely needs an upgrade. Inwardly, I'm wondering if the pair of them are suggesting this instead of rent which, as usual, has been thin on the ground lately.

Carl jumps in immediately. 'I'll need to check the attic out for access electrics and things like that, of course, and it will need a more substantial staircase – a spiral one would work well – but I don't see any issue, Janet. There's plenty of room.'

'That sounds good,' I reply cautiously.

'It's sort of in lieu of rent, Janet.' My sister says it as bold as brass. She must be able to read my mind. She goes on: 'Of course, when it's done it will add considerably to the value of the property.'

I remain silent, thinking about the pile of credit-card bills I'm paying off with the minimum amount every month, left over from when I did up Lavander Cottage. My tummy tightens up whenever I think of the sums I owe.

Chloe looks at me. I think my daughter can also read my mind, but she always has my back in situations like this. She opens her mouth. 'How long it will take?'

Good question, Chloe.

Carl shrugs. 'I'll fit it in around my other jobs, but I'll try to complete it as fast as I can.'

'I see.' So no idea, not really.

'There's only thing we need to know, Carl,' Mitzi is on one, holding court. *'Are you insured?'* We all laugh at this.

It's a lot of excitement for one evening. I want to be happy about it all but I'm feeling really nervous about money. I'm in bed going through my spreadsheets, working out how to keep the credit-card people and the utility people happy now with minimum payments, and fretting. Can I even cover all those? I try to sleep. Worrying never helps and I've been moving pence around between columns now for hours.

Yawning, I plump up my pillow, turn off the light and have just settled down when I hear Mitzi's voice from the landing. 'Janet?'

Eurgh. 'What?'

'I forgot to tell you, some walkers rang earlier. They're doing the Pennine Way and they want to stop in the cottage tomorrow.'

I'm fully alert. 'Right. What time? How many?'

'I can't remember exactly. Morning? Afternoon? Four, maybe five?'

'What – people? Time?'

'Not sure.'

'Thanks, Mitzi. I really appreciate you saving this information till now.' *I could kill her.*

'No problem.'

I need to re-set the alarm. I adjust the time to an hour earlier. Plump the pillow again, turn off the light again. I need to sleep. Two minutes later, the sound of loud knocking is coming from upstairs. It lasts for about five minutes.

I shout out: 'Do we need to put the ensuite in now?'

'Yes!' comes back with a cackle from Mitzi.

The banging starts up again. I try to ignore it but it's loud and distracting, and after five minutes a bit of dust drops from the ceiling. I turn the light back on and end up reading an old copy of *Good Housekeeping* for the recipes. Hmmm. Hope this is going to go OK. Do we need planning permission? Thank God it's a day off tomorrow. I have set the alarm for six, so I can be in the cottage changing the beds for half past.

No rest for *this* Superhost.

The banging goes on quite a lot of the next day, and I notice layers of dust arriving everywhere. I escape to the calm of the cottage where everything is pristine and quiet, awaiting its new guests. I am sitting at the kitchen table there, rearranging takeaway leaflets, when they finally arrive. So much for Mitzi's morning – it's late afternoon. First up is an oldish guy looking harassed.

'Hello, I'm Brian. I'm not doing the walk, I'm just providing back-up. I go ahead and make sure you've got heating on and organise food plans, et cetera, et cetera.'

He scurries backwards and forwards between the car carrying a range of lumpy rucksacks, pillows and duvets. He must have done several thousand steps as I'm watching him. Then he drives off, to return forty-five minutes later with the three ladies. Oh dear. A sorrier and more sullen-looking bunch it would be hard to find. As they tramp towards the cottage, the weather meets their mood. It's that soft drizzle that can drown out hope, gentle but never-ending as if the skies are constantly holding some back so they can keep it going as long as possible to test everyone's endurance-wear.

It's a grim day to have been out on a muddy moor. I go outside to say hi and am met with a row of exhausted frowns.

'We're knackered,' says one. 'It's much harder going than we thought.'

'My hip's playing up,' groans another.

'And I didn't bring the right socks,' the youngest one of the group adds sulkily.

As the weary travellers go inside the cottage, Brian stays outside for a few minutes, chatting to me. He explains that the ladies had decided to do a leg of the Pennine Way. He sets off with them, he says, then he goes back to the car to travel to the next meeting point, then he walks out to meet them with provisions to see how they are doing.

'It sounds like you're the one doing a lot of walking, Brian.'

He laughs awkwardly. 'No, no, I'm just the support.'

I reckon Brian will have done the Pennine Way twice by the time they've finished. Quite where he fits into this group I can't work out. Is he a husband, a brother, a father? I'm not sure, but the devotedness suggests family.

I have gone back to sorting out the washing when I get a call. It's Brian the Back-up.

'Would you like to come and tell the ladies the best places for food?'

Not really. I can think of a lot of things I'd rather do, like finish wrestling with a bedsheet and get to grips with the endless mountain of odd socks – where do they all come from? And where are their other halves? I'm tired. To think I alphabetised the leaflets for all the local take-outs and restaurants just before they came – you'd think they'd study them, but no. Honestly, it just goes to show, a Superhost's work is never done. I give up and go over to Lavander Cottage.

Parked in front of me I find a row of miserable women, all overcome with exhaustion, sitting around the kitchen table as Brian fusses with the kettle, suggesting and being turned down for a range of drinks. Tea? No. Peppermint tea? No. Camomile tea? No. Glass of wine? No. Dandelion and burdock? No. Ginger beer? No. Fruit juice? No. On it goes.

'So what are you thinking for food?' I intervene. 'There's a great pizza/pasta restaurant you can ring and they'll deliver, or a couple of great Indians? Or how about an award-winning fish and chips place, perfect after you've worked off all those calories on your walk.'

'Is there anything modern or healthy?' A snotty, unpleasant tone from the youngest one.

Deep breath, Janet. I don't remember 'come in and get a grilling' as part of the service we offer at the cottage.

'There's the Thai place in Hebden if you want to go out? And a vegan restaurant that's sometimes open.' (Does entirely random hours, I've passed it open *once*.) 'Or there's the Chinese supermarket, you could maybe buy some ingredients and cook yourself something? I'll leave you to it. Well done, ladies!'

'Thank you, thank you very much, I appreciate your help.' Brian follows me to the door, almost clinging to me for comfort.

I turn to him. 'They look shattered, Brian. If I were you, I'd give them fish and chips and a glass or two of wine, get the telly on, and a couple of foot baths later they'll be smiling.'

'I wish.' He looks wistfully at me.

As I close the door on Lavander Cottage, I feel as if I'm banging up an innocent bystander on a guilty crime charge. Poor Brian. Half an hour later, I notice them all trooping down the drive in fresh, clean cagoules. When they return a whole two hours later, it looks like they're carrying fish and chips and there's a bit more chatter.

I try for an early night. *Try.* Chloe, who doesn't have to get up early for college or work has, as a result, gone nocturnal. Only the trail of hot-chocolate-stained mugs and toast crumbs give away that she's alive and feeding during the day. Ten p.m. onwards, her bedroom becomes the social equivalent of a Friday night at the Acapulco night club in Halifax. The chatter and laughter never stop, and the music is relentless. I am repeatedly woken out of a deep sleep by the sound of a beat drop, followed by a whoosh and a roar of acknowledgement.

After this happens at least five times, I find myself shouting at the top of my voice outside her door at ten past three in the morning, 'Turn that flaming music off or I'm going to take your bloody phone off you and you won't be getting it back until bloody Christmas!'

Things quieten down enough after that for me to get some sleep, although Harvey is in at 6 a.m. mewling, despite my putting him into the kitchen and locking the door the night before. Either he's a feline Houdini or Chloe has been on the search for midnight snacks and forgotten to close the door. By six-thirty, I'm drinking tea and compiling a small list of reasons to murder my daughter. Out of the window, I spot Brian on the first of endless trips up and down the drive to the car, and give him a wave. I want to persuade him to write the review for the cottage. To achieve Superhost I need a run of Five-Star reviews, and given the walkers are prime miseries and don't look like they'd give anything in life one star, I'm hoping he'll help.

I pop outside and say cheerfully, 'Good morning, Brian. How did you all sleep?'

'Joanna slept on the sofa-bed, she was dead to the

world when I came past her at six, so I think she slept well. I was in with Catherine who was tossing and turning and moaning about her ankle, or was it her back all night? As for Lydia, she was up not long after me complaining about sleeping longer than normal.'

'Well, sleeping longer than normal has to be a good thing, I think, don't you? Super-comfy bed. Lovely bedding. Peaceful surroundings.'

'Yes, Janet. You're right. Peaceful surroundings and lovely bedding.'

'Worth a Five-Star review, Brian?'

'I er . . .'

'I'd *really* appreciate it.'

He smiles. 'Whatever you say, Janet.'

Result. But, oh gosh. Now I feel like *I'm* bossing Brian about.

When Brian has the car packed, he approaches the patio with a little knock and presses an envelope into my hand.

'Cash one hundred and twenty – that right, yes?'

'Perfect, thanks.'

'You've got a lovely place here.'

'Thanks, Brian. Five-Star review lovely?'

This time, he laughs. 'You don't give up, do you? Yes, Lavander Cottage is definitely worth five stars.'

'Great. Will you write the review, Brian?'

'Er . . .'

'You see, I'm going for Superhost, so every review needs to have five stars. It would mean a lot.'

'Very well. I'll mention it to the girls.'

My heart sinks. That's that review down the pan. I'll be lucky to get two stars from that parade of gloom merchants.

'Do you know, I could stay here for a week,' Brian says dreamily, looking around.

'On your own?' It just pops out. I didn't mean to actually *say* it. What a faux pas. I can hardly look him in the eye.

He does a big sigh and tells me, 'They're pain in the arses, Janet, but they're my pain in the arses.' He then gives a rueful shrug and disappears again into the cottage.

I get it. It doesn't do to judge people you don't know, their quirks, their grumpy ways; that's basically how we all feel about family. On cue, our bathroom window opens and a chain of smoke circles drifts out of it. I have an absolute ban on smoking in the house. Mitzi knows how much it annoys me.

I shout up, 'Outside, please, Mitzi – if you have to smoke.'

'Sorry, Mum.' The lit cigarette comes flying out, almost hitting me, as the bathroom window is slammed shut.

MUM! *Chloe?* My hair stands on end. *Smoking.* It's disgusting, so unhealthy. What is she thinking? I'm raging with disappointment. The lit cigarette, like a torment, continues to smoulder at my feet and a snake of smoke peels up and hits my nostrils. It must be the lack of sleep that makes me do it, but I'm jumping up and down, stamping on the cigarette as the cottage door opens and out lurch the walkers.

They limp, hobble and drag themselves down the drive, and Brian has his arm supporting one of them. *How far did they actually walk?* You'd think they'd done back-to-back marathons, the way she's milking it. The youngest one is a bit more energetic; she's oblivious to everything, scrolling through her phone – looking for vegan sushi, no doubt. The sun breaks through the clouds and it's the perfect weather for a walk, though I wouldn't dare suggest it, and none of them seem inclined to notice.

I give them a wave off and Brian is the only one who responds in kind. Bye bye, misery chops. As they drive away I can hear the distant whirr of mechanical diggers and angry voices coming from Laura's property. I've got that red velvet cake in the oven I plan to take down to her. I curl my fingers around the brown envelope of lovely cash and contemplate what it might buy: the week's shopping, a trip to Gordon Riggs for a plant or two – but let's face it, it's basically money for Chloe's cig habit. *Eurgh.* She needs to get a job. *Today!*

I insist she helps me turn the cottage around. It's a bloody tip. There are muddy boot-prints everywhere, every sheet, towel and pillow-case has been used, there's shampoo all over the shower and the toilet needs a bleach. They've left two grotty gaiters under one of the beds and another odd woolly sock to add to my pile for the chuck. The take-out boxes are a mixture of fish and chips, Chinese and pizza, so they must have been walking and waiting for hours, tramping round Hebden collecting these. All the leaflets with details of delivery services are spread across the table too. Strange folk.

Chloe adds to the hard work, needing instruction every five minutes, whatever the task. I can't help nobbling her about her smoking.

'It's a one-off social thing. I'm a social smoker.'

'Is that right? Yet you're smoking in the bathroom, on your own, in the morning. Which bit of that event is social?'

'Mum! It's leftovers from the night before.'

'You were home last night.'

'When I was being *social* last night. Anyway, I was practising smoke circles, that's all.' She grins. 'They

47

look cool, you must admit.'

'No. They look grubby and they smell awful. Smoking is a killer, there's nothing cool about it.'

I'm struggling to find ways to reason with her as I mop down the stairs into the kitchen. Chloe is half-heartedly wiping round when she opens the fridge and pulls out a large unopened bar of Milk Chocolate. My heart does a little leap. I go to take it from her, but she pulls it out of my reach.

'No, Mum. You can't have this. Sugar is the silent killer. If I give you this chocolate it is the equivalent of passive smoking three cigarettes.'

She gloats, a big smile on her face. Pay-back time. I grit my teeth while attempting to appear unruffled, though my desire to rip the foil off the bar and demolish it whole is acute.

'That's fine, Chloe. I'm on a diet anyway.'

'Since when? You were eating madeira cake last night.'

'Are you going to finish wiping so I can get on with mopping?'

She smirks at me in an infuriating way, as if she's won or something, and I have an urge to push the dirty mop into her face. I'm not proud of myself. I take the mop bucket outside and pour the grim brown slush down the drain, my hopes for Superhost and Super-mum disappearing down the drain along with the dregs.

REVIEW

*** Three Stars

Clean. Only 1 bathroom for four people is hard work though. Quiet. The walk into Hebden is more like 25 minutes than 15.

TIP FOR RUNNING A B&B

Some guests are miserable and like it that way. It can be hard if you're a people-pleaser. You have to let them get on with it.

TIPS ON LIFE

If you are planning to go walking, maybe decide if you actually *like* walking first. Check the weather, as walks can be miserable in the rain.

Get yourself a Brian.

Patience is a virtue. If anyone has any going spare, could they please send me some via Lavander Cottage, Hebden Bridge. I'll pay for the postage.

CHAPTER 4

The Translator

W ake up with horrible feeling I might be falling for Miles. I'm looking at my phone all the time waiting for his call or a text. It's getting on my nerves. We've not seen each other in work this week and he hasn't been in touch. One minute he's all over me like a rash, next minute I'm dropped like a stone. I don't like it. I've obviously been too easy and this is my punishment. I begin unpicking what we last said, what we last did, what were our last moments. I can't even remember them all that well, to be honest, because it's been so busy at Valley Dental. I suppose I'll have to bump into him in work at some point.

I'm a trained receptionist, I remind myself, and I could always leave Valley Dental. There are lots of other reception jobs in the world if that's what I need to do. So I instigate a plan: the next time I start obsessing about Miles, I shall put on *The Archers Omnibus* and start scrolling through planting designs on Pinterest or looking at other self-catering cottages in Yorkshire. Works a treat.

A lovely woman called Sumi, her husband and three small children are in Lavander Cottage for a week whilst he is here translating for a case at the local crown court.

'We may need to extend if the case goes on,' they told me.

I'm secretly praying the case will go on for weeks. I'm seriously rocked by the mean Three-Star review from the bloody walkers. In their heads that will be generous I'm sure, but for me it puts Superhost out of reach. There's not many bookings for this year yet and the spreadsheet has way too many red numbers, while the bills under the egg-hen are growing.

Sumi asks me for places to take the children and I suggest Eureka! The National Children's Museum in Halifax. It has exhibits to suit all the ages and once you've paid entrance you can return free all week. I think getting them out is the best idea, as the kids all seem a bit on the hyperactive scale. Watching them race around the garden this morning I was on pins as they pulled at the decorative flower heads I'd left for structure through winter. Then they gleefully trampled on all the bulbs shyly peeping out of the ground as if they were engaged in an enthusiastic game of Whack-a-Bulb. I was glad when Sumi came out and called them in, as I was very close to having a go at them. I'm feeling wound up regularly at the moment, even with the HRT. It might be the building work, as the house is lathered in dust. I was on the landing this morning, watching as Carl, having ditched the old pull-down ladder and replaced it with a big metal builder's stepladder, climbed up into the attic. I heard him moving around, then he shouted down to me, 'Did you know there's a cupboard up here with an old boiler inside? That will have to come out.'

'No,' I shout back. 'Or if I did know when we bought the house, I've forgotten.' I've always tried to spend as little time as possible up in the attic. It's got a light switch, but I've never liked climbing up and down the pull-down ladder. The new temporary stepladder looks even more precarious.

'Don't worry, Janet, I'll sort it. I know what to do, I'm not an idiot. Not like Frank, haha. Right, I'm coming down.'

At this precise moment he drops his phone, which comes flying out of the hatch, followed in quick succession by both legs, knocking over the stepladder. His legs are now flailing around in mid-air. Presumably his elbows are wedging his body from collapsing all the way through – well, that and his size, as he's no lightweight, put it that way. Having quickly retrieved the stepladder, I guide his feet to the top step, then excuse myself so as not to laugh too loudly. It's the only laugh of the day, unfortunately.

Mitzi has turned into a project manager; she's waltzing around in trouser suits and low-cut blouses and is arguing with suppliers about every screw, every scrap of wood, every hinge, every bit of skirting, the paint and silicone tubing. I feel like I'm living every moment of this project with her.

Meanwhile, Chloe has got herself a job waitressing at a restaurant in town, *thank God*. She's only just getting used to working life and when she comes in she's in a mood and flings herself about the house.

'I'm absolutely exhausted, that was a full eight hours of work. *And* I had to get home and get there as well. I'm on my feet all the time. Plus, I had to be nice to people I don't know, *and* get on with the other members of staff that are all cliquey idiots. *And* I'll have to do the same again next week.'

I keep my mouth closed and my face expressionless to try very hard not to be judgmental or share a thought about this in any way. The thing with Chloe being a server, I've noticed, is that it's then *my* job to wait on her and clean up after her, endlessly. She's suddenly getting into cooking, so the kitchen is a permanent bombsite. It doesn't matter how tidy I leave it, it will soon turn into a collection of dirty cups, pans, knives, chopping boards, cake tins, Tupperware containers . . . you get the picture. What is nice is that I get endless shared photos of her cooking creations sent to my phone, and quite often I come home from work and a meal is ready. My daughter is a great cook – it's just she's messy as hell and I miss my kitchen. My quiet stir after a stressful day.

Oh well. It's going to take a bit more than a stir to tackle the stresses at the moment. The electricity bill has come in and I owe two thousand pounds. *Two thousand pounds?* I can't make head nor tail of it. I've gone round checking everyone's room for electric heaters. I'll have to spread the payment, of course, but across the year? 'How about ten years?' I suggest to the utility guy, but there's no reaction coming back down the phone.

What with fuel costs going up, there's the Council Tax increase and the food prices are through the roof. Worst of all, my fixed-rate mortgage comes to an end this year and I'm dreading what it's going to go up to. I'm getting scared to open a bill at the moment. Every brown envelope feels like a loaded threat and I'm demolishing Jaffa Cakes at a ridiculous rate. I have to face it and ask for help.

After I hear Carl go out and Mitzi gets off the phone I brace myself and grab my moment.

'Mitzi, can I have a word, please?'

'Bathroom World are checking for copper mixer taps, they might ring me back at any time.'

But I'm on a mission. 'Well,' I reply, 'we can stop talking when they do.'

'Go on then, what is it?'

'Mitzi, I'm really struggling with bills. I've got a

two-thousand-pound electricity bill and I'm piling up credit-card bills and the cottage isn't really busy enough to cover everything, and what with food prices and sorting Chloe out and being only part-time at Valley Dental, I'm getting really worried and,' *go for it, Janet,* 'I need some rent.'

'But we're building you a new bathroom.'

'I know you are, and I'm very grateful, but I can live without your attic bedroom having a bathroom. I can't live without rent.'

'Well, we can't. It's a nightmare when Chloe goes in there for hours and we're all busting. Carl's using the drain round the back as an ensuite.'

Charming! 'I know it's not ideal, but we've coped so far and we'll have to continue to cope because, Mitzi, and I'm deadly serious here, *I need some help with the bills.*'

'Well, this really screws up our plans, Janet.' And she stomps out, her heels clickety – clacking.

There's £124,000 left on the mortgage. It's such a lot. I'll never get there, not on my wages, not with these bills. I might need to take a payment holiday, for like . . . *forever*.

As I leave the house to go to work, we see each other in the kitchen. My sister has a face like a slapped arse. I've really annoyed her, I know. *But what can I do?* She needs to contribute: I've carried her for far too long. It's always been the way with Mitzi and me, she's always taken advantage of my soft nature. Whenever I'm about to lose my rag she'll always find something to trump things, like a bit of cash or a new job or a promise of something. The truth is, I've always been scared for Mitzi. She was homeless for a while after Uni, it was hideous to listen to her talking about the shelters and how close she was to danger all the time. I persuaded her to sofa surf with us, only that little bit of time has turned into . . . well, for ever. As for Carl, he's just sorting himself out from the divorce. His occasional night here has definitely expanded into most of the time, and once he's done the work on the attic, which has to be worth a few thousand pounds in kind, I know he'll be happy to contribute.

It's a miserable gloomer of a day and as I'm wandering through Hebden I notice there's loads of graffiti everywhere. It's so disfiguring, it ruins things. I wish there was an easy way to get rid of it. I'm walking past the third lot when I take time to actually read it, and realise it's obviously all written by the same person.

Squat the Airbnbs

I read it and it's like my brain needs a moment to take it in. It's a punch in the gut. My heartbeat runs up by about a hundred beats a minute. I go red. I feel insulted, *personally*. After all the effort and the aggro of getting my garage done. Why? Why are people so mean? So ungenerous? What have I ever done to them? I try to make a little bit of extra cash, cash that I've worked hard for and put myself out to achieve – all that time and effort to earn that tiny bit extra. At the moment, I'm putting up a translator and their crazy kids – where are they supposed to stay?

I'm fuming. I go into work and I'm brooding on it like mad. I make a mess of two appointments and knock over the Oral B toothbrush display Tony spends hours arranging in the back-lit glass cabinet. This is not a good day. I'm packing up when Miles appears in reception. He has had a haircut and is showing a bit of stubble, and I hate to say it but he looks very good.

'Where have *you* been hiding?' he says grumpily.

'I was going to ask you the same thing.'

'Fancy a drink?'

'I fancy two.'

Miles laughs. 'Let me get changed, five minutes.'

I'm feeling weak. I'm feeling down. I'm feeling alone. So when, a whole hour later after those two drinks, Miles suggests going back into the building to do some extra hours training, I go willingly. I'm grateful for the distraction, and though there's a part of me that thinks I'm being easy and this doesn't feel like the healthiest thing I've ever done, I don't really care. I'm enjoying the attention and God knows I need some fun.

After the 'training' session, he offers to give me a lift home but I want the chance for fresh air, so tramp along the cycle path getting wet through from the mist. Miles is texting me with his favourite poem about clocks for some reason and I'm half-reading it when I spot another *Squat the Airbnbs* graffiti on the wooden lamppost. I look around to see if there's anyone close by, and no one is. So, feeling reckless from the drinks and the training, I take a biro out of my bag and pull myself up onto a wobbly bit of fence. Balanced with one leg on the fence and one arm wrapped around the lamppost, I dig into the wood and scrawl:

Get a bloody job

It's pathetic, I know, and it doesn't address the issue. Miles recently and very eloquently explained the pressure second homes are having on locals who are trying to get on the property ladder – hence the frustration with Airbnbs. But so bloody what, I think tipsily.

'Mine's my garage,' I tell the graffiti. 'It's never even been a home, in fact it's still part of my home and I'm sharing it with even more people, bringing money into the town. Surely that's increasing the dwellings in the area, which is a good thing?'

I secretly think it's a lot of jealousy. Hebden is full of people who say they hate the state but don't mind living off it. Not that that opinion would go down well anywhere, not least in my house with Mitzi for a sister. I'm admiring my handiwork with the biro in my hand, back on the ground, when a figure appears out of the mist. It's a wretched-looking Laura Watson being dragged along by her dog.

'What are you doing, Janet?'

Oh God, rumbled – and by Laura. 'I'm er . . . just looking at this lamppost.'

'Have you just put *Get a bloody job*?'

'No.'

'Janet?' She is actually smiling.

'Possibly.'

'You like having your little B&B, don't you, Janet? Remember, you inspired me. It's not your fault, but at the moment, I don't think I'll even have a house by the end of this fiasco.'

Her voice gets tearful and I go to give her a hug but she puts her hand up.

'No, no. Don't encourage me. I'm a mess. I ate all your cake, Janet. All of it. Do you know how many calories there are in a complete red velvet gateau? I'll have to starve myself for a few days now. Again, not your fault. Planning are coming round next week. From the council. I may lose my house. There we go. Again, *not your fault*. I'm taking all other calories in through wine.'

Despite her past sneaky actions of trying to crush me and close me down in several devious ways when I first started up with Lavander Cottage, I can't help but feel sorry for her. I want to find a way to help.

'Y'know, maybe you should get Carl to come and sort it out,' I suggest rashly. 'He will know what needs doing. He's a very good builder is Carl, Laura. If anyone can do it, he can. Plus he knows the lad you've used, so he might be able to come to an arrangement about money, I don't know.'

'Do you really think he would do that . . . come to an arrangement? What sort of thing?'

I've said it now. What was I thinking? I try to backpedal somewhat.

'Well, obviously I can't speak for him, Laura, but this lad Frank is sure to want to put things right – it's his reputation at stake, after all. And Carl might be willing to help you both out and maybe they can agree to off-set labour on another job or . . .'

Shut up, Janet, I urge myself. You don't know a thing about what Carl will or might do. What about the improvements to your house if he does help Laura? Stop your mouth running away with itself, engage brain!

'I don't know what Carl would charge, of course,' I manage feebly. 'That's up to him.'

What on earth am I getting myself into here?

'Oh, I see, some sort of a *quid pro quo* arrangement. So I might get my B&B after all?' She is considerably cheered up, whilst I am feeling a tsunami of sheer dread.

I give her a weak, 'Yes.'

'Give me that.' She grabs the biro off me and heaves herself up onto the wobbly fence. Under *Squat the Airbnbs* she grinds something into the wood – I can't see it until she jumps back down.

'Wow. O-*kay*.' I look at her: she's wearing the ferocious expression of a wildcat. I wouldn't want to mess with her. Her message says:

Just you effin try

At that moment, two walkers come into sight and stroll past looking suspiciously at us. Laura hands me the incriminating biro.

'Thanks, Janet, good chatting to you. Excellent suggestion re Carl. I'm going to call him,' and she sets off running with her dog.

After one last look at the lamppost, and a slightly raucous chuckle, I plod on. And when a wave of anxiety floods through me, I know what it is: a delayed case of Big Gob.

Chloe has sent me a pic of a lemon drizzle cake she's made, which is lovely, and Carl's van is in the drive so he's probably working in the attic. I sigh at the prospect of drifts of plaster dust and baking paraphernalia that I'm going to have to clean up.

Miles texts me.

Would you like to go for a cycle at the weekend? Don't worry, we won't risk the rusty wheeler. I've got a spare bike. XXX

I've no reason to refuse so I send him the thumb-up emoji. Though quite what it might involve has me really giving it the thumb down. I reckon ten miles is my absolute maximum. But I'm glad it's something over and above a shag, a thing to do together beyond the bedroom. Maybe there's reason to be hopeful about Miles.

I open the front door to find the house is a blare of noise. There's electric saws, vacuuming, hammering and loud music blasting out of the kitchen. I feel like going back outside. When I pluck up the courage to go into the kitchen, Chloe is pulling a lasagne out of the oven, and to my surprise the kitchen is in a very reasonable state. Mitzi wanders in and she's wearing overalls. Her hair is up and covered in plaster dust, giving her a wise old witchy look.

'Come and see,' she instructs me.

I clamber gingerly up the builder's ladder to the hatch, where Carl helps me up inside. It's astonishing. The floor is boarded out and there are two metal lintels supporting the roof, leaving enough space to comfortably stand up. Mitzi climbs up after me and points out the drawn outlines on the floor where a loo, a bath and a shower and a sink will be.

'A bath?'

'If we can support it.'

'Wow.'

'We'll punch a hole through Wednesday when the weather's good and put in two Velux rooflights.'

'Right.' I'm almost speechless. 'How will you get a bath up here?'

'We'll make the hatch bigger. We'll have to anyway as we've got to build a proper staircase up from the landing.'

'I'm impressed.' And that's true. How could I not be? It's incredible.

Later, back downstairs, I'm sitting over dinner just revelling for a moment in the changes afoot in my life. I'm eating a delicious meal I haven't cooked. I'm getting a new loft conversion I'm not paying for. It's all a bit much really. I'll manage those bills somehow, I decide. I'll keep things ticking over, I'll use the cottage cash to pay this month's credit cards, and if I swap credit cards and move some stuff onto the zero interest one, all will be well . . .

I'm working it out in my head when there's a knock on the patio door. It's Sumi, looking agitated.

I open the door to her, saying, 'Hi, is everything all right?'

'Well, yes and no. Can you come round? Sorry, you're eating.'

I was, but now I'm speculating. What can be up?

I tell her, 'I'll finish and come round.' I go back to the table and scoop another portion of lasagne onto my plate as Chloe raises an eyebrow.

'I was going to freeze that for another meal.'

'Yeah, not today though, eh?'

I eat at record speed, risking indigestion. I have to know what's going on. I knock on the door of Lavander Cottage. It quickly opens, and as it does so, a solid yellow pool ball whistles past my ear and out into the garden.

'Come in, come in.'

It's chaos. The kids are racing around the main entrance bit where I've put a pool table I got on eBay. They manically chase around and under it, throwing everything and anything they can reach at each other: pool balls, chalk, shoes, clothes, towels. Sumi seems oblivious as she heads into the kitchen and puts the kettle on. I see that prawn crackers are scattered everywhere, a carpet of crunch. I'm attempting to hide my horror at the state of the place. The doors slam and I wince, that one has a glass panel. Now it's open again, now it's closed again, smashed against the wall, the handle chipping into the plaster with the force of the slam.

The three boys pile into the kitchen then start chasing each other around the table in here, one windmilling with his arm scattering all the magazines and leaflets, No Smoking signs and air fresheners onto the floor. Nothing from Sumi. *Nothing.* I'm given a weak tea I didn't want and politely slurp at it whilst trying to distract myself from thoughts of the pain of the clean-up I'm facing around me.

'The case has been abandoned. We would like to go

back home, if that's OK with you, so only two nights not six?'

'Right, yes of course, no problem.' Bloody hell. I'd got the cottage blocked out for a week, and now there's no one going to be in it. A pool ball whizzes past me again. I can't stand it.

'Be careful with these pool balls, lads, they're very heavy. Back on the table, please.'

Another bounces across the floor.

'Pick them up.' At last Sumi summons up some parenting, but it's so feeble they take zero notice.

Two, three more pool balls are now bouncing around the kitchen floor, smashing the prawn crackers into smithereens. I get down on the floor and pick them up.

'So when do you want to leave?' I ask, wishing it was right now.

'Tomorrow morning, early. We need to get back now.'

'I see.' It doesn't give them much time to tidy up, is all I can think.

'Give it back.' The smallest of the little crushing crew wanders up to me and holds out his hands for the balls. I refuse.

'No. They're not for bouncing on the floor, they're for the table only.' I'm holding five of them in my hands.

'Do we cancel through the site, or are you able to refund?'

'Oh no, you'll have to cancel through the site.'

With less money than I was planning for, this is going to be spreadsheet hell. I'm slowly reversing out of the place, pool balls in hand, when *boing!!* I register a pain on my forehead. I have collided with a pool ball thrown at head height. It hurts like buggery and I stagger from the force of it.

'Sorry.'

Sumi yanks the arm of the youngest and throws him into the kitchen, closing the door on him. The other two scream with laughter at his plight. I stagger out of there, almost slip on the other pool ball resting on the patio, and manage to get back into my own kitchen. I collapse on a chair, letting all the pool balls roll onto the kitchen table where they come to rest between the dirty plates, the empty lasagne dish and the jug of water.

Mitzi wanders through smelling fragrant, long spirals of wet hair down her back, in a matching silk nightie and flowing Chinese-style dressing gown. She pulls some cash out of her pocket.

'Fifty pounds a week until we're done?' She slips it under the water jug.

I'm in a daze from pain; the rent doesn't seem to matter any more. Mitzi grabs a bottle from somewhere and disappears with two glasses.

I tentatively touch my forehead. 'Ow.'

Mitzi reverses back into the room. 'Was that an ow?'

I point at my forehead. 'A pool ball hit my head.'

'Who did that? The little gits in the cottage?'

'Hmm.'

'Let Dr Mitzi take a look.'

'Could you get me some paracetamol?' The low hum of pain like a wave grows on me.

Minutes later, Chloe is down rubbing butter on the bump. I try to explain to her that we tried this in the old days for burns and suchlike, and it never worked, but it's a TikTok medicinal theory now so it looks like we never learn. The washing-up is done around me, someone runs me a bath. I wake up, still in it and freezing cold, an hour later, Chloe knocking on the door.

'You're not dead in there, are you?'

'No, I just fell asleep.'

'Mum! You shouldn't go to sleep after a bump.'

'Too late now, I'm awake.'

My daughter tuts loudly and I hear her stomping away as if I'm deliberately not looking after myself. I reflect that my cold bath probably won't do me any harm – Wim Hoff has made a fortune doing ice baths. I am relieved when I wake up early the next morning. There is a sore, apple-shaped bruise on my forehead, and I hit the Ibuprofen for a change of painkiller.

The translators have gone by the time I'm up and dressed. I brace myself for the anticipated mess. It's bad. There's a crack in the glass pane of the kitchen door, the wall is chipped from the slams it has had. I notice a faint felt-tip line around the entire perimeter of the wall, but the prawn crackers have been swept up and an attempt has been made to swipe around the kitchen surfaces. Carl sticks Sellotape over the cracked pane, he reckons that will hold it, whilst I fill and sand the hole in the wall. The only bonus is that I get a lovely review from Sumi on every site imaginable. Chloe is adamant we should slag her off in return, but I can't summon up the nastiness. Even with a multicoloured forehead as reminder.

Bloody kids.

REVIEW

***** Five Stars

Amazing cottage, lovely host, great location, *sooo* clean!

TIPS FOR RUNNING A B&B

Reflect on how big your place is going to be. Do you want to attract families? Children are lovely, but I've yet to meet a tidy one.

TIPS ON EVERYTHING ELSE

Watch after-work drinking. It makes you do stuff you wouldn't do sober.

Avoid flying pool balls.

FYI butter doesn't help a bump.

CHAPTER 5

The Hot Boys

Six of the fittest young men we have ever had in the cottage are staying for a week of training before a huge overnight fell race at the weekend. They are up and out at all hours, stretching, jumping, running up and down the lane doing 'intervals', timing each other, goading each other.

If I've ever wondered what it would be like to have sons or quadruplets this, I imagine, is a bit like it. They're always bringing me into conversations when I'm in the garden or putting out the recycling; they start arguing about something and want me to offer a thought. It's that type of thing. They're loud, fractious and *so* competitive. Mitzi does her best to restrain herself until Carl disappears in a morning and then she is out there in her Lycra gear doing outdoor yoga . . . as if any of these twenty-somethings want to see a forty-plus woman doing Downward Dog.

That is very judgy, Janet – she's gorgeous, is my sister, and I'm sure they love it. I'm definitely not into them in that way. To me, they're boys and they bring out the mother in me, not the cougar. OK, out of the corner of my eye I can spot the odd good bicep curl, but I'm not going to stare. Plus, what would we have in common? Fitness, I've realised over the years, is something I admire, but it's like a foreign country to me. I've arrived at the port but never had the time or the money or the inclination to catch the ferry.

Here's my personal fitness regime: I can manage Zumba once a fortnight if the weather's all right and Chloe's had her tea and Harvey the cat doesn't need defleaing. I cycle a mile down the road to work when the weather's decent. That sort of thing. It's pretty much the bare minimum. So though Miles has kindly organised to bring a bike to the house for me, I can't help but feel nervous about what he's expecting from me today on our cycle ride. It's officially winter, for goodness sake: who does fitness outdoors in these temperatures?

Miles arrives exactly on time. He seems a little bit rattled to find me laughing with one of the lads about the latter's hairy calves. They really are the hairiest I've ever seen. He is the loveliest of the lot, called Reiss. He's twenty-four and as he explains he has no hair on his chest, I make a little joke.

'It's travelled down with all the running.'

He is laughing at this as Miles wrestles uncomfortably with the bike rack.

'All right, mate?' Reiss asks in a friendly manner.

Miles nods, but it's on the rude side and I cringe a bit. He turns to me, says curtly, 'Are you ready?'

I mean, clearly I'm not, since I'm still in my dressing gown. 'Not unless we're going in pjs?' I say. 'Give me five minutes.'

A grin from Reiss, barely an acknowledgement from moody Miles.

I squeeze myself into leggings I haven't worn for quite a while. The fact they say *Zumba Lite* on them pegs them to at least ten years ago. An old Benetton T-shirt goes on top. I don't need a sweater or tracksuit top. It was a frosty start this morning, but once I get moving on that bike I know I'll be too hot. I overheat very easily. I hope Miles hasn't planned a route with lots of hills. I dig out a luminous yellow wind-catcher thing and a pair of knitted gloves. It's not a very coordinated cycling outfit but then I'm not a very coordinated cyclist.

Gulp. I'll have to do.

'Are you wearing a pair of cycle shorts under those?' It's Miles, looking disapproving.

The idea that anything could fit under these gives me the giggles.

'No, Miles, I don't have any and I'm not sure I could fit anything under these. They're a bit tight.' I smile, he doesn't return it.

'We're doing twenty miles, you'll need something.'

I don't like this. Miles is being stern and it's rather intimidating.

Reiss, who is doing press-ups in the background, turns to us in a perfect side plank, 'I've got some cycle shorts you can borrow, Janet.' He returns moments later with a large pair of red knickers with a giant padded bum.

'God, they're hideous.' Mitzi is hovering in Tree pose.

'It doesn't matter, she'll need them.' Grumpy Miles again.

The way he is behaving suggests this cycle trip is taking a serious turn. Meanwhile I pack a couple of Kit-Kats, a flask of tea and two packets of Seabrook Ready Salted crisps into a little rucksack. I go into the living room and peel off the leggings and slide on the cycle knickers. Getting the leggings back on is quite a feat. I notice Mitzi walk past and call out for help.

'Give me a hand.'

She takes one look. 'Haven't you any others?'

'No.'

'Any that actually fit? What size are they – zero?'

I feel quite proud that I once squeezed into an eight. The fact they don't actually fit is not the point. Maureen returns with a pair of leggings that I can actually pull on, and though they're not perfect they do actually go over my tummy *and* the cycle knickers so they are much better. The cycle knickers are so strange; they turn walking into a Wild West cowboy-style experience, putting a gap between my thighs I haven't had for years. I pull on my wind-catcher jacket to try to disguise everything and go back out into the garden. Miles is engaged in a press-up challenge with Reiss, with the other lads shouting them on and Chloe filming it on her iPhone.

Mitzi lights up a fag. 'I hope he has got life insurance and hasn't got a dicky heart. He's at a funny age, Janet.'

Miles *is* becoming very red in the face and I decide I need to get him out of there.

'Oh Miles, come on. What time are we setting off? I thought we had to get going if we want to be back for that thing?'

'*That* thing?' Mitzi raises an eyebrow.

Miles takes the lifebelt I throw him and collapses onto the ground whilst Reiss continues to finger-press himself up into a plank, to the roar of the lads and the coos of Chloe.

Fifteen minutes later Miles and I, seats adjusted, gloves on, helmet on, brakes tested, are on the road. It's a bright winter's day which is lovely, if a bit blinding, and it isn't long before I'm hoofing like a good 'un, attempting to keep up with the dot on the horizon that is the rapidly vanishing figure of Miles. I catch up with him eventually and find him sitting at the side of the road looking at his phone.

'Sorry,' I gasp, and know I'm bright red in the face. 'I can't keep up. It might be easier to say where we're going and I'll meet you there.'

'No, it's no bother, I'll slow down the pace. Right, let's get going.'

Miles's slow pace and my fastest ever pace are so far distant from one another that it's embarrassing. I'm going full whack and I'm *waaay* behind him. At one point I even get off and push the bike up a really steep hill and only catch him up on the downhill ride, when my weight against his skin and bone gives me much-needed extra momentum. As predicted, I'm so hot by now that I've taken the wind-catcher off and wrapped it around my waist. I've taken my gloves off too, and they are in the pocket of the wind-catcher. If I could take off my top and travel in my bra without causing a major pile-up, I would.

The road is so busy and the cars are so fast and so close it's terrifying. I'm concentrating on avoiding the pot-holes when I notice that Miles has veered off the road into a pub car park. *Thank God.*

'Hurrah, are we done?' I've got just enough breath for the following words: 'I could kill for some chips.'

'We're not even halfway there yet, Janet.'

My heart drops to my boots and suddenly every-thing starts to hurt, my bum, my wrists, my head itches, my legs are shaky. I take off my helmet.

'I think I need a sit-down.'

'We've been sat down for the last hour.' Miles seems determined to be unpleasant.

Something kicks in. Annoyance. This isn't a nice romantic ride, this is a bloody endurance test and I don't remember signing up for it. I face him, my hands on my hips above the strange knickers.

'Well, Miles, I'm going to go inside that pub, get a drink and order some chips and relax for half an hour.'

'*Half an hour?* That means we won't make Brighouse for one o'clock!'

'No. *We* won't but *you* will. I can't keep up, Miles. These are horrible roads to ride, the drivers are all way too close and fast. You're travelling at ten times my speed and I don't want to hold you back. You carry on and I'll see you later.'

'I'm not going to leave you.'

'You're not, *I'm* leaving *you*. Go get your time in. I've come easily far enough if I've to turn around and get home again. Read my lips, Miles: I'm done.'

I'm resolute. Miles looks unsure, but I push the bike against the picnic table, go inside the pub, order half a lager and some chips and when I come back outside Miles has gone. I'm glad. I don't like feeling that I'm holding someone back. I eat my chips slowly, savouring every salty mouthful. I slurp my lager and try to work out where I am on Google Maps. My backside is sore and my thighs feel chafed as I eventually summon all my courage, mount my steed and wobble off.

I take the first road off the main road that I can and slowly pick my way down onto much quieter lanes. I get off and push a couple of times where it gets a bit hilly and eventually I find the canal. It's not as if it's all that peaceful, with walkers and prams and dogs and the Canadian Goose population terrorising me at every opportunity. Though there are moments where it's just me and the absolute quiet and the turn of the wheels, the trees reflected on the water and the odd floating duck. I forget about my bum hurting and my legs straining and my wrists stiffening, and it's bliss.

Then the rain hits. Didn't he check the bloody weather? It's an absolute deluge. I'm getting battered by machine-gun-like drops, I can barely see where I'm going and my fingers are numb with cold. My windcatcher is now stuck to me like a drenched second skin – nothing, absolutely nothing, is waterproof. My trainers squelch, rain runs down my face as if I'm being sprayed with a hosepipe. It's horrible. I'm frozen stiff. There's nowhere to shelter on the canal so I dig in and plough my way home, almost hysterical with gratitude when a familiar landmarks pop up. Slowly, slowly, I drag my weary self and the bike onto the drive. The patio door opens and out pops Miles.

'Shall I put the kettle on?'

I try to hold myself together. 'Can do,' I manage, resisting the urge to throw his stupid bike as far as I can.

I stumble exhausted into the house where Mitzi is gliding around in a floor-length purple dress with a purple-plaited bodice and matching purple-plaited headpiece, and she's chanting whilst holding what looks like a smoking wooden frog. Her chanting increases in volume over the noise of the kettle. I'm defeated and peed off and tired and wet and cold. I'm not by any stretch of the imagination my best self.

'Bloody hell, give it a rest, Mitz.'

She gives me an iron stare. 'I'm tuning into my shaman self.'

What the heck is that? Later, much later, I look it up in the Collins Dictionary, where it explains: *shamanism is a religion which is based on the belief that the world is controlled by good and evil spirits, and that these spirits can be directed by people with special powers.* The shamans, no doubt.

But at that low point in my day, all I can say is a narked: 'Do you have to do it in the kitchen?'

'I've nowhere else, Janet, not whilst the building work is being done. According to the new census, shamanism is the fastest-growing religion in the UK and I, Janet, have done three weekends down at that camp in Surrey studying shamanic ritual. I might possibly be an expert. Oh, and Carl's here. He wants to speak to you about—'

'Give me a minute, can you,' I interrupt. 'I'm piss wet through here.'

'Er . . . Janet.' Miles is trying to say something but I ignore him.

I couldn't give a monkey's, I'm past caring. I pull off my trainers, strip off my gloves, drag off my socks, wrestle with my T-shirt and wriggle out of my leggings. I chuck everything on a pile and am standing dripping in wet soggy bra and cycle knickers, my hair plastered across my face, when Carl enters the kitchen with Oliver and Laura Watson in tow.

'Ah Janet,' he says, 'Laura here needs a word.'

Never, I swear, has a moment lasted for so agonisingly long. Chloe saves the day. She pushes through them, takes one look at me and says, 'Fuck's sake, Mum, go and get changed.'

I reach out for the tea-towel hanging over the kitchen chair and hold it in front of me, and I can't decide which bit of me to try to cover up. I'm shuffling sidewards out of the room when the patio door opens and Reiss and his mates put their head through.

'Wish us luck.'

Everyone is grateful for the excuse to look anywhere but at me. There are lots of 'Good lucks!' and 'Best wishes!' when, I've no idea what possesses me, I shout out, 'Good luck!' and I wave the tea towel like a banner, revealing all.

'You can keep those pants, Janet,' says Reiss with a wink. It is at this point I drop the tea-towel and run.

Twenty minutes later I'm dried off after a hot shower,

wrapped up in my woolliest cardigan and rocking a pair of Chloe's sweat pants. I'm sitting in the front room, drinking a huge mug of hot chocolate, topped with cream, a chocolate flake and some hundreds and thousands courtesy of Chloe, and I'm listening in shock to what Laura Watson is telling me, in between bouts of weeping.

'They're saying your house is not safe?'

'Yes, Janet, not just the extension, the whole bloody house.'

I've no idea what to say. Oliver pats her gently on the shoulder but she shrugs him off with a blast of contempt.

'I *told* you not to use him. Didn't I? Didn't I? "Twenty grand less," that's what you said. "Twenty grand less." I said he was very young and I didn't like the look of him. You totally ignored me, refused to listen to me. And look where we are now!'

Oliver sighs. 'Not this again, Laura. This gets us nowhere. We don't need to do this again and definitely not in front of Janet.'

'But it's your bloody fault. We'll have to strip out all our savings, fund the build ourselves whilst we wait for the bastard insurance to come through, all because of you and your tight penny-pinching.' She takes a deep breath, turns to me. 'Janet, could we stay in Lavander Cottage whilst all this is going on? Hopefully with Carl and the Planning Officers keen to help we can get through this as quickly as possible. Obviously, we'll pay whatever your going rate is, but the ability to pop down, supervise the build, keep an eye on the property and be around my own special things whilst this is going on would be of massive psychological benefit to me as I endure this TRAUMA.' She pivots to hard-stare at Oliver at this point.

As Mitzi wanders in mid-chant, there's a momentary glance between her and Oliver that Laura and I both clock, but I pretend I haven't seen. The room crackles with tension – or it could just be Laura's long nails clicking together as she flexes her knuckles. Mitzi closes her eyes, resumes her chant, turns and walks straight back out of the room.

'Obviously, it's far from ideal.' Laura throws an evil look towards Oliver.

Carl then comes into the room with Miles. They are talking winter tyres by the sound of it, and Oliver makes a big effort to join in with their conversation.

'What's that, lads?' he says jovially. 'Tyres?'

I need to give Laura an answer. 'Of course, if it will help the situation.'

Gulp. *Is this really a good idea?* I think Laura might end up killing Mitzi. Does she know that she and Oliver had a thing? A Christmas bonk? I get the feeling she does know. There's never been an open acknowledgement, of course, only an underlying hatred that bubbles to the surface every now and again. So why, knowing that, do I feel absolutely obliged and on a train track I can't escape with the destination firmly fixed at 'Yes'?

'How soon are you thinking, Laura?'

'This coming Monday, if you please, Janet.'

After what feels like an exhausting day I'm now lying in bed thinking about Laura Watson moving into the cottage on Monday. Practically Perfect Laura bloody Watson. Living next door. I don't know how this is going to play out.

Chloe was not at all happy about it. Once the Watsons and Miles had departed, and Carl had gone to the pub with a friend, she spat out: 'That Laura was a right *biatch* to you last year.'

Very black and white, is my daughter. She doesn't get neighbourliness or forgiveness. I tried to explain to her.

'I'm channelling my inner Joanna Lumley, Chloe.' She looked blank, didn't have a clue who Joanna Lumley is, so I tried again. 'Think of someone with a big heart and a sense of humour.'

'Er . . . you're describing yourself, Mum. I certainly wouldn't put up a cow who's slagged me off and tried to close my business down.'

All true. But these are desperate circumstances for horrible Laura.

'It's not for long,' I said feebly. 'Just to help her whilst this building work is going on.'

'Mum, what about *our* building work? Who's doing that if Carl's round at Laura's? I can NOT continue to wake up every day with dusty hair.'

Oh God, I think now. What a mess. In doing someone else a kindness I have made all my own family miserable. Mitzi went pale when I told her.

'Laura and Oliver Watson next door in the cottage?'

'Yes, just whilst her house gets sorted.'

'Janet, you know she hates me.'

'Oh, I think she must be over that.'

'No, she's definitely not over that.'

A bit of me shrivelled inside, but I had another go. 'We're doing her a favour, Mitzi, it's an emergency situation. She'll owe us after this and she asked me outright, which made it awkward. I don't have any bookings either, plus I need the money, so . . . To be honest, I couldn't say no.'

'You know that Oliver still contacts me.'

'Er . . . no.' I was gobsmacked.

'And you know that Carl has no idea?'

'Er . . . no. Sorry.'

My sister then swept out of the room, saying, 'I'm going to have to do some incantations.'

And the chanting started in earnest and is still going on. I feel like joining her.

Face it, Janet, you've upset everyone to please Laura bloody Watson. What an idiot I am. I'm feeling panicky about the cottage now too. It's a nice welcoming space, it's homely, but it's not up to her snooty standards. I'll have to try to lift that burn stain off the hob. The grout in the bathroom's going a bit black in places and I haven't managed to touch up the paint in the entrance where the kids ran round it with felt tip. Oh Gawd. It's hardly Superhost standards. I might have to insist as part of the arrangement that she doesn't leave a review.

What on earth have I done?

REVIEW

***** Five Stars from Reiss & Co.

Janet and fam are boss hosts. Fun times. Great place for training. We won!

TIPS FOR RUNNING A B&B

Sometimes guests are hot young things. Try not to notice. Or even better, treat *everyone* as if they are hot young things ☺

Remember that having guests around can impact on your personal relationships. Your nearest and dearest can resent the attention given to others. Looking after guests whilst looking after relationships takes some managing, that's all I'm saying. Not sure how you prepare for that one, good luck.

TIP ON LIFE

Keep an eye on the weather when planning a cycle ride. For goodness sake make sure at least one thing you're wearing is waterproof.

CHAPTER 6

The Way Too Many's

My ex-husband Franklin has left the cracker factory where he had been promoted to foreman, and is now a Gas Engineer. Well almost, he has to finish his training but he's two-thirds of the way through and he's loving it.

This is the news in from Chloe. She went out for dinner with her dad and his new girlfriend Mousy. She's actually called Minnie, but because she has a squeaky voice Chloe is calling her Mousy. I'm not making any comment. The longer I can keep my mouth shut, the more information comes my way. I can't help but want to know. I feel a mixture of relief and a burning resentment. He's doing something – really? Great news. At last he's doing quite well for himself, so *why couldn't the work-shy arse do that for us*? He'd stayed here for months, mooning around, eating us out of house and home, not lifting a finger – until I had to ask him to leave.

Let it go, Janet, I urge myself. *Let it go*. After all, it's nice to think he might be able to help me out with my boiler if it plays up. I wonder if he gets discount on new ones . . . I'm sure I heard mine groan last November when I switched the heating on.

It's weird to be penny-pinching whilst I'm still sort of seeing Miles, who thinks nothing of spending two hundred pounds on a meal. We were out last Friday at this new posh place called Heather's on the tops, and the food was lovely – so pretty, so flavoursome, so bloody small a portion. We came back to mine, as Miles's flat in Hebden has nothing in it, as per usual, and had three rounds each of tea and toast. I tried to say it was a waste of money eating out so often but Miles was having none of it. He doesn't skimp on anything. He showed me an electric bicycle he was looking at – *sooo* much money. I kept my face straight, but really I'm thinking, That's nearly my salary for the whole year!

I'm on a savings push. I wonder if Miles will notice I've worn the same dress three times now? I've put a filigree metal gate I've had in the back garden on Facebook marketplace to see if I can raise a few quid. 'Look after the pennies and the pounds will look after themselves,' my dad used to say. At the farm, he never spent a penny on anything. We girls and our mother had to put up with holey shoes, holey tights, no holidays, no windows that didn't have icy draughts, no curtains, nothing. It's no way to live. I do *try* to look after the pennies but the pounds don't seem to have got the message yet.

At least I've stopped offering to go halves on bills with Miles; he always says no and looks a bit offended if I get my purse out. I'm trying to just enjoy things as they are and not project into the future. It's hard. I don't think we're remotely compatible really, but we have a good time together and the sex is pretty bloody fabulous. He's fun, is Miles, and lively and he does like to go out quite a bit. Though trying to be a let's just have a fun relationship-type of person is an effort when you're secretly quite old-fashioned.

I remind myself that it's a blessing to get out of the house. The building work in the attic has come to a standstill now that Carl is full-time over at Laura's. She moves into Lavander Cottage on Monday. This is my one last weekend of peace. It does mean there's an arctic breeze from the attic, where Carl had optimistically created a hole in the roof for a new velux window. It's currently taped up with fabric and gaffa until he has a moment to fix it in. Mitzi is hardcore and has taken to doing her yoga and shamanic stuff in the half-realised attic space, still only accessible by the stepladder on the landing. I've no idea what her shaman stuff involves. There's chanting, dried flowers, full-moon rituals. I've had to have words about the incense as the smell of it drifting into my bedroom at night has me gipping, it's so strong. She swears she's incanting and needs it permanently on burn. I've bravely climbed up there during the day on the quiet, when I know she's not in, and stubbed it out, stolen a few of the sticks and cones and thrown them in with the food waste hoping she won't notice.

She's up there chanting away when I notice three cars reversing and nudging past each other on the driveway outside our house, and out of them are pouring a lot of people and a lot of luggage.

Oh Gawd. Flashback. I was in a rush, a week or two ago. I was racing about as I was due in to cover reception, but had agreed to drop Chloe off at work and Mitzi at Job Club. She must be their longest-running member – do they give out medals for long service? Now I remember, I was parked in the Job Club car park when I opened the app on my phone and clicked *accept booking*. I didn't really think. Or read it properly. I just said yes to a booking for this weekend. Damn it. What exactly did I say yes to?

I throw open the laptop with shaking hands and

frantically scan the messages. I've set up a template with the address on so I've obviously sent that to them. Panic sets in with the grinding sound of wheelie cases making their way up the drive. Thank God I cleaned Lavander Cottage this week and set it up with fresh bedding. The message reads: *Bernard and guests, here for a wedding, might be up to eight of us, possibly nine.* NINE? Oh dear God no.

I dig out a loaf from the freezer, my fresh milk, ten of the mini-butters and a bottle of wine and sling it into a *So Hebden Bridge* jute bag. I am gingerly opening the patio door when one of them, a short rotund guy in a snazzy waistcoat and expensive shiny brogues, notices me and waves.

'Hi darlin', you Janet? I'm Clive. Which way to Lavander Cottage?'

I paste a smile on my face. 'Hi, Clive. Just head straight down the drive, and it's the door in front of you. You'll see the sign.' I hand over the key with the jute bag.

'Oh nice, ta very much, darlin'.'

He strides off, and I cringe as the parade of people passing by begins. They are all middle-aged Londoners, friendly, slapping each other on the back, up for a good time and very noisy. The amount of luggage they've brought will fill the downstairs entrance. I don't know what to say to prepare them, or what to say once they've explored the cottage and found it inadequate for seven people never mind nine! I make myself a giant cup of tea and hide behind the kitchen island. I'm slowly demolishing a pack of Maryland Cookies when Mitzi peers around the island at me. She is expertly shuffling a pack of Tarot cards.

'Where have they parked the coach?'

'Ha ha. Don't ask. There's *so* many of them. And I'd forgotten all about them.'

'I counted eight.'

'Nine. There might be nine.' Why did I agree to take them, when the cottage only sleeps six maximum? I've really screwed up here.

'Where are they all going to sleep?' Mitzi wants to know.

'I've no idea.'

'Hmm.' My sister throws down three cards onto the floor beside me, then expertly flicks them over one by one.

She gives a nod. 'It's going to be fine.'

I seize on her words. 'How do you know?'

'One of them is a Coin card.'

'What does that mean?'

'The cards are all positive. Their message is: just take the money and run, Janet.'

There's a knock on the patio door and I nearly jump out of my skin. I am glued to the lino. I shake my head frantically at Mitzi.

'I can't face them.'

Mitzi sighs, gets up and strolls over to the patio door, opening it to reveal a handsome silver fox-type gent. He is in casual pale chinos with his shirt unbuttoned a bit further than you might get away with normally. Unless you were in Benidorm or, say, Essex. Mitzi seizes the opportunity and hits the charm button.

'Well, hello, how are you? I'm Mitzi, and welcome to Hebden Bridge and to our Lavander Cottage. Everything OK? There's quite a few of you. Are you going to all fit in there? The cottage does say "sleeps six maximum" but I could make room over here if there's a bed-shortage crisis.'

I can just picture the flirtatious look on her face.

A shout of laughter greets this.

'That sounds great, love, but there's no need for you to put yourselves out. By the way, my name is

Bernard, and yes, we do seem to be a bed short. We're wondering if you can organise a folding bed and maybe a duvet? Our mate Tommy was in the SAS – he's a tough geezer, hard as nails and can sleep anywhere.'

'Thank God for Tommy, eh? Well, I'll leave my offer open. Janet, you'll sort an extra bed, won't you? Will one be enough, Bernard?'

I crawl out from behind the island pretending to be looking for something.

'Hello there, Bernard. Of course I can take over a spare Z bed and duvet for Tommy. Apologies that there's been some misunderstanding about the size of the group. I'll get that organised for you as soon as possible.' I give him a nervous smile, wondering how fast I can get to Argos? At least I have some single fitted sheets, and duvets with matching pillowcases that Chloe uses. And I've loads of spare pillows.

A voice pipes up. 'Maybe two might be better if there's eight of you.'

Shut up, Mitzi. I feel the profit drain from my bank account as I react like a nodding dog with a fake smile on my face. What will two top-quality Z beds cost?

'You're right, mate. Yes, there's eight of us so two would probably be a good idea. Here, are them your actual Tarot cards?'

'Yes, I'm a professional Tarot reader,' my sister lies with a smirk.

'Are you really? Oi, Trudi, *TRUDI!*' Bernard bawls and I nearly jump out of my skin.

A glamorous-looking pink-haired woman teeters over from the cottage on high heels and sticks her head in the door. The first thing she says is: 'We need more wine glasses, dear.'

I reach into my cupboard and pull out four and hand them over.

'Ta, love.' She takes them, and I can't help noticing

her nails, which are about an inch long and covered with bright pink varnish to match her hair and which glitter with tiny stuck-on jewels. 'And prosecco glasses if you have them?'

I'm scrabbling in the back now, to find four non-chipped prosecco glasses. I'm sure there are four already in the cottage. I give them a swipe with the tea-towel.

'Trudi,' Bernard intervenes, 'you'll never guess. Mitzi here is a bona fide professional Tarot reader. What d'yer make of that, eh, gel? Fancy a go? Get yer fortune told?'

Trudi is dead excited. 'Oooh, yes, you must pop over and do mine. What do you charge?'

Quick as a flash my sister switches to sales mode. 'Usually forty-five cash on a traditional spread, but if I'm doing more than one I'll take it down to thirty-five.'

'Come on then, let's do it. Have you got some cash on you, Bernie?'

'You know I have, you minx. Lovely jubbly.' He rubs his hands together. 'Well, thanks for the glasses, missus,' addressing me then turning to my sister. 'Will you have a glass with us, Mitzi?'

'Yes, I most certainly will, Bernard. Alcohol is an ancient and revered technique to encourage the lubrication of the third eye to smooth our journey to the universe.'

Bernard guffaws. 'Get that, Trudi! I thought we was in Yorkshire but we're heading to the universe.'

I can't help but smile as I watch Mitzi walk across to the cottage arm-in-arm with Bernard, who herds Trudi like a sheepdog into the cottage. At least one of us is going to benefit from this stay. I'm still in shock from the surprise arrival of the group. Where am I going to go to buy these folding beds? And how would I get them home? Plus, am I fit to be seen anywhere in sweatpants and a too-tight *Back to the Future* T-shirt that belongs to Chloe? At this point, Harvey pads into the kitchen, mewls at high volume with a gagging sound I recognise, and throws up at my feet. Back to the future? *If only.* It's Back to Reality here.

By the time I've dug out two duvets and the rest of the bedding, found one decent Z-bed stored away and been to Argos for another, then delivered it all to the guests, it's getting on for teatime. I've a lovely recipe for a suet herb-crusted vegetable tagine but I keep being interrupted by requests from the cottage. More towels, more milk, more little soaps, takeout advice (it's all there on the leaflets, you lot), taxi numbers, more chairs, tea-towels, do we have a dartboard? This is a definite downside of being so close to your guests: they have easy access to bother you. Why look in a guestbook for the information you need when you can knock on next door and annoy the owner?

After what must be the sixth interruption, I give up on a herb crust and get on with just making a tagine. It turns into more of a healthy chunky soup and all a bit boring, and I end up soaking up half of it with a sourdough loaf.

I flick through the TV trying to settle down, but nothing is catching my attention. *Emergency in A&E*, *Motorway Emergency*, *Emergency Sea Rescue*. What is it about emergencies? I want to relax, not worry about some other poor beggar. I pray I am never in an accident, because more than likely a camera will be shoved in my face and I'll be too poorly to say, 'No thanks, I don't want to be famous for having a mini-stroke on the pirate ship off Bridlington.'

I'm feeling worn out and ready for bed when I notice I have some notifications on Facebook marketplace.

King Louis

I'm interested in your gate, where are you based? Is it heavy? Will it go in my car?

I'm about to respond when I notice another message underneath.

BobbyB

Remove my gate from your For Sale items, it is NOT for sale.

I can't quite get my head around this and have to read it again. Eventually I respond – I mean, I have to.

JanetJ

It's not your gate, it's mine and it is for sale.

Immediately there's a response.

BobbyB

It is NOT your gate to sell. Remove this ad immediately or I will report you to the site for selling stolen goods.

I'm proper fuming now.

JanetJ

The gate has been in my back garden for the last five years. I am perfectly at liberty to sell my own gate, and the fact that it looks a bit like yours does not give you the right to accuse me of stealing. I've never stolen anything in my life and I will report YOU to the site for going around making public accusations that are completely unjustified and frankly libellous.

King Louis

I'll leave the gate.

Seriously. The rage. They need to come up with a new show. *Internet Anger Emergency.* All the people getting wound up by idiots online. I'm thinking about what a great show that would be when Chloe comes in and collapses head first on to the sofa.

'Fourteen hours I've worked today. I am wrecked. Feed me, Mum.'

The tagine does not go down well so I'm rustling her up a mini-baguette pesto mozzarella panini-type thing when Mitzi staggers in through the patio door.

'I've been talking to Grandma Irene.'

'Who?' Chloe perks up.

'Have you been in the cottage the whole time?' My turn.

'Did you hear me? *Grandma Irene.*'

'Who is Grandma Irene?' Chloe demands as Mitzi slumps into a seat at the kitchen table.

'She was our grandmother,' I explain. 'Our mother's mother.'

'Oh. Right. What was she like?'

'We don't know, Chloe. We never met her.'

Mitzi props herself up on the table. 'Irene's happy on The Other Side.'

'Good to know,' I say briskly, followed by, 'But how about the guests – how are they?'

Mitzi grins. 'They're the real deal – proper Eastenders. Friendly, got all the chat.'

'I gathered that, and they're nice with it, aren't they? So . . . they're comfy, no complaints?'

'We did a séance,' Mitzi confides. 'They have *a lot* of relatives in Sweden.'

At this point, Chloe does a very loud burp and it feels like the perfect moment to encourage everyone to go to bed.

'Right, I'm locking up,' I say firmly. I've had enough.

'What is a séance?' my daughter wants to know.

'It's not a chat for bedtime,' I reply, giving my sister a warning look that she ignores.

'Communing with the spirits that have gone before us,' Mitzi tells her.

'Oooh, sounds spooky. Can *we* have a séance?'

I'm literally pushing them both out of the kitchen and up the stairs, turning lights off as we go.

'No, thanks,' I tell her. 'I've enough on dealing with the people turning up who are alive, never mind encouraging the dead to visit.'

'Janet?'

'Yes?'

'Mum also came through. She sends her love.'

My heart does a teeny tiny sigh. All I can say is, 'Are you going to be all right, climbing that ladder in your merry state?'

'Perfectly fine, thank you.'

Mitzi makes her way precariously up the ladder. When twenty minutes later I hear a loud bang, my worst fears are realised. I leap out of bed and onto the landing, where Mitzi is lying at the foot of the ladder.

'Are you hurt?' I'm really worried.

'I needed a wee. I think I've broken something.'

'Well, don't move, OK? Stay perfectly still and I'll call an ambulance.'

Four hours later in A &E, it turns out that Mitzi is not seriously hurt. She has minor bruising, having bent back her thumb, causing cartilage to strip a tiny bit of bone. She needs to wear a thumb casing for the next six weeks and avoid further damage.

The next day, the London lot pile out of the cottage en

masse dressed up to the nines in wedding-guest outfits. I offer to take a photo and it turns into a free-for-all; can I do singles, pairs, this trio, these four, more endless group variations. It gets so convoluted I'm grabbing phones as they come at me, posing their owners and shouting at them to change position, readjusting hats and buttonholes. I even bring out chairs for them to sit on.

One of them, granted one of the most elderly there, is constantly going, 'What's she saying?' in the most irritating way. I make sure we get a shot of her with her gob open and her eyes shut. Mean Janet, *stop it*. Eventually they pile into taxis that I had to order because they couldn't pronounce Mytholmroyd, and off they head to the wedding. That's another hour of my life gone that I won't get back.

Mid-afternoon, Carl turns up with a spiral staircase in his truck, to replace the step ladder that was going up into the attic space. It makes the landing a little more snug but still accessible and is the best solution to not eat up much of the attic bedroom. Our house is alive with drills, banging and sawdust. Mitzi sits in the garden in dark glasses resting her poorly thumb on a large wine glass. Chloe moans about the noise and threatens to go back in to work to avoid it. I'm vainly attempting to enjoy my Sunday, supposedly a day of rest, but there is a huge list of chores in preparation for Laura coming in tomorrow. I cannot get rid of the London posse soon enough.

I go to bed early and am having a very confusing dream about Laura reorganising my fridge into good and bad shelves, when I get woken up at 2.30 a.m. by the sound of taxi doors crashing open and shut, and the chorus of 'Parklife' being belted out at the tops of my guests' very drunken voices. The combination of food fascist Laura and the very merry loud Londoners all feels pretty surreal to me, Janet Jackson, half-awake in my bed in Yorkshire, and I struggle to get back to sleep.

The smell of bacon coming from the cottage starts at 7 a.m. The visitors are eventually all out by 11.40. Lots of dark glasses. Bernard, looking sharp in a tan ankle-length Crombie and matching flat cap, winks and blows me a kiss as he strolls past the patio propping up a fragile-looking Trudi. I'm blowing him one back just as Chloe and Mitzi walk into the kitchen.

'Mum! Janet!'

I don't know what comes over me, lack of sleep probably, as I then attempt to do a twerk, saying in a muffled voice, 'Mi Yorkshire Puddings bring all the cockneys to mi yard.'

Mitzi immediately joins in with a dance move Beyonce would be proud of.

Chloe is horrified by us both.

'Ugh, stop it, please, *stop*, you're hurting my eyes and giving me a headache.'

We take no notice. I refuse to be outdone and Mitzi and I end up bum to bum in a twerk-off that Chloe refuses to judge. Eventually she puts her coffee down and shows us both what an actual twerk looks like.

Oh, to be young again . . .

REVIEW

**** Four Stars from Trudi

Janet is a lovely very Yorkshire host. Cottage bit small for 8 of us. Tarot reader service excellent.

TIPS FOR RUNNING A B&B

Don't accept bookings when you're in a rush.

Avoid the phone app. It's too easy to forget what you've done when you're in the supermarket ticking off frozen peas from your list on Notes, whilst responding to a text from your kids asking for Little Moons. Before you know it you've said yes to a coachload of pensioners from Anglesey.

Like I said, worth repeating, avoid the phone app. The writing's so small you might miss the request for 20 wine glasses and the chance to really think, Do you want the sound of a bunch of raging alcoholics in the cottage on Sunday after *Countryfile*?

TIP ON LIFE

The internet is full of nutters. I've no tips to offer. Please send me your ideas for dealing with this one.

TIP ON MID-LIFE ROMANCE

It's tough. There are no guarantees, no obligations, nothing is safe. Tune into your inner Rizzo, be cool and enjoy the ride ☺

CHAPTER 7

Laura Bloody Watson, Part One

I'm regretting the decision to let Laura stay in the cottage about forty minutes after she arrives.

'Janet sweetie, I'll replace the bedding if you don't mind? Oliver's *so* used to 400 thread, anything else scratches.'

'The television, Janet, it's very small. Oliver's going to bring up the flatscreen – is that OK?'

'Janet sweetie, I can't manage with a polyester throw. I hope you don't mind but I'm going to bring up our wool ones.'

'Isn't the kettle slow? I suppose I'm just used to our Quooker tap.'

'I've found three chipped plates. They're good for plant-pot crock, should *I* put them outside?'

'Janet, does the vacuum cleaner need a new bag? I've started on the upstairs and it's very slow going.'

'Janet, have you tried Method cleaning products? They smell so good, are carbon neutral and actually work. I've managed to shift the stains on the shower door using my daily shower clean, I'll keep them here now.'

It goes on and on, all morning. I'm gutted I'm not in work. To think I'd spent last night blasting through the place. It was immaculate. Only a Laura would think it acceptable to tell another woman that she's cleaning, when she knows damn well that the other woman has bust a gut to get the place ready. Are these the little tyrannies middle-aged women inflict on one another? *Your house stuff isn't very good quality, is it? Your cleaning's not up to scratch, is it?* The awful thing is, mean comments like that hurt. They really bloody sting.

By now, I'm so wound up my tummy's chewing bile. I need to find some zen because she's here for a month and I can't let her get to me. Not when I've persuaded everyone it's going to be fine, and everyone's relying on me to keep everything and everyone pleasant.

I decide I need a walk and make the unusual decision to reach out to Miles on text. He's usually free after 2 p.m. anyway; he doesn't take on many patients on a Monday so he can catch up on paperwork. I feel quite vulnerable, taking the risk to treat him like a confidant and a friend, and know I need to keep it light.

Hey, the dreaded Laura Watson has arrived and it's as bad as I imagined. In need of dental emergency rescue ☺

I get up onto the hills above the valley for a bit of fresh air and to enjoy the wonderful view up there. It immediately feels better to escape the house. Clomping about in old boots through mud and puddles, wind blowing a hooley, my hair all over the place, I lean over a wall to watch some cows as they tug at the grass and gently nuzzle each other, and memories crowd into my mind.

I was born on a farm. The thing I miss the most is the long views, letting the eyes rest on distant places. The huge patchwork spread of fields, criss-crossed by a snake of walls dividing up the mini-kingdoms. It's been a while since I've climbed up here, and it helps to remind myself I've come an awful long way from my farm days. Mum and Dad, what a pair, rough as houses, not many gentle loving moments from either of them. It's as if they were scared they'd make us soft. Well, that backfired, didn't it? I'm a bloody pushover. I'd do anything for anyone really. I suppose it leaves you needy when you don't get nourished as a kid. Ever afterwards, you're always on the look-out for a cuddle or grateful for scraps of affection. Or desperate to give all the love and affection you've got in your heart to anyone who will have it.

I reach over and give a curious calf a scratch on the head. Seeing this, his mum is over sharpish, but I don't panic, just reach down and pull her a handful of juicy grass up from the verge and feed it to her. Feeling much calmer, I realise that by the time this calf is a few weeks older, Laura and all her irritating ways will be well gone out of my life. In the meantime, I decide I'll come up here as often as possible to watch the calf's progress, knowing that this will help me through the ordeal. I take in big, deep breaths, flooding my lungs and filling up my heart.

I'm a different woman by the time I head down the drive – good job, because all hell's broken loose.

'He's only gone and broken the bloody telly.'

Laura, her arms full of cushions and blankets, is rolling her eyes at Oliver who is vainly attempting to gather up the remnants of a large TV that lies in a smashed pile on the drive. He yanks in anger at the cable, and when the screen smashes into more danger-ous fragments, he swears, 'For fuck's sake!'

Carl's head pops out through the patio door. 'Do you need a hand there, Oliver?'

'Shouldn't you be down at the house sorting out the pilings?' is the furious response.

Now Carl looks annoyed. 'Look, mate, I've been on site since seven-thirty this morning when I was hoping to talk to you about the drive materials, *only you weren't up*. So now three hours later I'm having my fifteen-minute break. That all right with you, boss?'

Oliver growls acknowledgement, but without looking up. The atmosphere is all very feisty. I need to get involved. Blimey. And it's only Day One.

'Morning, Oliver,' I say calmly, and give him a smile. 'What do you think if I bring a blanket? We can wrap it all up in that and I'll drive it straight to the tip.'

'Thanks, Janet,' Laura replies savagely. 'Take these, Oliver.'

When she throws a cushion that lands him full in the face, Carl smirks and I push him into the house through the patio door to avoid the bloke's pride being hurt any more than it already is.

'Oliver is such a prick.' Carl paces the room. 'I'm doing them a bloody favour and his attitude stinks.'

My sister is in the kitchen making herself a coffee. Her eyes flick to me and for a moment we register then move on.

'Can you put that kettle back on, please,' I say. 'I'm in need of a very strong tea. And Carl, would you like a sausage butty? I've extras and they need eating.'

'Yeah, go on then, if there's one going, ta. I'll take my time to eat it an' all.'

If I could pass one piece of advice to Mitzi, it would be that food makes people happy. She avoids it, which is why she's so slim whereas I love it and have the figure to prove it. A lifetime of cake abstinence to fit in a size eight dress is not my idea of a life well lived.

The to-ings and fro-ings continue all day over at Lavander Cottage. Laura's flashy BMW screeches up and down the drive, and she jumps out and stomps into and out of the cottage with endless amounts of stuff. Chloe is watching her antics whilst she cuddles a huge marshmallow-topped hot chocolate, her comfort drink before a shift.

'Exactly how long is she staying for?' my daughter asks, licking her chocolate moustache.

'We agreed a month,' I tell her. 'Carl said that would definitely cover it.'

'Looks more like six, all that stuff she's bringing in,' Chloe humphs.

'No way.' Mitzi swishes past in a Scottish Widows advert-type cloak combo. 'Carl wants it over and done with as soon as possible. He's agreed a fixed price, so he's going to be working all the hours God sends to try to get it finished in three weeks. He's even organised for Planning to come early, so he's definitely going to hit that date. Just don't tell *them*.'

We all watch as Laura marches ahead with Oliver trailing behind her, both carrying piles of bedding and pillows, and what looks like a rug and possibly a foot bath.

'He's a broken man,' Chloe says thoughtfully, as she slurps up the dregs of her drink.

'He's married to Laura Watson,' Mitzi puts in, 'and she'd break Genghis Khan. She's got chronic perfection-ism issues and is so uptight she squeaks when she walks.'

'Oh come on,' I feel I have to say. 'She's not that bad.'

'Don't defend her, Mum! She's currently turning your cottage upside down with all her stuff that's more perfect than your stuff – or hadn't you noticed?'

Yes, of course I'd noticed.

'She can't have kids.'

I don't know why I decide to throw in this emotional grenade, but I suppose it's something I've always been aware of with Laura and it pretty much mitigates anything negative I feel for her.

'Really? But did she want them?' Chloe asks.

'Yes, she did. I was walking back from taking you to school one day. I'd forgotten your PE kit and was annoyed with myself and was telling her so and she came out with it. Three rounds of IVF and three miscarriages.'

'Oh, I feel sorry for her now.' Chloe gets up and comes over to me and offers herself up for a hug, the simple act of a hug from a daughter that poor Laura was never going to get. I'm so lucky.

'That's why we shouldn't be too judgmental about other people, as everyone has their burden to carry.'

'Ugh. Save me from the bleeding-heart bollocks. Everyone has a burden? That doesn't mean they have to become one to everyone else they ever come into contact with. That woman is a pain in the arse, and she's living right on our doorstep.'

That's Mitzi, ruthless as ever, chomping her way through a breadstick. She's so tough, I think, then I remember she has her own issues with childlessness to deal with.

Bloody hell, this day feels like a minefield. And Mitzi hasn't finished.

'Right, Janet, I've three white witch trainees coming into the shaman room tonight, so just for this evening can you please not disturb us by asking me if I want a cuppa or shout up about turning off the incense.'

'What's a white witch?' Chloe raises an eyebrow.

'It's pagan philosophy, it's all about living in harmony with nature.'

'Thank you, David Attenborough. What's the witch

bit about?'

My sister is on a roll. 'It's about understanding what nature has to offer us, what nature can do for us.'

Chloe grows impatient. 'Forget the nature bollocks – what's the witch bit?'

I giggle at that and even Mitzi has a smirk.

'Look at it this way: I've been practising as a shaman, healing, using crystals and doing earth mystic stuff since I was what, Janet – thirteen?'

'Er . . .' I am lost for a moment.

'You know, remember the perfumes we used to make and the stone circles and that time I set fire to the gorse bush as a warning to Thingamajig's mum?'

'Oh yes.' It's all coming back. 'The straw doll up the chimney.'

'God yes, I'd forgotten about that.' She guffaws. 'When Dad lit that fire for a treat on Christmas Eve and nearly burnt the house down.'

'Yep.' Boy, is it coming back.

Mitzi turns to Chloe to explain further. 'The thing is, Chloe, I'm inclined this way. I carry a weight of experience of the alternative universe. I've spent decades immersed in this way of life and what I've recently realised is that lots of people can benefit from my wisdom.'

'Really?'

'Yes, really.'

'Like who, for instance?'

My sister's not having any cheek from Chloe. She says sternly, 'Shamanism, I'll have you know, is the fastest-growing religion. People want answers to life's mysterious questions.'

'Right.'

Mitzi is in full flow now; the cape is flapping around her and her arms are raised as she projects her voice, staring into a dreamy distance.

'And I, Chloe, am very well placed to teach them. The fact is, I am on the cusp of a breakthrough career moment.'

Oh my Gawd, I think – not another.

'You mean, lots of gullible idiots want to sit around in a circle and learn about dried fruit and nuts?'

I start laughing at this point. Mitzi is unapologetic.

'Exactly. And you might be interested to know, Little Miss Cynic, they are very willing to pay a reasonable amount of money for the experience.'

'If you can get people to pay you for that stuff, you are a genius, Auntie Mitzi.'

'Thank you, Chloe, it's time you realised.'

Out of the window I see Laura walking down the drive with her arms full of jars. She does a right turn and heads towards the patio door.

'Bye bye, you two.' Mitzi pulls a sprig of healing lavender from somewhere and waves it around liberally as she hastily backs out of the room.

'My shift starts in forty minutes.' Chloe hands me her empty mug, opens the patio door and walks out of it as Laura arrives.

'Morning, Chloe,' Laura says stiffly.

'Morning, Laura. Hope you get settled in. Bye.'

'Janet, you don't have any oat milk, do you? I'm desperate for a coffee.'

'I don't think so, sorry. I could do you a black coffee.' I look though the cupboard and pull out a jar of cheap supermarket instant coffee and hold it up for her to see.

She looks horrified. 'No, no, I won't, thank you, Janet. I'll ask Oliver to get the machine going. We're both *so* fussy when it comes to coffee.'

She scurries out of the kitchen at high speed, and I giggle to myself. That's one way to get rid of someone like Laura: cheap supermarket standards. It's like I've been gifted a key. I'll cling on to that for when I need it. Thanks, Universe. Maybe this Mitzi stuff is wearing off on me.

I pretend I'm not, but the reality is I spend the night hanging around my phone. No message from Miles. Not a text not a smiley emoji, nothing. All the usual emotions make an appearance: anger, embarrassment, jealousy. They're like mini-menopausal hot sweats as they sweep through, flaring up and down as I try to rationalise the hurt I feel. I'm not worth an acknowledgement? What am I doing, seeing this guy?

I go to bed early, berating myself for having anything to do with him. Though I regret it ten minutes later when the bells start chiming and the incense billows into my room. I can hear Mitzi chanting and her followers repeating whatever she says loudly and out of tune. After what feels like ten piercing and repetitive chants I've had enough. I go downstairs and find Carl in the kitchen eating a bowl of cereal. He looks shattered.

'How's it going?' I ask. 'Are you hungry? I can do you a sandwich.'

'Well yeah, if you're doing one, Janet, I'm starving.' He takes another huge spoonful of Frosties. 'We're getting there. I've stabilised the foundations, which is the main issue. Another concrete load tomorrow and the groundwork's done.'

I am frying some bacon when Mitzi sweeps in. She gives Carl a cuddle and a sloppy kiss I'd prefer not to have to witness.

'The attic space is amazing for teaching – they're loving it,' she tells him. 'Mind, we could do without the smell of bacon percolating up there, Janet. It's not exactly conducive to concentration. I've left them up there meditating but I heard more than one tummy rumble as I came down.' She turns back to Carl. 'You had a good day, love?'

I present Carl with the sandwich and hear him say, 'It's getting better now.' He wolfs it down and I stick another couple of slices in the pan.

'You know, I'm not sure we can use the attic as a bedroom and a bathroom.'

'You what?' Carl explodes. 'We've done half the bloody prep.'

Mitzi puts her hands on his shoulders and kisses him on top of his head. 'Darling, after some minor tweaks, you will also have created an amazing zen space.'

Carl growls.

'We can talk about it later,' Mitzi says. 'Give me five minutes and we'll be done.'

True to her word, five minutes later, there's a clatter of feet down the metal spiral staircase and Mitzi leads three women, one in her twenties and two women closer to my age through the kitchen. They are all decked out in an arrangement of scarves and beads and floaty skirts that wouldn't look out of place in 1973. Carl and I give each other a look and watch them trail through the patio door and out to the lawn. Once there, Mitzi leads them on some sort of spin-dance thing whilst chanting, 'Om . . .'

She is in her element and when she returns without her group fifteen minutes later and plants sixty quid in notes on the table, she is chuffed to bits.

'That was their first session. They loved it.'

'Well done.' Carl grabs her round the waist and pulls her to him. 'Cash in hand too, that's great.' Mitzi glows from his approval. It's lovely to see.

'That's for you, Janet. Rent for this week. I've upped it a tenner.'

'Thank you.'

I don't blink or do any fake modest 'no, really I couldn't' type of thing, I just take it. I put it in my pocket because I don't want anyone to know where I keep the cash. The brown pot egg hen clucks at me and I give her a wink in return. *Laters, chuck.* I'm pretending this is normal – that Mitzi gives me money rather than the other way round – and decide I can cope with a bit of incense if it means I get some help with the bills.

I suddenly recognise how tired I am. The shock of Mitzi giving me money must have tipped me over the edge. I go back upstairs and collapse into bed, promising myself I'll change the bedding tomorrow. There's a pair of Miles's boxers screwed up at the bottom of the bed and what feels like a faint layer of builder's dust on top of the duvet cover. I don't care – well, I do care, but I'm too tired to do anything about it. Standards are definitely slipping.

I wake next morning to a message from Miles.

Hey. On the slopes for the week. Good luck. Followed by a little ski emoji and a wine-glass emoji. I look at it and feel as if I've been high-fived across the face. Though of course I know I'm not really allowed to feel anything. I'm not Miles's partner. He owes me zero explanation and zero invitation. It hits me hard though. I feel like an idiot. A needy desperate idiot.

Zombie-like, I get ready for work. I decide to walk in to try to clear my brain but I'm clumsy and struggle to fasten my trainers without getting into a tangle with my laces. My face looks grey with stress and I'm sure I can feel a breakout on my lip of a cold sore – the sort of thing I only get when I'm run down.

At Valley Dental I hurry behind the reception desk, throwing my coat and bag down under it to avoid the social areas. I feel so humiliated and embarrassed. I can't help it. I assume everyone at work knows he's away, everyone except me, the woman he's been sleeping with. With no proper conclusion about what's appropriate to feel, think or say in these circumstances I make a decision to confide in Judy. She's the longest-serving dental nurse here, works exclusively for Miles and knows *everything* without ever really saying anything. Plus she's a friend. There's absolutely no point pretending to Judy and I need to know what she knows.

I catch her in the kitchen when I go in to make a camomile tea for a nervous Lisa Smart who hasn't been to the dentist in ten years. Judy is not remotely judgmental, totally on my side and is a machine of information.

'You didn't know he was going?' she asks me.

'No idea.'

'He's had it booked in, a month ago. I didn't want to take any leave then, so I'm here doing anything that comes up – cleaning the bloody fish tank and getting Tony coffee mainly.'

I don't know how to say it, but I try. 'You know that Miles and I were . . .'

'Oh, he never stopped talking about you. "Janet gravy this", "Janet looking lovely the other" . . .'

'Right.' A tiny bit of me relaxes. It wasn't just a figment of my imagination. He did like me and we were/are getting on.

'Oh yes, you were lovely – and so was bouncy Bella and needy Nina.'

I can't quite process what Judy has just said. I get a full-blown hot flush from my scalp to my toes, a wave of nausea hits me and I reach backwards to steady myself on the kitchen counter.

'Sorry, Judy. What did you just say?'

The look on her face says it all.

'Oh my God, don't tell me you didn't know?' Judy is mortified. She can see I'm shaken. 'Oh Janet, Janet love. I'm so, so sorry. Let me get you a chair.'

I am wobbly, I can't deny it. I sit myself down on the metal bin for a moment, wrestle in my bag for a tissue and find myself unexpectedly crying. Judy is beside herself. She rings through to Tony and says she's taking me home because I'm not feeling well. I explain we can't go home, not with me in this state and with builders and shamans and Laura and everything. We retreat to one of the grottier pubs somewhere I'd never normally go ever, but it's dead and discreet and we find a hidden corner. Judy returns from the bar with a pint for me and an orange juice for herself.

'I'm *so* sorry, love. I didn't know anything was still going on between you. I had no idea you were still keen on him. Oh shit, me and my big bloody gob.'

'Don't worry, Judy, I know you didn't.' As I calm down from the shock, I begin to slowly seize on threads of myself, my dignity, my pride, my self-esteem, and attempt to weave them back together across the conversation. It's not about you, Janet Jackson, I tell myself. Don't take this personally, don't let this hurt you. It's Miles being a two-faced twat, that's what this is about. Nothing to do with you.

Gently, once she's decided I can take it, Judy shows me his Insta account. *Foxdentist74*. It's Miles showing off on his various machinery and activities: water skis, Strava timings, pot-holing, quad bikes, racing cars, Segways, ski slopes. And in between, over the last few days, a woman is always in the background of every other ski-slope shot. All in black, she has dyed blonde hair and giant sunglasses that hide everything bar the pouty mouth.

I down the pint. Order a bottle of wine. Judy sips at her glass, speculating that it could be needy Nina. Cheshire set, waiting list for *Real Housewives of Cheshire*, born rich, married rich, divorced rich, specialises in doing nothing in life bar booking spa retreats. According to Judy, Miles hates spas and finds them, and Nina, boring. Then Judy runs out of time. She has her Keep Fit class to get ready for and it's gold dust to get in with Clive GoGo at the gym as he's *sooo* good. 'You should come,' she says. 'Blow your cares away.'

I'm too weak to know if or why she's suggesting it. My confidence has taken such a battering that speculating if it's because she reckons I'm plump, fat, dumpy, whatever, is not a sensible idea. I take her hand as she prepares to leave.

'I'm glad you told me. Thank you, Judy.'

She gives me a hug and wags her finger at me, saying, 'You, Janet Jackson, are far too good for Miles. He's a boring posh idiot going through a very boring post-divorce mid-life crisis. He's going to be very skint and emotionally wrecked by the time his wife Miranda's done with him. Believe me, it's not even started and *you do not want* a Miles post-Miranda. Run for the hills, Janet, if he comes knocking. *RUN!*'

She's lovely, Judy. I fill my glass with the last of the wine and sit there quiet and nurse it. The hot shame has gone. Judy has helped with that. So down to earth, so matter of fact. No judgement. It helps me not to judge myself too harshly. The fact remains that I'm an idiot. A too-easy-to-have-sex-with idiot. But I'd never hurt anyone intentionally. I wouldn't be cavalier like Miles, would I? Not with someone's emotions. You hurt Peter the librarian, I think, and my heart sinks. Here comes the Karma.

I stagger home. I quite like it when the rain begins to dash against me. All that daft renewal baptism stuff kind of makes sense when you're soaking wet and everything that you put on that day, all the make-up and the hair stuff, gets literally washed away. I pile in through the patio door and Chloe is there looking anxious with Mitzi.

'At last! Where have you been? We've been calling you since four o'clock!' Accusations, angry faces.

'Oh, sorry.' I dig out my phone and find there are lots of messages and phone call notifications. It's now after 7 p.m.

I feel a bit cornered. 'Sorry, I lost track of time.' It doesn't help that I'm still drunk.

'You OK, Mum?'

Chloe puts her penetrating eye radar on me. I shrivel under her gaze and her instinctive understanding of me. I've nowhere to go and I'm not in a good place to be able to hide it. Mitzi is on me now too, looking me up and down.

'Something's happened, Janet. What is it?'

I can't escape my daughter and my sister. I don't even want to. I fall open like a book to the final page.

'Miles is cheating on me though we weren't a thing anyway, so I can't complain, but I didn't know and now I do. It makes me feel like a tramp and an idiot.'

These are my people and they smother me in love and tea and a bath is run and Chloe gets me set up on Insta which I can't decide is a good thing or not. She spends the evening scrolling through Miles's Insta page with Mitzi. They locate, they say, three other women and at least two of my home-made pies. I don't know whether to laugh or cry.

'I don't get featured but my pies do?'

'They are good pies though, Janet.' This comes from Carl who is glued to *Top Gear* whilst Mitzi and Chloe 'doom scroll' – that's the term apparently.

'I have to say, Mum, he's pretty bloody boring.'

Mitzi nods. 'There's not one funny meme on here.'

'Judy says if he comes knocking, to run.' I manage a chuckle.

'He better not come bloody knocking, I'll have his ballbags for earrings and his dick for a coat hook.'

'Mitzi, *please*. Honestly.' I shake my head.

Carl, who is engrossed in the action on TV, doesn't turn his head but adds, 'I'll make some room on the back of the ensuite door.'

Well, that's it, we are howling. Howling. And if there's anything that makes the pain and shame of being cheated on when you're not allowed to really call it cheating, it's having the support and laughter of your own little family. I am blessed. I'm also exhausted. I drag myself upstairs and suddenly remember I need to change the bedding. I sigh and go in to start the process but there it is, all done for me. A hot water bottle has been put in the bed, and there's a love heart on a Post-it note on my pillow.

Love you, mum. Best mum in the world.

If I had any doubts about how lucky I am, that settles them. I collapse into bed where, just before sleep overwhelms me, I wonder where Miles's boxers are. In the bin?

TIP FOR RUNNING A B&B

Try to avoid agreeing to host the Lauras of this world. The

domestic goddess is impossible to please and it will be a nightmare trying.

TIPS ON LIFE

To find love you have to be prepared to take risks. Sometimes they backfire and it's horrible and embarrassing and you're humiliated and that's all there is to it. You will survive it. All you can hope is that you'll be a bit smarter next time. Don't give up. Being loved is lovely. Be grateful for every scrap.

CHAPTER 8

Laura Bloody Watson, Part Two

Harvey the cat has taken to running into Lavander Cottage whenever the door opens. I can't help but feel insulted. It's as if he is constantly awaiting his chance to enjoy the luxury lifestyle afforded to him by Laura's upgrades. Fortunately, Laura seems relaxed about it. Harvey is on full charm mode with her, lots of purring, rubbing up against her leg and looking handsome on the windowsill. They both seem to enjoy the attention. I try to suppress my feelings of rejection, as I moon over at him preening in the window there. I suppose I am feeling a teeny bit sensitive about everything at the moment.

I'm going into work today for the first time since I found out about Miles. I'm expecting him to be in. We have had no communication since his emoji text. I am feeling generally quite relaxed about it all and decide I am almost over him. I have reminded myself every day that we were never going to be anything serious. After all, we have very little in common, and I always knew we were ill-matched. I've zero plans to become a Lycra bike lady. So it's over. Done. He has also not been honest about seeing lots of other people at the same time as seeing me. 'Everyone's at it, Mum,' Chloe informs me. Fine. I understand this is the world we live in. But not to say or hint or explain is neither very nice nor is it honourable. I've known Miles a long time, and I deserve better. I will have better. Or I'll not bother at all. This is what I keep saying to myself endlessly on repeat.

Chloe has put together the outfit I'm to wear. A tailored skirt with a pussy bow blouse, court shoes, a blow dry and lipstick. It's a lot of effort, this so-called revenge dressing, but Chloe insists it's essential for my self-worth and progression to closure. I'm just wondering if I've brought a blister pack as my shoes are already rubbing and all I've done so far is walk to the car.

As I'm leaving, Mitzi pops her head out of the window of the Velux. I can barely make out what she's saying but she's holding what looks like a starfish.

'What's she waving?'

Chloe looks up. 'Oh, I think that's her mini-Miles.'

'Her what?'

'Yeah, she told me about it. She's doing some sort of spell thing.'

There's a muffled cry from above and then something comes sliding down the roof tiles over the gutter and lands with a dull plop on the drive between us. It's mini-Miles, now looking very much like a small broken figure.

'Was that meant to happen?' I wonder aloud.

Chloe shrugs and Mitzi joins us, looking out of breath in a sequin bikini.

'Aren't you cold?' I ask her.

'Well yes, Janet, I'm not dressed yet, I was doing a morning incantation.'

'Is that thing really supposed to be Miles?'

'I was going to save it until tonight but he launched himself.'

'You let him go deliberately.'

She shakes her head. 'I swear he leapt. I was showing you him for a bit of moral support.'

'He's not looking too good,' Chloe notes. She nudges him with her foot; the crude figure has a stick pointing out where it joined the leg to the body.

Mitzi picks the figure up. As it dangles, looking vulnerable, the wool wrapping unravelling in the breeze, she considers it for a moment.

'He's good. Stay strong, glamour puss.'

I cringe. It will be obvious to everyone at work that I'm making extra-special attempts to look good, which will give the game away. Then I reassure myself that, since I've had no further communication with Miles, he has no idea where I am at. Tony is oblivious to anything and Judy knows anyway, and no one else matters. As I reverse out of the drive, I turn back and see Mitzi hanging the broken figure on the outside light, which she then turns on. Gosh, I think. Now he's going to get roasted. Poor mini-Miles.

The first half of the day flies by and without a spare moment to think. There's a run on emergency appointments and so many new people asking to join the practice that I've had to create a second waiting list. Lunchtime comes and I'm starving. I'm microwaving some home-made moussaka I'd brought in, having discovered three portions of it hiding under some tortellini in the freezer. I've no idea how long it had been there. It's taking an age to warm right through and I'm peering into the microwave to see if I need to give it another minute. I always go by smell with a microwave; looks are one thing, a bubble is obviously a good sign it's cooked through, but you can't beat the aroma. Once the smell is there, it's done.

There's the ping, so I open the door and am handling the pot very cautiously in case it's hot, when a hand rubs itself right up my thigh and on to my backside. Well, as you can imagine, it's a shock and causes me to drop the pot. I stumble backwards to escape getting burnt, the pot hits the floor and its contents are splattered everywhere – across the doors, the worktop, my pretty blouse and the kitchen lino. I turn around to see who was mauling me and there's Miles, grinning inanely.

'Whoops,' he says.

'Whoops?' I'm seething. 'You caused that. Groping at me when I'm holding a hot pot, what a stupid thing to do. I could have got third-degree burns.'

'I know who *is* the hot pot around here.'

'Oh, shut up, Miles, and pass me some bloody kitchen roll.' I'm so angry.

He laughs and unravels a ream of sheets. I turn and give him a hard stare.

'Do you see me laughing?'

'OK.' He makes a face, like I'm not being fun, then he fidgets and I can tell he's trying to decide how to pitch things.

Finally, he comes out with: 'Janet, I'm sorry. That was totally my fault.' He takes the dirty sheets of kitchen roll from me and puts them in the bin, then unravels some more and reaches with it to wipe my blouse. I snatch it off him and continue the job, working my way around the kitchen.

Through gritted teeth I hiss: 'Can you move, please, so I can get this cleaned up.'

He kneels down next to me and makes direct eye contact. 'Let me make this up to you and buy you some lunch.'

I stand up, stuff the bin with the kitchen roll and wash the bowl and my hands. His apology definitely helps. I'm feeling calmer but I don't turn around to him. I face the sink, and say, 'No. I don't want to do that.'

He's approaching me from behind again; I can literally feel his body heat but I ignore the temptation to turn.

'Please let me, Janet, I feel awful for ruining your lunch.'

I take my time with the tea-towel, dry my hands with it, fold it and put it back on the drainer. I then take a deep breath and turn to him.

'I said *no*, Miles. I don't want anything from you. I regret that I ever let things become so unprofessional. And now, if you'll excuse me, I am going back to my desk.'

I have to wriggle past him, since he deliberately doesn't move to let me pass so I'm forced to touch against him. I don't look at his face. When I take my seat, my heart is going 100 miles an hour, and I'm sure I look flushed though I try composing myself. A raft of grumpy-looking clients are seated in reception, all of them seemingly looking in my direction. I rummage in my bag under the desk where I find half a Wispa and a small box of M&S No Sugar butterscotch sweets. Not the healthiest lunch but it will stave off the cravings.

Miles doesn't come through the main reception, preferring the back route presumably. I'm trying to decide if I made myself clear – and did I do OK? I didn't cry and I don't feel too upset. I think getting angry sort of cauterised the other emotions. You can't feel soft and vulnerable when you're ready to slap someone round the chops with a dishcloth. Shame about the moussaka though, I love that recipe.

I've nearly finished the whole box of butterscotch

mints and I'm rifling through my coat pockets to see if there's anything else to chew on, when I see my phone has missed messages, lots of them, all from Miles.

Hey gorgeous, sorry about lunch again.

Hey, don't go quiet on me, let me make it up to you.

Janet, you're playing very hard to get and I don't know why. I said I'm sorry.

Janet, what did you mean about regretting being so unprofessional?

Are you in a huff with me?

Come up, let's talk about it. I'm free after 3, come up and let's discuss.

You look hot today by the way. That blouse is smokin'.

The messages go on and on – a mixture of apologies, demands and sexy stuff. I am battered trying to manage the reception and cope with the messages. He must be typing them in between every patient. What must Judy think, I wonder? Maybe he's always on his phone and she's used to it. Yes, that's probably it. If he's not texting me he's texting someone else. Trying to keep us *all* sweet.

It's coming up to ten past three and the last client, Tanya Monks, has come downstairs and rebooked for a month of veneers treatment. She must have money to burn, I think, since her teeth already look lovely. I'm wondering what to say to Miles. I dread the thought of him coming down and having to face up to him again. He's a mixture of good looks, charm and persuasion. It's hard work resisting him even though I know he's a rogue and all that. The thoughts of sex are hard to dispel too.

I need to get out of here. I'm not due to leave until 4.30 p.m. as it's usually my job to lock up, so I can't just up and go. I abandoned my post last week with Judy because of Miles-related trauma, leaving reception in the lurch, and I can't do it again. Focus, Janet. The downstairs loo has run out of toilet roll, I should put some in. I pull two toilet rolls out from the utility cupboard and put them into the loo. It's a shame, I'm so good at this job. I know what to do and can deal with most everything that presents itself. But not this, I tell myself. *This isn't going to work*. I can't face seeing Miles every day.

I put the phone on to answer-machine mode and place my trusty metal Paperchase pen into my bag along with my matching diary. I look at the mini-succulent I brought in years ago when I first started the job. It's barely grown, pot-bound, but it's sturdy and happy enough and it's been with me here for ever. I'm wondering whether to take it or not. *Am I leaving my job*? I'm not sure.

My phone buzzes and I can see it's Miles texting me again. I ignore it. I pick up the cactus and put it in the bottom of my bag. Throw my coat over my arm and without saying anything to anyone, I leave the building. Gently closing the door behind me.

I'm home in minutes, I don't know how, driving on absolute auto-pilot. My head is a blur of questions. A glass of wine will be nice, I decide. A nice big glass of Sauvignon, with some crisps, maybe. And then how about a box set. That thing I started watching that was a bit boring but everyone says it gets better if you get past the second episode. Am I on top of the washing? Do we have any clean towels? No one's complaining. I'm home, I tell myself. I'm safe now.

I get out of the car, only to see Laura stride out of Lavander Cottage as if she's been watching and waiting for me. *Arghh*. Come on, Superhost. Dig deep. Brace yourself.

'Hi Laura, how you doing?'

'You look smart, Janet. Can I have a word?'

My spirit takes a deep dive into the wheelie bin. I

should do a Miles on her – say 'yes, but keep it quick as I'm tired after work'. Instead, I do my people-pleasing thing.

'Of course you can. Is everything all right?'

'Well, it was. Apart from your cat.'

'What – Harvey?'

'Yes, Janet, Harvey.'

'He's not scratched you, has he? He can be quite unpredictable.'

'No, nothing like that. There's been – a smell.'

A smell?

'I wasn't sure what it was and I turned everything upside down looking for it.'

Great. She's seen everywhere the mop has never touched.

'It took me quite a while to locate the source.'

Everywhere, she's been absolutely every-bloody-where.

'To put it bluntly, he's been doing his business in the blanket box.'

'What!' Harvey hasn't pooed indoors for years. Not that I know about it. He doesn't have a litter tray or anything.

'He's been using the spare blanket box as a toilet, Janet. Would you mind taking a look?'

A bit of me wants to laugh. He wasn't visiting Laura for luxury throws and perfumed cuddles, he was looking for a comfy litter tray. The little bugger. I head into the cottage, braced for the worst. That's the thing, I decide, about wearing nice clothes. They're good for standing still and having your photo taken. Otherwise, they just get ruined by the everyday stuff. The spills, the splashes and let's face it the rolling-up of your sleeves, hitching up your skirt, kicking off your shoes and dealing with the turds. There's never a single day that doesn't come without some mess or mishap or worry to give that Perfect Life stuff a run for its money. Not one day without some little whiff of manure.

I pick up the blanket box that, sure enough, contains a number of offerings from Harvey and take it outside to deal with. More kitchen roll filling up the world's binbags. *Have I seriously just walked out of my job of the last seven years?* What on earth am I doing?

I go into the main house. Harvey rubs himself around my legs as I wash out his water bowl and refill his food bowl with cat biscuits. He's a swine. Males are all bloody swine, Janet Jackson, as you well know. So what's the plan, genius? What exactly are you going to do now?

TIPS FOR RUNNING A B&B

Keep your pets away from guests. It might start with a nice stroke but that's not a guarantee it will end well.

Mop everywhere you can. The Lauras of this world look for the muck.

TIPS ON LIFE

Not qualified. Ask elsewhere.

Second thoughts. Jamie Oliver does a lovely moussaka recipe.

CHAPTER 9

Bye, Bye, Laura

I'm having lunch with Judy. We are in a discreet corner of a not very popular café in Hebden. I feel for her. She has ordered a pulled pork sandwich that looks like it was resuscitated just hours ago; a damp gherkin hangs out of the side like the tongue of a knackered Spaniel. I go for soup from the Specials board. I have a rule: if there are leftover crumbs on the table and a bashed-up menu, then the only thing safe to eat is the Specials, since they are the only things that are likely to be fresh. Having said that, the beef-bourguignon soup with massive crouton is taking some chewing.

I've brought my hand-written resignation letter with me. It's taken me hours to write. I've done three different versions, one explaining I could no longer work with Miles, one explaining that for circumstances it's difficult to explain I could no longer work there, and the last one simply reads: *This is my notice of resignation. Thanks, Janet Jackson.*

Judy is trying to talk me out of it. 'Even Tony has said out loud that he misses you. Tony – Mr Misery himself!'

I've been off 'ill' for ten days. Miles made numerous

attempts to get in touch for the first day or two but that stopped when I sent him the following text:

Miles please stop bothering me. You have plenty of other women to keep you entertained. I'm no longer one of them. Janet 'no more gravy' Jackson.

I appreciate it wasn't my greatest literary moment, but it has done the trick. He's left me alone. What has been touching is that the rest of the staff have been unbelievably nice; they've sent flowers and Get Well cards. It feels horrible having to lie, but given the circumstances, what else can I do?

'I just think you're being too hasty, Janet,' Judy advises me. 'You don't need to leave. You can ignore Miles.'

'I can't ignore him, Judy, it's too awkward. What happens when he brings his new girlfriend in, what then?'

'Oh, he already did that on Tuesday. She's called *Franny*. She's a complete air head, twenty years younger than him and desperate for kids. He's fifty next year, Janet, he has two grown-up daughters. I'm telling you, he's off his nut. He's losing the plot. It will be fun for you to watch, I promise.'

'No, not for me, Judy.' The news about Franny decides it. I pull out the letter. I feel a bit shaky handing it over, wondering what I'm going to do next.

'Will you give it to Tony for me, please, and make sure to thank him for his flowers. What am I talking about? Thank *you* for the flowers, Judy. I'll miss you all.' I have to leave, before I start to cry. I put some cash on the table for my awful soup but she pushes it back into my hand.

'No. Don't be daft, my treat. What are you going to do?'

'I don't have a clue.'

Judy's face sours, as if she's found a mouldy strawberry in a still-in-date expensive punnet from M&S.

'He's such a twat. I'm going to deafen him with the vacuum all afternoon.'

I laugh, give her a hug and leave. I need to, quickly, before I change my mind and snatch the letter back. Blimey. *It's done.* I'm knocked out by a whoosh of fresh air as I step outside. A whole new unemployed Janet era awaits. I've worked at Valley Dental for seven years. *Change.* Here it comes, ready or not.

I'm at a loss as to what to do with myself. I wander aimlessly until I reach the cheap supermarket in the middle of town and go in. Onions and apples are on the reduced pile, so I buy them all. I soon regret it. I'm carrying my own bodyweight in shopping home before I've even hit the canal. *Eurgh.* I seem to enjoy making life hard for myself.

I'm a sweaty mess by the time I get back and hit the kitchen. Then, though, I have a glorious afternoon in batch-cooking heaven. Cheese and onion pies x three, apple turnovers x eight. The house is alive with the smells and even Mitzi comes down begging a corner of a turnover.

'I've quit my job,' I tell everyone over a cheese and onion pie.

Carl is in like lightning. 'I need a labourer, if you're interested.'

'Thanks, Carl. It's not number one on my career list but I'll put it on there for emergencies.'

Chloe stops eating. 'Quit as in quit?'

'Yes, as in quit. I'm done with Valley Dental.'

'Because of Miles?'

'Yes, I suppose so, because of Miles. I can't face him, not every day.'

'Oh Janet,' Mitzi sighs, 'he's the one who should be embarrassed. You can take the higher moral ground, sneer at him for the next six months and then you'll have another fella and you won't give a damn about him.'

'No, I can't do it, it's too awkward. He's bringing other women in, it's too much.'

'Workplace romance, always a disaster.' When Carl throws in his two penn'orth Mitzi seizes the opportunity.

'Like you'd know, working with twenty hairy-arsed builders.'

'Office girls and brickies, the things that go on, let me tell you.'

'Save it till bedtime, love.'

Mitzi, Carl and I share a laugh at that but Chloe cuts in deadly serious.

'I think you're missing something here, Mum. This is a sexual harassment case. You are being forced out of your workplace, so you should sue him.'

'Don't be ridiculous, he hasn't harassed me' . . . *much*. I immediately think about all the texts and the fondling and the not moving when I tried to get past, then put it firmly out of my mind.

'Chloe, get this straight,' I tell her. 'I'm not suing him. I'm not suing anyone. Right, I'm off to bed as I'm really tired – it's been quite a day. Could someone please fill the dishwasher.'

I'm overcome with exhaustion. The shock of it all is sinking in. Upstairs, I turn on the laptop to look at jobs. There are hundreds of them: care assistant, retail analyst, chef, cleaner . . . my head is soon whirling. I move out of jobs and into my spreadsheets, where the cliff edge of the end of next month looms ominously.

I close the laptop. Turn off the light and attempt to sleep. After two hours of wrestling with the bedsheets I get up and go down for a glass of water I don't really want. So as not to disturb anyone, I don't put the lights on, though Harvey pricks his ears up immediately, and comes to rub around my legs. He's obviously still hungry. I'm knelt down in the dark twirling the food round in his bowl with a fork to freshen it up and adding a few cat biscuits to it when I hear low chatter and giggly whispers. I stay bent down, thinking, Oh God, I hope this isn't Carl and Mitzi getting frisky.

The patio door then opens and there's a stumble and some laughter before I hear someone tramping noisily down the stairs. The main kitchen light comes on like a beacon, followed by a bellow.

'What the fuck is going on?' It's Carl, loud, grumpy and confused in a pair of Union Jack boxers, his hair smudged against his head, his face a crumple of anger and hurt.

The scenario before Carl and me is revealed in all its lack of glory.

Oliver is standing in the kitchen in his royal-blue velour dressing gown holding a bottle of red wine, with Mitzi beside him clutching a large goblet that is full to the brim. My sister is wrapped in a sparkly sheer two-piece that has its own train.

'Nothing's going on.' Mitzi is cool as a cucumber, as if she knows that to give away anything here would be to fall off the tightrope to sudden death. 'I went outside to have a smoke, bumped into Oliver having a sneaky drink outside the cottage, and he offered me a glass.'

Oliver is unbelievably nervous. He puts the bottle down on the side, asking Carl, 'Would you like a glass?'

'No, I effin' wouldn't. What time is it? Thought I was asleep, did you?' The angry accusation is pointed at Mitzi.

My knees can't take it any longer. I stand up and face them all.

'Sorry, it's all my fault. I must've woken everyone

up when I came down—'

'Janet.' Oliver almost throws himself on me. '*You* have a glass.'

'No, thanks. I'm on peppermint tea and I'm going back to bed now. Oliver, Laura must be wondering where you are. I'm sure she would like a glass of wine, so you'd better get back to the cottage.'

'You're right. I'd better make a move. Night night, everyone.' Oliver can't move fast enough and, leaving the bottle behind, he gets out while the going is good.

I can't look at my sister and Carl. It's all too much 'cat on a hot tin roof' with these two. Carl is giving off gamma waves of barely held back emotion like a Yorkshire Marlon Brando and Mitzi is staring into his eyes all unhinged and teary, hanging onto her glass like a desperate Blanche clinging to her sanity. I lock the patio door and leave them, and as I creep up the stairs, the voices start to erupt.

The next morning, I sleep in for the first time in ages, after a rough night spent fretting about everything. I'm barely awake, wrapping my dressing gown around me on the landing, as Carl slides down the metal spiral staircase and comes past at high-speed wielding two bin liners with his clothes spilling out of it.

'Good morning,' I say tentatively.

'The only thing good about today, Janet,' he replies grimly, 'is if I get this extension signed off at ten, then I'm free as a bird to fuck off for a bit.'

He throws the binbags by the front door, drags hi-vis and other jackets from the hall wardrobe and adds them to the pile of his stuff that's already there.

'You sure you're not—' I was going to say 'over-reacting' but he interrupts.

'Sure I'm not what?' He stops and stares at me, and I decide it's too early for this kind of confrontation. I've not even had a cup of tea.

'Sure you don't want a sandwich, Carl?' I manage.

'I've already had breakfast, Janet, thanks. Can this lot stay here? I'll be back for it after dinner.'

'Of course you can.'

He's out of the door full of purpose, slamming it hard behind him. I pick my way through the pile of coats and boots into the kitchen where Mitzi, never intentionally awake before midday, is sitting at the table nursing a coffee. She couldn't look more miserable. Her face is pale and free of any make-up apart from a dark red lipstick to accentuate the drama. There are tearstains on her cheeks. She's drowning in a huge grey sweatshirt that has a *Howdens Kitchens* logo on it. It's definitely not like Mitzi to be anywhere near leisurewear, so I presume it must be one of Carl's.

'How are things?' I ask, putting the kettle on.

She gives me the eyes. 'What do you think?"

'It's a bit OTT for Carl,' I say. 'Why is he reacting like this? *Was* there something going on between you and Oliver?'

'No way. It was a ciggie and a glass of wine.'

'Does he know you've . . . y'know . . . with Oliver?'

Her lip quivers and she goes to the fridge and pulls the temporary cork out of a bottle of white wine I was saving for cooking.

'Yes. I told him last month, in a moment of eclipse-induced honesty that I'll regret for the rest of my life.'

I can almost see her slip and drown into self-defeat and depression, hopelessness washing over her. I can't have it happen, *I can't* – my infuriating but much-loved older sister is the happiest I've seen her for years with Carl.

I snatch the bottle from her. '*No*. You are not having a drink before lunchtime, and you are *not* letting this one go. You can persuade anyone of anything, Mitzi Jackson, if you put your mind to it. Go and tell Carl right now how much you love him. Let him know he's the only one for you, that Oliver is a prat and a wally you regret sleeping with, and say you'll do anything he asks to prove your love. Do it! Right now!'

She looks at me. I can tell I've lit something in her as her eyes flash and her face flushes. I can see her mentally drafting scenarios already. I know I'll have to bully her to get going, so I physically push her out of her seat.

'Go on! He's only at the bottom of the bloody road. And get dressed, for God's sake. I can't cope with looking at you in a hoodie.' I soften my tone. 'You can sort this, Maureen Jackson.'

I pray she's taking it in; the emotions on her face are moving faster than clouds across a windy Pennines sky. How is this penny going to fall? She stands up.

'You're right, Janet. What the fuck – I'm in a bloody sweatshirt.'

She rushes out of the room and I give a huge sigh of relief. I don't know what I've done, but I've done something and it's better than letting her give up without a try. Thirty minutes later, Chloe and I are eating a frittata I've knocked up from an old potato, an onion, and a half-box of mushrooms and tomatoes that were going soft. I like a frittata. Heavy on herbs and well done with some kale thrown in at the end, it's incredibly moreish and we are demolishing it between us when Mitzi powers into the kitchen dressed in the kind of outfit that would give a Kardashian goosebumps. It's a soft, orangey-red jersey dress, skin-tight, and drops just below the knee. There's impressive cleavage and her bare yoga-toned arms are on show, her hair is shiny, waved to perfection and pulled to one side, and she has on strappy wedge sandals that tie around her slim ankles.

'Wow, good look, Auntie,' Chloe says.

'Thank you, gorgeous.' My sister downs a pint of water in one go, wipes her lips, does a tiny burp and announces, 'Refreshed, renewed, resurgent, here I go.'

'Where are you going?'

'To the mountain, Chloe, to the mountain.'

I shush Chloe after that, as I don't want her to interrupt the mountain momentum, but curiosity compels us both to follow Mitzi into the hall. After grabbing the two binbags that belong to Carl, one in either hand, she strides out onto the drive and heads in the direction of Laura's house.

An hour and fifteen minutes later, the X-rated noises coming from the attic suggest there has definitely been a renewal of vows between Carl and Mitzi. Chloe, who could not resist the drama, had followed Mitzi at a distance until she got to Larkspur House. Then she had hidden in the bushes, racing back up to gleefully regale me with the details whilst I empty the dishwasher.

'So there's a really tall, like, official-type, glasses-wearing guy there, and he's talking to Carl, right? Laura and Oliver are sort of behind them in the background. The official bloke gives Carl a handshake and a pat on the back and everyone is looking pleased and smiling. That's when Mitzi turns up with those two bin bags, looking well fit.

'She walks straight up to Carl, holds the bags up then drops them, really dramatic like, and says straight to him, "I would never, *ever* choose a washed-up prick like Oliver over a god like you. If you want to leave me, you are gonna have to get these bags off me first, 'cos I'm going nowhere, and neither are you." Then she grabs the bags again.

Chloe giggles. 'Well, the official bloke takes one look at Mitzi and turns round and says, "Well, I know you're not talking to me, love, 'cos no one's ever called me a god. Except maybe Sheila Cross when I passed her Orangery. Job well done, Carl. I'll be seeing you."

'He nips past Mitzi who's totally obliv to him and he does, like, a salute to Oliver and Laura and he's gone. Now, keep up, Mum. Carl at this point doesn't know what to do with himself. He ums and ahs for a bit and then he grabs hold of Mitzi and she leaps on him and that's it then, they're, like, in full snog. Except, *get this*, now Laura and Oliver are going at it full blast.'

'*Eurgh* – what, snogging as well?'

'No, arguing. "Choose a washed-up prick like you, Oliver? What does she mean?" Laura is on one. Oliver's trying to, like, bring her back down.' He's saying, "I don't know what she's talking about, darling." Then he tries distracting her. "What's the important thing here, hmm? The house has *passed*, Laura, we can move back in."

'Oliver's, like, hopping from leg to leg like a mad-man, so I start laughing and they both turn and look towards the bush. So I thought I'd better get out of there before, y'know, they find me or something. Though it's a street and it's freedom of speech or whatever, but, y'know, I *am* spying.'

'Excellent work, Poirot.'

'Yeah, I think I'd make a good detective or private investigator – get all the cheating bastards.'

I'm closing up the dishwasher and trying to leave the kitchen clean when I hear a car screeching up the drive towards Lavander Cottage. Laura Watson is at the wheel, storming past with Oliver chasing after her, still pleading.

'The house has passed, Laura – come on, we should be *celebrating*!'

Laura pulls the car to a halt and gets out. She whirls around, her teeth bared. 'Oh fuck off, Oliver.'

Blimey.

Laura doesn't acknowledge me once all day. Her face is rigid as she schleps backwards and forwards from the cottage to the car, heaving stuff about like a machine. The energy required to keep that level of rage going is genuinely impressive. Oliver looks fit to drop after lunch and I feel sorry for him. I take him out a cup of tea and a bit of millionaire's shortbread I've made.

'God, Janet, that is so delicious. I'm going to sit down and enjoy this.' He perches on a lounger, and after another mouthful he has lifted his legs up and is now lying back, eyes closed, savouring every mouthful.

'That's so good,' he says dreamily, licking the last crumbs from his lips. 'Laura doesn't allow this sort of stuff in the house. She says it's because I'm an emotional eater. She's right, of course. If I'm happy I eat, if I'm miserable I eat. When I see something nice, I want to eat it. Why not? Life's short – eat the bloody lot, I say, Janet.'

When Carl and Mitzi appear hand-in-hand out through the patio door, loved up and ruffled, I gulp. I don't know what to do or what to say. I needn't worry, as Laura's piercing nasal voice powers down from an open Velux window on the first floor of the cottage, which dispels all the unknowns in a flash.

'You haven't time to sit down, Oliver, if we want to be back in our own home before bloody midnight.'

Oliver leaps up from the lounger as if he's been prodded with an electric cattle prong. Unfortunately he leaps straight into Carl who stands like a solid brick wall above him. Poor Oliver, he collapses back down on to the lounger.

'Better get a move on, Oliver, or you're gonna be in trouble.' Carl can't help himself. At that, Oliver whirls himself around on the lounger and rushes into the cottage at whippet speed. I try to create a distraction.

'Can I get you a cup of tea, Carl, or some millionaire's shortbread?'

'Yeah, I will if you don't mind, Janet. I'll have a brew and then get stuck into your attic.'

'Great.'

I'm heading inside when Mitzi steps up.

'Stop. *I'm* going to make this drink. Strong builder's, Carl, not a lot of milk, right? Can I get you one, Janet?'

Er . . . Mitzi never asks me. Not that I'm a martyr or anything, but well, it doesn't happen very often.

'All right, thanks. An Earl Grey, please, not a lot of milk, and leave the tea bag in.'

Carl pipes up, 'And get us a piece of that millionaire's shortbread, Mitz. You want one, Janet? Make it two.'

Carl and I both perch on a lounger each, and before we know it we are both lying with our feet up relaxing, enjoying some milky sunshine, being served by Mitzi in a strange turn of the tables.

'Make sure they pay you before they go,' Carl says to me as he struggles with trails of caramel around his fingers. 'There's a lot of red bills coming through the door at that Larkspur House.'

I frown. 'Really?' I'm shocked to hear that and I'm still taking it in as Laura appears at the door with armfuls of dresses all bagged up in dry cleaning covers. I need to use the opportunity.

'Let me help with those.' I jump up and reach out to

grab a couple, and she reluctantly hands one or two over. Massimo Dutti, Karen Millen, Ghost, Jasper Conran. All immaculate pastels. I follow her to the car.

'So, you're definitely leaving today?'

'This is the last of my things.'

I take a deep breath. This is hideous, I'm sweating with embarrassment.

Handing the outfits over, I say, 'We should . . . er . . . probably settle up then, if that's the case, or will Oliver be dealing with i–?'

She's in like a blast before I've even got all my words out.

'Definitely Oliver. His mess. His to clean up.' She throws the dresses into the back of the car, and it's now I notice that it's packed with expensive-looking shoe boxes and shopping bags.

'OK, I'll talk to Oliver then. I hope you've had a nice stay, under the circumstances, Laura.' I'm being a bit obsequious, I know I am, but Superhost status is glowing like a neon light on the horizon and the Watsons have been here three weeks. I really need good reviews if I'm to stand a chance of making anything out of Lavander Cottage now – and God knows, with my situation at the moment, I need every scrap of cash and good luck going.

Laura, now sitting in the car, clicks her seatbelt, pulls on her impenetrable designer dark sunglasses and slides down the electric window.

'Between your crapping cat, uncomfortable bed, grubby shower and nymphomaniac sister, it's probably been one of the worst times of my life, Janet. That answer your question?' She hits reverse at speed, does what is almost a handbrake turn and screeches off down the road. I'm left as one of those figures hit by an arctic blast from the White Witch of Narnia, frozen to the spot, gobsmacked by the ruthlessness of the character they're dealing with and foolishly naïve to the danger.

Oh my God. *What is the review going to say?*

REVIEW

*One Star

Cottage needs an update. Uncomfortable beds. Women guests: watch out for your husband.

TIP FOR RUNNING A B&B

Don't do it. It's so bloody hard. Soul crushing. And expensive. No one's ever happy. You barely make any money. You have no control over what people say or do about you and your cottage. I don't know why I bother. Sorry, I'm being a miserable bugger. I can't help it.

TIPS ON LIFE

Don't sleep with the boss. It will go horribly wrong. You'll end up paying the price.

If someone, say a neighbour, is not very nice, maybe they'll always be not very nice. You can make an effort to get on and it might feel like you *are* getting on. But inside, the truth is, they're still not very nice. So don't be shocked when they prove it by being horrible.

CHAPTER 10

Chloe

Chloe is going to be eighteen and has asked if she can have a party in Lavander Cottage instead of in the house. She has officially booked the cottage through the apps, so at least all being well, that will be the first positive review post Lauragate.

Laura's terrible review after everything we had done for her, rescuing her home and build with Carl's help and putting her and Oliver up for three whole weeks, has felt like a gut punch that has gradually spread into a slow sadness. All my dreams and plans have been thrown to the horizon. It's almost impossible to imagine getting Superhost this year after that blow. I'd need so many Five Stars to compensate. The bookings have disappeared too, and that can't be a coincidence. Who wouldn't read that review and conclude, *I don't think so*. And the Watsons still haven't settled their bill.

I have been a bit depressed after that, and after the Miles situation. These last few weeks, I've gone around in slow motion. Not much energy to do anything. It's fair to say I have had an official case of The Doldrums. Hey ho. Spring's coming, the bluebells are out, it's time to get myself going again. *Make a plan and get a job, Janet!*

Chloe, the darling, has started giving me fifteen pounds a week toward her board. I didn't ask for anything, she just gave me it one day. I was head deep in spreadsheets and receipts at the kitchen table, trying to work out who else I could call to try to bring down monthly payments. I'd managed to persuade pretty much every credit card and utility to accept lower monthly amounts. They all sounded very used to the requests and the call centre staff were very sympathetic – once you'd got through to them. I got on so well with Sue from Water that I told her what had happened – that I'd had a fling with the boss in a weak moment and now I was out of a job trying to decide what to do next. She was very nice and told me how she'd once slept with the boss's son as a young woman at a Christmas party, and how she'd been given her notice on Christmas Eve and never saw him again.

'Are you on benefits?' she asks kindly.

'I can't face it,' I tell her. 'I've never claimed anything in my life, Sue, except child benefit. And now my daughter's coming up to eighteen, so that will stop too.'

She is so kind and sympathetic. 'My advice is, get yourself something bearable part-time and take tax credit top-up. It's the only way to do it these days. Most people are struggling, love. They might put on a good show, but we talk to everyone and they're all just keeping afloat.'

Sue managed to negotiate my monthly payment down by twenty quid a month, citing difficult circumstances and single-parent status.

'You're a diamond among utility call agents, Sue.'

'I know, Janet.'

I'll have to get a job soon, but what? It's scary really, when you have to think about jobs and careers in mid-life. It's not something I've had to do for nearly a decade. I had my run of really grim jobs as a teen and a young woman and then I gravitated towards admin in some type or another, bank, post office, dentist. Clean jobs behind a desk, set hours and not too taxing, not something I'd ever have to take home with me. Boring but reliable, a job that would allow me to get home and sort out Chloe. The difference now is I don't really need to do that any more. She's a grown-up, earning, giving me money! I'm the one who's drifting and unemployed.

I'm paralysed about what to do. Scared to commit to something and watch another decade slip by. Do I retrain? As what? Do I try and do something I might actually enjoy, such as part-time home help, cook, gardener? Right, yeah. I'm already doing that here. Chins up, Janet, I tell myself. Something will come up. Chloe, bless her, giving *me* some cash. Her positivity is what's keeping me going at the moment.

'Mum, I'm earning OK at the moment, so this is toward bills and everything. If you could get in a few more snacks, decent crisps, more chocolate, smoothies – y'know, the sort of stuff I like.'

I do, and they cost at least fifteen pounds a week on their own. I can't begrudge her though, she's trying to be supportive, and I appreciate the effort, so the party is definitely on and it's the least I can do. It's not as if I can take her on the long-promised holiday, not this year anyway. What's great is that one mention of the party idea and everyone, including her dad Franklin, wants to help Chloe have a fantastic time.

Carl digs out some old party lights, climbs on his stepladder and wraps them around the inside of the beamed entrance to Lavander Cottage, which looks great. I bake her a two-tier chocolate and lemon cake with lemon butter-cream icing. I make some white chocolate shards and stick them onto the cake, which is tricky, then add on different-coloured hundreds and thousands, with chocolate ones on the lemon cake and multicoloured ones on the chocolate. I'm well chuffed with it. Chloe loves it and takes a load of photos for her social media.

Mitzi writes her a poem that she reads out to her as Chloe listens, hair in a turban, one false eyelash on, waiting for her fake tan to dry, as she munches on a pot noodle. It's called 'Listen Up'.

'Tell me, what does eighteen feel like from there, sweet niece?

At eighteen, I hitchhiked to London, set my sights on the universe.

My heart hungry for heartbreak, my back broken from the baggage of a wicked home.

'Tell me, what does eighteen feel like from there?

'At eighteen, I danced my way around the world, set my sights on the stars.

Your beauty, sweet niece, will carry you to a million places,

your clever brain will get you in and out of them all.

'Tell me, what does eighteen feel like from there?

'Let me tell you what to do:
Eat the peach, drown in love, dive into the sea of
possibility.
Grab your year, Sweet Eighteen. Grab your year.
Grab your year.'

'Ah, that's good, that is, Auntie Mitz,' Chloe says. 'Love it. Thank you. I don't know how much drowning in love I'll be doing whilst I'm working forty hours at Moloko's in Halifax, but I promise I'll try to grab what rears I can.'

She's so funny, my daughter. No wonder she's so popular. She has a huge social media following, apparently. The photos of the cake she shows me get over two hundred likes. I'm a bit surprised – two hundred people? I don't know two hundred people. I don't *want* to know two hundred people. Keeping up with Mitzi and Chloe keeps me busy enough. They share a hug, it's so sweet. Mitzi is definitely warming up as she gets older and Chloe is such an open-minded girl it's lovely.

Mitzi gets a bit giddy after we have an early glass of celebratory fizz. She demos sixteen possible outfits in order to choose what to wear to the party. Mitzi's wardrobe is a kaleidoscope of wonder. Thanks to years spent trawling charity shops and car boot sales, markets and jumble sales, she has accumulated the most spectacular collection of weird and wonderful clothes. How can I describe the look? If Sarah Jessica Parker time-travelled via Glastonbury festival and morphed into a member of Bananarama sort of sums it up. Mitzi settles on a butterfly costume: a dip-dye sequin tube dress with these huge sheer rainbow voile panels that hang off both arms and a headpiece with two black glittery antennae, like pimped-up deely boppers. She looks amazing.

Chloe wants her to stand at the door and welcome every guest with a glass of prosecco.

'I'll do it with pleasure, Chloe, but I won't be able to accept anyone who looks as if they haven't made an effort. It's about standards.'

I disagree. 'For some people, a clean pair of trainers is a major effort. Or if they bring a bottle, that's a five gold stars effort. In fact, how many people are we expecting, Chloe?' A little flush of fear rattles through me, contemplating boys with bottles rampaging around the cottage.

'Oh, it's dead exclusive, Mum. Twenty max. Close friends only.'

'Girls and boys?'

'Of course.'

'Right, right. Do their mums and dads know? I mean, you're eighteen. No one can object if you drink alcohol. And I'm not objecting, I'm just sort of saying. Is it a good idea?'

Both Mitzi and Chloe pile in at this stage to object to my not objecting. I've clearly crossed a line. I leave them to their arrangements and get on with some more cooking. Chloe has asked for cupcakes, all different colours, which will then be put into the shape of a giant C. I absolutely love making them. I've got to be a pretty dab hand at icing over the years and I've gone for a pastel-pink themed rainbow effect, adding extra food colouring over time so it goes from a really creamy pastel pink through to a deep lilac. I'm arranging them in the cottage on a table we've set up for food, and they look pretty blooming good. So I take photos that I pass on to Chloe for her socials. Get me, I'm really with it!

Mitzi and Chloe disappear to get ready, so I use the opportunity to remove anything particularly precious from the cottage. I'm on my way out with a favourite vase and pretty sofa throw when Carl arrives, lugging a giant speaker.

'Where we putting the sound system?' he wants to know.

'Sound system?' I'm trying to compute what's happening when in comes another giant speaker, carried by a sweaty Franklin.

'Hiya, Janet, where's this going?' he puffs.

'I'm not sure. I didn't know we were doing this.'

'Chloe, she asked me to sort a sound system. It's my old mate Jacko's, you remember Jacko?' My ex-husband stares at me, as if of course I know Jacko. Trying to remember the name is like batting cobwebs away down an old corridor in a house I long since left and can barely remember living in. He's there somewhere, but right now I can't place him.

'Er . . . not really.'

'He sends his best. We're gonna have to make some more room. Can we put this pool table down?'

Before I've opened my mouth to reply, Carl and Franklin have dismantled the pool table then put it back up outside on the drive. I hope it's not going to rain. I've removed the last of my ornaments and am tweaking the icing on the final cupcake when the speaker blasts out. The icing shoots across the worktop as I leap out of my wits. It's one of Franklin's old

Trojan Records classics and boy, does it have a bass. I can remember us bumping and swaying to that tune so much as a young mum and dad, not having a clue about what we were doing or how we were going to manage. 'Never mind, don't worry, the baby is fine, let's put on another tune.'

I can't help myself and go into the cottage where Chloe, Mitzi, Carl and Franklin are dancing away. I join them and it's such a good laugh. Franklin wanders over and takes my hands one at a time and we do a little bit of swaying, I can see Chloe watching us from the corner of my eye. When Franklin twirls me round under his arm it's such a blast of the past, like slipping into a warm bath. I'm grateful when the song comes to an end and I can make my excuses and leave, *quickly*.

Upstairs in my bedroom, I dig out my electric-blue jumpsuit. Chloe made me buy it last year. It's bold for me, but Mitzi's butterfly gives me courage, since literally no one is going to be looking in my direction whilst she's in vision. Chloe is going bodycon, fake tan, contouring, eyelashes that could literally sweep up the yard, lips that seem as if they've had multiple bee stings. It's quite the look. Not as Chloe, you under-stand, but an attractive someone else. I barely recognise her when she totters downstairs. She looks amazing.

A van arrives at five to six with a balloon arch she has ordered. It has a light-up sign that says *Birthday*, so people can do their social media photos against it. Apparently everyone has them now. It takes up half the reception room, so Carl, Franklin and I hump even more furniture out of there into the main house to give her some more space.

Franklin approaches me as we drop the console table into the kitchen.

'You want me stick around, sort of thing? Make sure everything goes OK?'

Parties were always his thing, and I can't deny him his daughter's eighteenth. Plus, if there is trouble, I decide, he will know what to do.

'Yes, please, if you don't mind. Want a cuppa?'

'I've brought some beers and even a little rum.'

I smile. Franklin makes a mean Mojito. We're an hour in, and I've already had two. The music is loud but not too loud. There's quite a few of Chloe's old school friends in the cottage, and it's all feeling very civilised and fun when the question comes: have we any more ice? Now everyone looks in my direction, but I've had a drink and can't drive. Of course she'll need ice, why didn't I think of it? Plus I want to keep everyone's drinks watered down, so I volunteer to get some.

'I'll walk down to the Co-op.'

I set off before anyone notices or can get involved. I'm strolling down the road with a couple of jute bags as a couple of cars go past me up towards the house. I know they're party friends as I can hear Chloe shrieking when they pull up. As I pass Laura's I notice she is out on the porch with a glass in her hand, but I don't let on. I haven't forgiven her for the review and they still owe me £1200 – twenty nights at £30 per person per night. I'm going to get heavy with them on Monday about the money, I've decided. I'm going to ask Carl to come down with me as I know Oliver goes to jelly around Carl. I've politely asked the Watsons three times now to settle their bill. I started off with an email that was ignored, then I texted, was ignored, then I saw Oliver in the street and mentioned it and he apologised and said things had been chaotic since they'd moved back in and he promised me he would get to it this week.

That was two weeks ago. Why do they need to make it so difficult? Pay your bills, you swine! If I wanted to make the mortgage this month, they were going to *have to* pay it. I'm sweating by the time I get back to our street, lugging eight bags of ice, having cleared the Co-op of their entire stock. I can't help but get slightly nervous due to the amount of traffic now clogging up our street. Every inch of the road is parked up and there are what look like streams of people heading toward Lavander Cottage. The noise of music, party chatter and laughter is hitting the high-decibel range.

As I hurry past Laura's I hear a door slam – I'm not sure how to interpret that. I get back to the party and it's crazier than I'd imagined. Mitzi is DJ-ing at a phenomenal pace to a cottage that is rammed full of teenagers bouncing up and down to 90s' club anthems. I get told by a random girl I have never met before in my life that a friend of a friend of the birthday girl, called 'Amelia', is apparently upstairs sound asleep in Chloe's bed having 'had enough'. I go to the bathroom to see what mess is in there, to find two girls are holding each other's hair back as they take turns to throw up in the loo. I run back downstairs where the party has now spilled into the garden, with teenagers raving on the lawn and on the drive. I can see a heavy-petting young couple splayed against my verbena, and completely oblivious to them a pair of lads are having the beginnings of a tussle, all whilst Carl and Frankin calmly continue playing pool.

'What's happening?' I ask them. 'And where's Chloe? This party is getting way out of control.'

As if my words are the ignition, the tussle between the two lads grows into full-blown fisticuffs. Streams of kids emerge from the cottage with shouts and screams that are a mixture of encouragement and their attempts to stop the fight escalating. Once punches start being thrown and the chants of 'Fight, fight, fight,' get going, Carl and Franklin put down their pool cues and wade into the middle of the crowd to attempt to sort it out.

Carl immediately gets punched in the face by one of the lads. He doesn't move an inch, which is hugely intimidating for everyone, watching and wondering what he is going to respond with. Whilst we are taking that in, the other lad does some sort of kung fu move and kicks Franklin's legs out from under him. Tall and lanky as Franklin is, taken completely unawares, he makes a dramatic drop onto the ground. Carl reaches down to help him up, and now like a scene out of a cartoon, someone shouts, 'Pile on!' and the kids immediately start to topple and throw themselves onto Franklin, Carl and the other boys, et cetera.

I survey the scrum of bodies for a few seconds when Chloe staggers out of the cottage, takes one look and says to me in a desperate way, 'Oh God! Sort it out, Mum.'

I take a fast decision. Attaching my hose to the outside tap and using the nozzle, I begin to spray the hill of mangled shouty bodies with cold water. It does the trick. The stack erupts, as people dive and roll to escape the spray. It's all calming down now, aggression turning to laughter and screams of fun as I make liberal use of the spray on everyone there. It sweetens up the atmosphere, but the tension is immediately ramped up again as we are all deafened and blinded by the sound of loud police sirens and neon-blue flashing lights as not one, but two police cars skid to a halt in front of the house.

I feel as if I have been caught red-handed wielding a weapon and do the only reasonable thing I can think of and start to use the hose now to spray the flower tubs. Of course this is perfectly normal behaviour at ten o'clock at night with a hundred teenagers on my lawn. Two burly coppers and two equally intimidating female officers stride menacingly up the drive.

I feel all shaky and do a nervous, 'Hello.' Of course I don't mean to, but as I swerve to acknowledge them, I take the hose with me and a swirl of cold-water pebbledashes all four of them.

'Oh my God, I'm so sorry.' I drop the hose and put my hands in the air as if I'm being arrested in a movie. The nozzle jumps off with the impact of the hose hitting the ground, and the hose, now completely out of control, flails on the lawn, spraying water everywhere, including over me and very annoyingly also over the police people. Thank God Chloe realises what's going on and the water finally stops.

'I've, like, turned off the tap,' she says breathlessly.

'Thank you,' says one of the officers, who I notice is dripping wet. Through gritted teeth she asks, 'Whose house is this?'

So, as Lavander Cottage is *my* home and the party is at *my* house, and I'm the one spraying four police officers with water, it's inevitable that *I'm* the one in trouble. I end up, wet through, steaming and a teeny bit tipsy still, at the police station. Only once everyone has dried off does the tea come out and the atmosphere lighten up a bit. Three hours later, I call a taxi and return home stuck with a caution for noise and disturbance in a residential area and told that any more incidents of this nature and I will be given an Asbo. I assure them that won't be happening.

Franklin, Carl, Chloe and Mitzi and a random stray teenager are waiting up for me when I get home. Chloe has knocked up a stack of blueberry pancakes with cream, and a giant pot of tea is being refilled as I arrive through the patio door to a cheer.

I explain that the police had been called by a worried neighbour, concerned that there was a party going on that had gotten out of control.

'Who would call?' Chloe asks, and I know she is feeling guilty that her party had led to this.

'I had pre-warned everyone around here that we were having a party and to expect some noise.' Any normal person would have done so, and I am normal.

Chloe is livid. 'Bloody Laura bloody Watson, any money.'

Of course it was, I'm sure she's right.

Quite how I am ever going to get revenge on that woman is beyond me. Mitzi insists on making me a police arrest-type card thing with my name on it and then takes a photo of me holding it. She and Chloe mess about with it on filters and turn it black and white and retro then print it out and stick it on the wall. It's hilarious. I look like a latter-day Annie Oakley. I can laugh because I'm so exhausted I'm beyond caring. I look around at the piles of rubbish and debris scattered about the garden and could weep. The general upside-downness of the whole night has left me feeling absolutely wasted.

The clean-up can wait until tomorrow. After all, I don't have a job to go to. Do I?

'I'm off to bed.'

I'm out like a light and wake up early, still tired, but fired up with the sense that there's a lot to do and there's no point putting it off. I pull on some scruffs and go downstairs, braced for what I'm to face, only it's not too bad at all. The dishwasher at home is full of glasses, with another stack ready to go in. I tiptoe into the cottage, where Franklin is asleep on top of the sound system. The balloon arch is down on the floor, with the neon birthday flashing intermittently. I turn it off at the wall and retreat to let my ex get in a few more zeds. I go back outside and find Chloe out there, still in her party dress. She's got a recycling bag and is collecting up cans and bottles from around the garden.

'I'll do that, love,' I tell her. 'Have you been to bed yet?'

She twirls around, one eyelash stuck to her cheek, her make-up gone, her hair a tangled clump, some sort of stain on her dress, and she's barefoot. She also has a huge beaming smile that could light up a dark room.

'Mum. I love you. Best party *ever*.'

She drops the bag and runs and throws her arms around me, and whatever I am thinking, feeling or worrying about evaporates with the love coming from this lunatic, wonderful daughter I adore more than life itself.

'Happy Birthday, love, Happy Birthday.'

REVIEW

***** Five Stars

Wonderful space for a get-together. Best-ever hostess. A huge big thank you. We'll *definitely* come again.

TIPS FOR RUNNING A B&B

Yes, you might have a wonderful space that is suitable for parties, but avoid if at all possible. Unless you really want to annoy the neighbours. *There's a thought.*

Try to get your paying guests to pay *before they leave*. This may be fundamentally obvious, but people are sneaky and unpredictable. The most respectable, they're the ones who can really take you by surprise. Be better at it than me. Hold someone or something hostage. Get a flaming deposit.

TIP ON REVENGE

Anyone got any?

CHAPTER 11

The Carers

The request email about the cottage drops into my inbox first thing Monday morning. What a nice surprise to start the week and a wonderful distraction from the tenth job application form I've half-filled in. A mid-week two-night booking – Tuesday through till Thursday – from an organisation called Dove-care rather than an individual. The group consists of two carers and a teenager, and they ask if we have enough beds. Everyone has a double: there's 'a large double bedroom next to the family-sized bathroom' – anyone else sleeps in a single in the bedroom or on the double sofabed downstairs. They were happy with that and having exchanged details, they have arranged to arrive tomorrow at 2 p.m. That £180 will come in very handy indeed.

The clear-up from the party has been an epic, and this email gives me the momentum I needed to get it finished. Sunday was a giant communal hangover, everyone bleary-eyed with stops every half hour for bacon sandwiches and strong teas. Monday, I promised myself, would be the deep clean. Two hours of solid focus on my job applications and then into the cottage for the belt and braces.

I have psychologically prepared myself. It was a big party, I tell myself, and it's not going to be pretty. I pull on my rubber gloves. Sure enough, when I warily let myself in, superficially things don't look too bad, but once I get going, it's a different story. I find some of those little gas canisters under the bed. Nitrous oxide – laughing gas. Not good. I'm sure it's banned. The parents would not like that. There's biro graffiti scoured across the bathroom door. I mean, do I really need to know that Willow fancies Gavin. Next I find two used condoms stuck between stained bedsheets, ugh! It's a party crime scene and I'm glad there's only me to clear up the evidence. I spend a long time sanding down the bathroom door and re-painting it, before mopping, polishing and airing the place, re-making the beds with fresh clean linen and looking into every corner to make sure nothing has been left behind. I put back all the ornaments and precious things I had removed, and gradually, after about four hours solid graft, Lavander Cottage is back to presentable.

Hallelujah!

Back to the job applications. I had started off being a bit fussy about jobs, only going for quite grand-sounding admin manager-type roles. Dental receptionist roles were nowhere to be found – wrapped up in the scarcity of dentists, I suppose. So this was my third week at it, and now I was knocking CVs out here, there and everywhere in a scatter-gun approach. *Had I ever worked in a shop?* Yes, as an underage teenager serving cigs when I wasn't even old enough to smoke them. *Have you ever been a Carer?* Well, I've had a lot of caring responsibilities. Looking after Mitzi and Chloe, does that count? *Chef?* I am never out of the kitchen, is that relevant experience? I've applied for everything going. *Wanted – landscape gardener used to heavy machinery.* Yes, I do all my own lawn, after all. *Department store fashion retail manager?* Why the heck not, I wear clothes, don't I?

The rejections are stacking up, but I've made a special email box for them. As soon as I spot any words like 'we're sorry' or 'unsuccessful' on the email I don't read any further, I simply slip it into the Boring Not For Me labelled special inbox. At some point, I know that my skills are going to match up with something somebody in a twenty-mile radius wants, and then it's all going to be OK. What's that saying? 'What's meant for you won't go by you' – oh, won't it? I try repeating that kind of guff as a mantra ten times a day, to absolutely no effect.

The fact is, gentle reader, I'm so busy at home I'm beginning to wonder how I'll fit a job in. The en-suite is coming on great guns. Carl is banging, screwing and sawing all hours, and so far there's only been one unfortunate incident, a leak through the landing ceiling as the tiles around the bath weren't sealed in properly. It was an epic getting the bath up there; it needed a hole cutting into the floor and six blokes heaving on ropes. We managed to cover the landing ceiling with stain block and re-painted it and now you'd never know unless you stared at it, which of course I do, noticing the minor ring stains *every time* I walk upstairs. Hey ho.

The amount of dust and muck is killing me. To save the carpet, I draped spare sheets all the way up the stairs, which meant that everyone thought it was OK to keep their mucky boots on, so there's trodden-in filth everywhere. When I find some clay in between my toes after I step out of the shower, it's the last straw. I have to repeat to myself, 'It's not forever, this isn't forever.' This is the other mantra I swap about with my 'What's meant for you, etc' one. It's not very exciting inside this head at the moment, that's for sure, but thanks to my mantras and an addiction to social media recipes *and fig rolls*, I'm just about keeping going.

We have reached a milestone with the ensuite bathroom/remodelled bedroom/attic where we need to agree on a paint colour. I'd seen a nice background in a magazine fashion shoot with Fiona Bruce, whilst Mitzi has picked up something from an architectural digest magazine featuring Carla Bruni or someone else French. After an hour of 'heated discussion' Carl gets sick of it and throws the local paint-shop's colour chart at us.

'Forget fantasy colours,' he grumbles, 'and try the actual colour chart.'

'Carl, the way things are going with my shamanic teaching, I'll be running three shaman classes a week from this space,' Mitzi snaps. 'I need it to reflect the inner journey, and I'm not going to find that at Dickie's DIY, am I?'

Carl gives it to her straight. 'Forget the bloody hippies, we need to be able to take a dump in peace and get seven hours uninterrupted.'

Mitzi storms out of the kitchen after that for a smoke in the garden. So rather than get involved in what has the potential to become a grumpy domestic I decide to capitulate. Midnight Blue. It'll be so dark up there, we might as well not have spent all that time and money opening it up and flooding it with light. But hey, I give it three months before there's a tub of whitewash up there.

The carers arrive separately, both in gleaming new cars. They're very nice and tell me that 'they're working in the area', 'they're doing a conference thing locally' and 'they're providing a change of scenery to their charge'. The girl they're responsible for turns out to be a teenager with a lovely smile. The carers are also carrying a lot of bottles of booze, is what I notice as the carrier bags chink on their way past. *Don't be judgy, Janet.*

Once they're settled in I relax a little bit. They love the cottage, or at least they say some kind things. The Laura review has really knocked my confidence, the b.i.t.c.h. I don't like calling anyone that, but she deserves it. I decide it's time to go and hassle the b.i.t.c.h. and Oliver about the cash they owe me. Carl is busy fixing taps and it's a 'bastard of a job' apparently, so I don't want to disturb him. I decide I can do this without him by my side. *I can do this.*

I put on a suit jacket and as I power my way up the drive, the front door of Larkspur House opens and Laura, immaculate in a head-to-toe merino camel cashmere twin-set and powder-pink Uggs gives me a huge smile.

'Janet. *Fabulous.* Just the person! Come and take a look at Vale Villa. You are going to be the first person to see it finished.'

Oh, lucky me. What is she on about? Vale Villa? Two minutes inside I realise this is the self-catering space she was dreaming of creating. *This* was the reason for the extension. 'Al for Laura and Ve for Oliver, of course,' she trills. Of course? That doesn't quite explain the Villa bit or the fact there isn't a Vale. Heck, I have a garage that I call a cottage – who am I to say anything?

Vale Villa is like something out of a Nicole Kidman movie. It is immaculate: glass banister panels, a million shades of beige, a sheepskin rug here, a velvet throw there, a rope swing, a chandelier, big mirrors, a foot-and-claw bath, rose-gold taps. Laura is on full transmit and I'm on full nosy so I happily glide along for the full tour.

'These are from Biddulph – you know, the designer brand all the Cheshire housewives use? I managed to source them locally, and I'm *so* pleased with them.' She smiles over at me, it's entirely genuine, so I smile back even though I'm not actually sure what she's pointing at. The lampshades? The rugs? The candelabra?

'What do you think, Janet? Will people want to come?'

'I'm sure they will, Laura, it's gorgeous.'

'Do you think so? That's nice of you to say. Yes, I'm really pleased with how it's turned out. We're going to be putting it on a very exclusive site, as we don't want *just anyone* coming in, you understand? It's going to be very upmarket. So we won't be competing with your little place at all. No competition to worry about, Janet.'

I feel the hairs on the back of my neck go up like a dog sensing danger; what new sly elbow in the jugular should I be expecting next? *My little place*. My little place was good enough for her when she was begging me to let her stay. Right. Enough already. She's lured me in for a kicking – why do I always fall for it? But I've not come here to take any of her nonsense. I've come here to get my money. It's bloody obvious she's got plenty of it by the look of this place, or she's been spending all *my* money making her blooming villa look top brass.

I seize the initiative. Say coolly, 'Well, talking of *my little place*, Laura, I'm here to chase up payment from when you and Oliver came to stay. It's approaching five weeks since you left and well, I do need that money now.'

'Oh darling. Yes, of course you do. Have you checked your bank account? I'm certain Oliver put it in this morning. We've just been *sooo* busy that we've let all sorts of little things escape us whilst we've had our minds on the extension. We're all caught up now. Do you have the app? Go on – have a check now. I wouldn't want you worrying or out of pocket, not when you've lost your job and your little business is all you have now.'

It's infuriating. I go onto the app on my phone, and yes, there it is – the payment went through this morning.

'Oh right, yes, sorry, thank you, it's there.' I'm apologising to her, it's infuriating. *That's all you have now. Argh.*

'Not a problem, *great* to see you. I hope Chloe had a lovely party, I heard that the police came. Dearie me – was it you I saw in the police car?'

'She had a fabulous time,' I say with sincerity, and I chuckle reminiscently. 'Yes, what a hoot – it was me in the police car. I was arrested for having too much of a good time. Stuck between four strapping young men doing "Oops Upside Your Head". Hilarious. They were fake coppers – you know, the stripper type? You should have seen me, there's footage somewhere. Bye, bye, Laura, good luck with your venture!'

I laugh and wave as I stroll back down the driveway, thinking, You utter bitch. I don't know where 'Oops Upside Your Head' came from. What was I thinking? And strippers? A genius touch, if I say so myself, and I'll say anything. Anything to thwart her spite and her nasty mean mind-games. She can take her bloody palace and charge the earth for it, having done her best to rubbish my poor Lavander Cottage with her horrible review. That's my bookings down some more.

Farewell to any chance of Janet Jackson Superhost. Who will want to spend time at my little garage when there's that fancy-pants Hebden Hilton down the road?

I grit my teeth, thinking fast. I'll have to come up with a plan to attract the crowds. *Yeah, right.* I've not got a brass farthing extra to spend anywhere to attract anyone. Oh well. Concentrate on the good stuff, Janet. Twelve hundred pounds are in the bank account, which will cover bills for the next six weeks, and add to that another one hundred and eighty in from the carers. Bonus. Everything is fine for now. I will not let Laura bloody Watson ruin my day. Then another thought strikes me: Nicole Kidman or not, Laura has no idea what she has let herself in for. Guests, as I have learned from my own bitter-sweet experience, come in all shapes, sizes and behaviours. There is no way she will get through this unscathed.

Bloody good luck to you, Laura bloody Watson!

Back home, I collect up my gloves, tools and trug and set off around the garden. I chop out the dead leaves from some leggy perennials, dig out and divide some unusual geraniums, pull back the bramble that's exploded behind the shed. I track the bulbs popping up and work out where I really need to in-fill with new plants, prop and train the roses, weed out the dandelions from the flower beds and after a couple of hours, I'm scratched to blazes, feeling proud of myself and desperate for a cuppa. I go into the kitchen where Chloe is making herself a giant hot-chocolate creation and is buzzing fit to burst when she sees me.

'Mum, Mum, guess what? I've got you a job!'

'Sweetheart, I'm way too long in the tooth to be bar staff at Moloko's.'

'No. Frida's mum, she's been in touch – y'know Frida, from the party? Jessica's mate?'

I've absolutely no idea, but smile encouragingly,

wondering how Chloe suspects her mate Frida's mum is about to solve my employment crisis.

'It's like this. She wants a cake doing, she saw mine on Insta and loved it and wants one for Frida's party next weekend, only all chocolate or something.'

I get Frida's mum's details and after a few text exchanges, where I explain I'm not a professional cake-maker and I can't guarantee it will be perfect, I eventually agree to do a two-tier chocolate black and white cake with a piano keyboard motif up the side. What am I thinking? Anything to avoid a job, is what I'm actually doing. At least I can pretend I'm doing something useful to justify all this time off actual work. It'll be cash in hand, seventy-five quid. She came up with the price. Chloe told me they're minted so I'm just rolling with it. It's a lovely excuse to sit back, relax and scroll through the internet looking at fabulous cakes made by some absolute geniuses.

I spend the evening nibbling at a grazing plate I've conjured up from jars in the fridge and a home-made flatbread and hummus, whilst half-watching some daft cooking show on the telly. I keep noticing the odd car coming up and down the road and think nothing of it. It gets to ten o'clock and I'm yawning. I drop some recycling into the bin outside the front door and realise there's not two cars there now, but four. I look up at the cottage and see that every light is on. Every single light. Blimey, don't they know anything about being energy conscious? The blinds are all drawn down so I can't see in but I can see that every room is lit up. Let it go, Janet, I tell myself. They're guests, they can do what they like.

I'm pottering around the kitchen doing the last bits of tidying up before bed when a text pops up on my phone.

Sofa bed broek. Sorry.

I take it they mean they've broken the sofa-bed. Maybe they just haven't worked out how to open and close it.

Do you want me to come and try to fix it?

No. No. well wedje it tonite. Sorry.

Hmm. Great. The sofa-bed is broken. They're going to wedje it? What does that mean? That was not a cheap sofa-bed. It's fully sprung with a memory mattress, not one of those foam-block things. How have they managed to break it? I sense the £180 in my pocket almost slide out onto the floor. I'm suddenly not looking forward to the clean-up. Do I need to tackle them about how many people they have in the cottage? Bloomin' heck, can I not have a single straightforward experience for once?

Here's how it should go: when people book Lavander Cottage, I prepare the cottage, they are the people they say they are, they treat someone else's property with respect, and in a well-established system they get a nice place to stay and I get a fair exchange of money.

But somehow, this situation doesn't bode well. It's the bad spelling. It's the number of cars. It's the booze.

I don't have the best night's sleep. I'm fretting about the cottage, then Chloe gets in late from work and what with the stairs creaking and the toilet flush I'm wide awake and over-heating like I don't know what, courtesy of Mrs Menopause. Eventually I give up and go downstairs to feed the cat and empty the dishwasher. When I look out onto the street, I see that both extra cars are gone. Maybe I dreamed it?

Later that day, the carers are walking past the kitchen

window looking very respectable, all blouse and skirt and guiding arm around their teenager. They give me a friendly wave and I wave back. I'm getting paranoid, I decide, and I need a job soon if I'm going to spend my time concocting nonsense. I get on and make a trial chocolate cake and then I can't help myself and make a trial lemon one. They both look pretty fancy by the time I've finished, though it's taken me a good few hours to get them looking perfect. I take a photo, and when they're done I head off for a walk down to the popular local café in the area, The Tasty Mug.

The lovely owner is clearing tables when I go in so I grab my moment, show her a picture of the cakes, explain that I'm making a birthday cake for a 'client' and that these are my trial runs, and ask if she'd be interested in buying them. It's cheeky, but it works and twenty minutes later I've dropped them off and have forty pounds cash in my pocket. Boy, does that feel good! So good I sit down and order a hummus, carrot and chutney sandwich and a cup of tea and sit for half an hour reading a crafting magazine that's lying about. I'm feeling happy. And I deserve a break.

I'm sitting there enjoying myself, relaxing, when the lovely owner brings me a little slice of the chocolate cake and a top-up of my tea, free of charge. Well, I'm in heaven. Very happy with the cake, which is so rich it's almost double fudge, whilst still being a light sponge. I congratulate myself on the ganache, which is delicious, and has a great consistency without being sickly. I got the cocoa bitterness just right.

I'm seeing a whole new career rolling out in front of me, cake-maker to the stars, cake-maker for Christmas, for birthdays, weddings and christenings . . . cake-maker for anyone who wants one really. I'm in a wonderful daydream of sugar balls, boxes tied with ribbons, homemade chocolate curls, gold-leaf decoration and fountain candles when a text pops through. It's from Mitzi.

Shit, come quick, bath collapse.

I get up in such a hurry I spill the tea all over my front; the cake plate hits the floor and smashes. Babbling, 'Sorry – emergency at home!' I leave one of her twenty-pound notes for the bewildered owner and I'm out, racing home as fast as I can go on a tummy full of food. No time to call, or think, I puff and pant on to the drive, throw myself inside – and am greeted by mayhem. I can hear Carl shouting, a couple of blokes I've never met before are on the landing holding the bottom half of the bath with their hands at full stretch, whilst Carl looks to be holding it up from the attic above. All around is broken plaster and split floor-boards, the metal spiral staircase is bent in two and Mitzi is looking horrified at the bottom of the hall stairs.

Carl has a sweat on. He shouts down: 'I'm not going to be able to hold on to this much longer. Mitz, Janet – go and find some wood, anything to prop this up.'

We race into the garden, *wood, wood, wood* – where? There's nothing strong or long enough. *Think, think, think.* We have an old stepladder I put plants on – the ladder might do it. We are both hurrying in through the patio door when we hear an almighty crash and the two blokes come pelting down the stairs, a look of fear mingled with excitement on their faces. The noise is tremendous.

After the dust and the shock dies down, we hear a quiet 'Help!' We drop the ladder, and scurry over to the hall to find the bath crashed through what was left of the metal spiral staircase and through the spindles and banister on the main stairs, leaving Carl left hanging by his fingertips to a half-smashed floorboard in the loft, legs flailing as he contemplates dropping onto the chaos. Running back up with the ladder, like an incompetent Laurel and Hardy, my sister and I manage to negotiate past the bath dangling over the staircase like the bus in *The Italian Job* hanging over the precipice on the windy Italian road with Michael Caine and the stolen gold bullion.

We prop the ladder against the top of the house stairs and then lever and support it against the safest-looking bit of hole. Carl wraps half a leg round the top of the ladder, then, making a lurch, he grabs hold of it for an instant and slides down like a pro to land with a thump at the bottom. The bump as he lands seems to unsettle the bath and we all leap back up onto the landing as the sound of splintering grows and the bath shudders through the handrail to do a heavy nosedive onto the floor of the hall.

'Fuckin' bath,' spits Carl.

'I have to agree,' I say breathlessly.

'I need a fag.' And Mitzi picks her way gracefully through the debris, to go and light up outside.

The evening is a blur of pulling and dragging the broken banister, floorboards, the distorted remnants of the metal staircase and the bath out onto the front lawn. When the carers pass by on their way to Lavander Cottage with their teenager and their chinking carrier bags around 5 p.m., I muster up the friendliest half-smile I've got in me and a weak question I don't really want any response to.

'Everything OK?'

'Wonderful, thank you.'

But the pretty teenage girl they are caring for looks

like she has lots of questions. Her eyes are almost popping out of her head at the bath lying on the lawn; she points at it and keeps staring as she's led away into the cottage. Normally, I might be tempted to have a chat, *but not today.*

Carl, Mitzi and I are nursing a bottle of wine and the scraps of fish and chips still in the paper when Chloe piles in through the patio door back from her shift.

'What's with the bath in the front garden?'

We're too tired and dispirited to reply. She takes one look at us and marches into the hall. It's cleaned up now, but the Do Not Enter hazard tape that's stretched across where the banister and spindles once stood to avoid anyone falling through is pretty dramatic. Added to which, the heavy grey plastic that is gaffer-taped across the hole in the ceiling that was attic floor and once supported a bath, but now only offers up an unappealing breezy gap to the Midnight Blue roof of what was Mitzi and Carl's bedroom and ensuite dream.

'Bummer.'

'Yep.'

'Was anyone in the bath when it came through?'

'No.'

'Shame, that would've been pretty funny.' My daughter is heartless.

'Yes, hilarious. I could have had a flood to clean up too. You always help me look on the bright side, Chloe.'

I'm almost being sarcastic, which sort of shows where I'm at. We traipse back into the kitchen, Chloe's head hanging down, and then she suddenly barks at the lot of us.

'This means there'll be more bloody building work now, I suppose. I'm bloody sick of it, I've got dust in my hair every single day.'

'Sorry, love. I thought those joists were solid oak: with an acrylic bath, it should've been fine. A chronic miscalculation. Back to maths school.' Carl is looking crestfallen and guilty. I want to hug him. It's not his fault, he's done his absolute best. Mitzi, who is propped against the half-open patio door smoking a fag, is half-listening, half-watching. It's her turn to grumble.

'I've got six shaman sessions booked in for next week – where am I gonna do those? When do these party animals in the cottage leave?'

'Yes, they are party animals, aren't they?' I agree. 'I've been thinking that. It's all a bit weird for carers on a work trip.'

As I say this, a man I don't recognise sheepishly wanders down the drive with another chinking carrier bag of bottles. I don't do my usual friendly thing since I'm not feeling very friendly after a mammoth day, a wrecked house and a brand new bath lying out on the front lawn.

All I can manage by way of a greeting is a curt: 'Can you ask them to keep the noise down, please?'

He nods weakly as he goes towards the cottage. The ladies must have been waiting since the door opens as soon as he arrives, and the pounding racket of house music leaks out.

'They're meant to be carers, looking after that teen-ager,' I sigh tiredly. 'God knows what they're really up to. I can't be bothered to have it out with them, but they said they broke the sofa-bed last night.'

'When are they leaving?' Mitzi wants to know.

'Tomorrow.'

'Good.'

Carl gets up and stretches with an almighty yawn,

telling us, 'Ladies, I'll get this sorted, don't worry. Just let me get a night's sleep and I'll have a plan when I wake up. Can I grab a pillow and I'll get me head down in the back room.'

'I'm coming with you.' Mitzi and Carl disappear arm-in-arm.

Chloe rolls her eyes. 'I hate building work.'

'Me too, darling.'

After making a sweep of the fridge, the crisp cupboard, the biscuit jar and the fruit bowl, to gather a carrot, some Hula Hoops, a handful of assorted biscuits and an apple, Chloe tells me, 'I'm off to bed.'

She slopes out of the kitchen, arms and pockets full, moody teenage-style. As I begin the process of locking up, I stare at the cottage and can see in the cracks where the blinds don't entirely fill the edges of the windows, the kaleidoscopic blur of multicoloured lights picked out against the night. I'm fuming. Disco lights? A party? It's not what you expect when you book a couple of carers in for two nights. I'm dreading the electricity bill, the sofa-bed replacement cost and above all the clean-up. My life is non-stop Mrs Mop at the moment.

Later, I lie in bed and try to relax and mentally send myself back to the café. To that last lovely moment when all I had to think about were cake ribbons and soft buttery icing, pastel-coloured hundreds and thousands raining down like a fairy-tale.

'*Muuum*, the hot water's not working.'

'No, it won't be. Sorry, love. It'll have to be a cat-lick wash tonight. We'll hopefully sort everything out tomorrow.'

'CRAP. My hair stinks of hot oil.'

Door slam, door slam, scream of frustration. Sweet dreams, Janet, sweet dreams.

REVIEW

***** Five Stars

Lovely quiet location. Friendly host. Shower a bit cold in the morning.

TIPS FOR RUNNING A B&B

Don't take bookings from Dove-care carers. Hand-marks streaked down the stairwell. Pictures at odd angles. Glasses broken. Sofa-bed jammed as someone has attempted to bend it the wrong way. Two pairs of dirty knickers and a bra. On the plus side they're gone by 8 a.m. and leave a Five-Star review.

TIPS ON LIFE

DIY disasters. Try to have some contingency cash put away for when they happen. *Yeah, right.* Or alternatively do a number of good deeds for a relative in the trades so they owe you big-time. That's a long-term solution but worth it. Start early.

CHAPTER 12

Echo

I am three cakes in and it's only 11 a.m. The lovely woman at The Tasty Mug has asked me for one each of the lemon and chocolate ones, on a weekly basis. Apparently the last two went down really well, and if I can keep the standard up, then it could become a regular order. I am determined these two will be even better.

Chloe has done the research and found that I need to do an online Food Hygiene certificate. She's already booked me on one this week, so now I'm swotting up like crazy so I can try and pass it. Most of it is taking me back to Mrs Babbacombe and her obsession with white scouring powder in Home Economics. OCD wasn't a thing then, of course, but I think it's safe to say on reflection that she probably fitted the diagnosis. The kitchens were cleaner when we finished than when we started!

The piano cake I did for Frida's birthday was a success, I'm glad to say. It was a labour of love, but I suppose the first time of making a cake like that is going to take an age. Anyway, the exciting news is, I've had another cake order! All off the back of the Insta pictures that Chloe took of the piano cake. Her mate

Lucy has a grandma called Sandra who's turning sixty, so I'm now doing a giant cake in the shape of an S for Sandra. She's having a big party in three weeks and apparently is a macchiato coffee fanatic. So it's a coffee cake S with tiny chocolate cups as decorations. I've decided I want there to be six coffee cups, two on top, four around the edge. I've been practising chocolate tempering via the internet for six hours and managed a half-recognisable coffee cup that collapsed soon afterwards.

I'm seeing it all as learning rather than failing. I've been watching the Ziggy Zen channel, and she repeats loads of stuff like 'all failing is learning' and 'please subscribe for more Zen'. Anyway, she's got a lovely room she does all her Zen talks in, she's got great hair and is seventy with the figure of a fit thirty year old, so I reckon Ziggy's on to something. I need all the Ziggy Zen I can muster at the moment.

Mitzi has taken over the cottage, *temporarily*, whilst Carl, bless him, is repairing the attic floor, installing a *very light* shower, restoring the staircase, banisters and spindles, and putting up a new, sturdy metal staircase. He reckons it's cost £3,500 just in materials. Insurance doesn't go anywhere near unfinished DIY. So I don't have it, Mitzi doesn't have it, and so he's stuck it all on the business credit card and we've agreed that's rent for the next seven months at £500 per month. Reasonable enough, considering he gets all his household bills thrown in, and lots of meals.

Meanwhile the cottage is being used as Mitzi's shaman space. From her earnings in there she has agreed to give me £100 a week. That's much better than nothing. As a matter of fact, she is getting a lot of interest in her shaman courses and is starting to advertise – well, I say advertise, but twenty flyers stuck on noticeboards around Hebden seems to be enough to generate a whirl of interest at the moment.

Whether she will keep it going or not, I don't know. I suppose she can always spread the shaman love a bit further and advertise in Todmorden then or Halifax. I reckon people love a new trend, and shamanism is it at the moment. Good for Mitzi. It's long overdue, her finding something she's skilled at and which she enjoys, and which actually provides her with an income of sorts. It's the nearest my sister has come to a permanent job in a long time.

Meanwhile I'm earning around £60 in total a week in cakes, and Chloe the little star has upped her board to £30 a week. I don't know if it's all going to be enough, but if I batch cook the heck out of every scrap of food and we don't put the heating on for another two months, we might just be able to keep our heads above water before I need to think seriously about getting another job. I don't really want to get another job, as I'm *sooo* enjoying making my cakes.

Carl is going to try and restore the floor and staircase at record speed, as he has an extension with his name on it up Elland and they want him to start in three weeks. That would see the shamans back in the attic and me able to go full throttle on the cottage again. With that in mind, I've tentatively left bookings open from three weeks' time, praying for everything to work out. Bring on the Zen, Zen, Zen. I think I'm mixing up religions, with my palms together and eyes raised to the heavens, but hey, that's modern life for you. Everyone is everything these days.

Mitzi has been so busy with her shamans that she's brought in a helper, Echo. The latter is about sixty with hair that's a mixture of dreadlocks and curls, ribbons and string. It's an alternative to hair extensions, let's put it that way. Her clothes are all natural fabrics, you know the type – the never-ironed, faded, washed-out colour, big, strange pockets, hessian-type of garb. It's a style. That's what it is, a style. Accompanied by wide flat shoes that curl up, with rubber toes. You get the picture.

I'm not too sure about Echo. On the surface she's pleasant enough, but she seems to hold something back, that superior air of 'I won't engage, you're not worth my time, my head is with the universe'. I overheard her say she can see into souls – what utter baloney! I can tell if someone is looking sad, I don't need to look into their soul. Echo is hanging around a lot at the moment. I caught her moving things about in the cottage kitchen, which felt a bit odd. She was meant to be bringing nettle tea through to a group Mitzi had got in to do a healing session together or something.

It happened like this. I was dropping off some mail to Mitzi, who'd been watching for the postman for hours – some incense or other she was desperate for. I'd surprised the postie with a version of 'scream' but he wasn't the usual guy so my namesake's song was lost on him. Anyway, post in hand and not wanting to interrupt, I tentatively knocked on the cottage door and Mitzi waved me in enthusiastically. She had a group of six shaman trainees all holding hands across a giant table.

'We're settling our spirits. Could you bring in the nettle infusion, Janet? It's with Echo in the back.'

I tiptoed past the group, who began to chant, heads bowed, and as I crept past them and into the kitchen, I found Echo in there, not brewing up nettle tea but moving the knife stand and the recipe stand around, swapping the tea and coffee pots. I watched her for a bit and then did a little cough.

'How's this nettle tea doing?'

Echo jumped; she definitely *hadn't* felt my spirit enter the room.

'What?' She looked flustered. 'I'm just getting organised.'

'Right, well, Mitzi needs it sharpish.'

I flicked on the kettle and cack-handedly tipped the leaves into the strainer; half of them went over the counter. I waited then poured over the boiling water so they could infuse inside the weird-shaped glass tea pot.

'I'll take over now, thank you.' Echo painstakingly gathered all the bits of dried nettle that I had let spill and pointedly put them into the strainer to reinvigorate the weak-looking infusion.

She took six earthenware mugs and arranged them on a tray around the tea pot. I reckoned they could do with a good wash but when Echo gave me a beady side glance, I decided to leave her to it. I was getting intense *get out of here* vibes, and in response I couldn't help but give her a *no I won't move it's my cottage* vibe in return. In the end though, I had to give in and leave, as I really did need to get on and check that my cakes weren't burning.

I usually leave this kind of thing to Mitzi or Chloe, but my intuition was really tingling, sending me warning signals. I've decided I really do not like Echo.

Over the next week or two the house starts to feel like Piccadilly Circus. Carl and his floating bunch of builder friends are constantly turning up at all times of the day and night. Carl is pulling in every favour he's ever had to get the work done cheap. They're a lovely crowd, but I can't get any of my own work done. They arrive and they always need a tea, and a chat, and yes, they'd love a butty if there's one going. The stories go on and on, the kettle goes on and on, I'm getting through two

litres of milk and a dozen eggs and a big, sliced loaf
every three days.

I hear about Tez, who inherited a small fortune off
his mum and dad and spent it within six months,
boozing and gambling. He's now taken to dog breed-
ing, only so far it's not going well as his dog 'Budgie'
won't perform when he's in front of people. So a bloke
and his missus from Manchester were really annoyed
after they'd travelled all that distance with their bitch
on heat for nothing.

'What can I do, Janet?' he asks, spreading his hands
helplessly.

Budgie is a big French bulldog-type thing with a
lovely silvery-grey coat and a heavy wrinkly face, and
he sits in Tez's van on the seat whilst his master works.
He wears a permanently plaintive expression, as if he
doesn't really belong in a builder's van in Hebden but
should be wearing a bow-tie and trundling around the
Palace of Versailles or something.

'Maybe he needs a bit of romance, Tez – some music, soft lighting. Do any of us perform well when
surrounded by an audience of four people staring at us?
Especially when one of them is a grumpy bitch from
Macclesfield who's probably got a bit of cramp from an
hour travelling on the M62?'

'Fair point, Janet, fair point.'

Then there's the builder called Fax ('cos he's from
Halifax); he's a very talented joiner but used to be a
jockey and has twenty-four broken bones so has to be
careful lifting heavy weights. He's also a serial dater
and has two women on the go currently as he can't
decide which one he likes best.

'I mean, I like Vee, Janet. She's got a steady job, her
own house, her kids are grown-up, we go for a drink
and we have a laugh.'

'So what's the issue?'

'I know, I know, it's just Renee, she's a bit wilder – you know, she's a bit rougher round the edges . . .' He smiles.

'Right.'

'You know.'

'Not really.'

'She's a demon in the sack, Janet. It needs saying, she's a bloody demon.'

'OK . . .'

'Yeah, it's a dilemma.'

I represent the female point of view in every discussion, Renee, Donna and Yvette, Vee, Katy and Lauren. You name it, I am them. Sometimes the stories are funny: 'she kicked me out because she said my feet stunk'. A lot of it seems to be 'my partner is complaining about the time I spend cycling' (thinking of Miles, I can identify with that), 'at golf, at work, at my mum's, at my mate's, with my kids, at the pub', etc. It does make me wonder what men are after. It seems to be: food, sex and comfort – but only when *they* want it, mind. Is it just a replacement mother figure they are looking for, I wonder?

The fact is, relationships of all shapes and sizes take work. For once I'm glad I'm not in one. I'm so busy working out how I'm paying for the next month's bills to be worrying or spending any time thinking about anything or anyone else. Though it is interesting listening to all these men and their relationship issues; it's like a college course on bloke-dom.

At this point, I must say that some of the stories are very sad though, shared over a cuppa in an early drizzly morning, and sometimes the men tell me they have never spoken about these things before.

For instance, Patrick explained to me how his wife Treena suffered from post-natal depression after she gave birth to their baby daughter Ava. One day, she told him she didn't love him any more and went away, leaving him to look after baby Ava.

'I had to give up work, which was very difficult at first,' he told me. 'Thankfully, a few good people helped me out with bits of money and we eventually got in the groove and got through. There were a tough few months but Ava was a good baby and we got on great. I loved her so much, Janet. We were so close. And then one day eight months later, there was a knock on the door and Treena turned up with her brothers. She took Ava and that was that. Done. I've seen Ava maybe three times since then. Her mother moved away, to the other end of the country. My daughter is about eleven now.'

My heart aches for him. 'I'm so sorry to hear that, Patrick. You did the right thing though, and hopefully you'll have a chance to tell Ava all about it, one day. Can I do you a double fried egg sandwich with a bit of brown sauce? Look, sweetheart, you're not old. You should go and find a career woman around thirty-five who's keen to settle down and have babies. There's plenty of women like that out there. Or how about a single mum, who needs a good man to help her?'

His face lights up. 'It's true that I'm lonely. You reckon?'

'A hundred per cent. Get on some of those sites, say you're interested in a relationship. I don't know, I've never done them, but get yourself out there. Say that you're kind, a grown-up – the right women would like that. There you go, love, double egg, brown sauce, strong cuppa.'

Heart-breaking. Then there's Mitch. He is a big guy with a deep brown Welsh voice like toffee that kind of soothes and slides over you, every word considered and thoughtful. His head is covered with a tangle of silky dark brown curls, peppered with a bit of silver here and there, that make you want to run your hand through them. He's got big arms and shoulders, and you can see the muscles ripple beneath his shirt. I can't help but look. I think I'm probably a bit sex starved; it's been a while since bloody bugger Miles. I find if I don't think about sex but concentrate on other things – like crochet, or recipes or stuff I need to wash or garden plants – I can get by. But suddenly though, big sexy Mitch with his soft heart and his strong arms and his big brown eyes . . . well, he's got me a bit distracted. His story too, is *sooo* touching.

His ex, Melanie, life and soul of the party with a great career as a travel agent, was really close to her mum, who died suddenly of a heart attack in her early fifties. Mitch didn't realise quite how badly Melanie had taken it. True, she'd gone very quiet and didn't want to see anyone or do much, which seemed perfectly understandable at the time.

'Only six months later, she still wasn't back at work and I was trying to say to her, "Let's go and do something nice" – you know, Janet, a walk along the canal or something like that, nothing to it, and she turned round to me really calmly and said, "You don't understand, Mitch. My life is over. I've nothing I want to do. I don't want to be in a relationship any more. I've lost my world and I want to be alone. No pressure from anyone. Please leave me alone, I need peace".'

He stuck with her, he told me, desperately tried to persuade her to go to the doctor, realising that she was depressed, but she wouldn't leave the house, not for over a year. He tried everything.

'It was tough. I'd go into work every day and she didn't seem to notice when I left the house nor when I came home. I managed eighteen months like that and then I had to give up as it was really getting me down.'

I feel for him. The guilt and the hopelessness. He's

not actually divorced, has never been able to face it. I'll never forget the trauma around my own divorce, when I was maintaining a face to the world as I dropped Chloe off at school, checking into work, staying upbeat and positive for the patients and the other staff at Valley Dental, pretending to join in with the chit-chat in the kitchen there while making a cuppa. When inside I was crushed. Constantly tamping down the gurgle of fear about the future that bubbled up every idle minute, nearly sending me out of my mind. At times like this, when the scaffolding of your life has collapsed beneath you, it seems you're still expected to wave and smile.

Mitch's big brown eyes welled up when he told me that Melanie has now got chronic agoraphobia; she is not a well woman. I gave him a double fried egg sandwich too, along with some mushrooms. He's an in-demand plumber, is Mitch, and he stopped the tap dripping in the kitchen whilst he was waiting for Carl to get out of the attic so he could go in there and plumb in the shower. Mitzi is, of course, quick to notice a hunk in the house and when Mitch has finished his sandwich and thanks me for it, once he's gone she gives me a wink and a very sly smirk.

'Double mushrooms? I don't blame you one little bit, sis. That Mitch can do my plumbing any time.'

'Shut up! He's nice, that's all, and he had a sad story about his ex being agoraphobic.'

'Then I dare say he needs a bit of comforting, Janet. A big warm bosom, a big warm hug.'

'Oh, do go away. Haven't you got a spell to cast somewhere?' She's really annoying me.

'Yes, a *love* spell.'

I throw a mushroom at her.

Mitch was around a couple more days, and when he came to leave, he stalled in the kitchen doorway, saying, 'Well, that's me done, Janet.'

173

I brushed off the flour on my hands and impulsively went over to him. Asked, 'You got another job on?'

'Oh yes, I've got loads on.'

'Right. Well, you've been great, Mitch. We all so appreciate you helping us in our hour of need. Has Carl sorted the money out with you?'

'Oh yes, don't worry. He owes me a couple of days, we'll sort it.'

'That's good to hear. Thank you again, Mitch.'

'My pleasure. You do a great butty, Janet.'

'No problem. I love cooking.'

'I can see, with all your cakes.'

I look at the kitchen table, which is stacked with plastic containers filled with different sponges for the sixtieth birthday party and The Tasty Mug, either ready for decorating or due a delivery.

'Yes, I'm trying to build up a little cake business.' It was the first time, I'd said it, *a little cake business*. I liked it. I liked the feeling it gave me, a feeling of *purpose*.

'Good for you, Janet, nice job.'

'Yes, so if you ever want some cake, or need a cake or just fancy eating some cake, well, you know where I am.' I also know I'm blushing. I'm smiling at him, babbling like a fool, willing him to *really want some cake*. Or alternatively, push all the cakes off the kitchen table and just lay me down on it and really give me a good . . .

'Yeah, I do like cake – a light Genoa is my favourite. I will think on, when I want some er . . . cake.' Can it be that Mitch is blushing too?

'Great.'

Mitch's big brown eyes pour into mine for a delicious moment, interrupted by the tinkle of a bell. It's bloody Echo, traipsing down the drive, chanting some gobbledygook, followed by a tribe of skipping, hopping women. And when I turn back, Mitch is gone, sharpish, and who could blame him.

The thing with the shaman stuff is that it goes on late. People are coming and going at all hours, and there are small groups on the lawn doing chanting circles late at night. The length of the drive is scattered with leafy debris, and when I ask Mitzi about it she explains it's the incantation setting. Good job I only swept a little bit of it up then.

Gulp. I've taken to ignoring Echo. It's very petty, I know. She's obviously getting to me a bit, but she's up and down my drive and it's not nice having a hostile force passing in front of your kitchen window every half hour – I swear she's curdling my butter cream.

She's always over in Lavander Cottage, she's never away, and then one morning I'm up ridiculously early as the cat has barged his way into my bedroom. I go yawning down the stairs, feed him and open the back door, because even though he has a cat flap he still prefers to be let out the side door by his handmaiden like the little prince he is. It's just after six and I'm wrapped up in an old fleece, bleary-eyed, feeling the stir of the morning weather and contemplating moving a buddleia that has arrived out of nowhere and taken over a bed.

There's a sudden rattle from the cottage and a window-blind shoots up – and there's Echo staring out, in what looks like a kind of nightdress. We are both surprised, it's fair to say. She takes one look at me and *bosh*, the blind crashes down. Hmmm. I'm a bit taken aback. It's too early to be arriving, isn't it? That was definitely a nightdress. No mistaking it. Is she staying in the cottage now? Mitzi hasn't said anything, but maybe this has been going on a while and I haven't realised. All my instincts are on hyper alert. Something doesn't feel right and I am pacing about waiting for Mitzi to get up so I can interrogate her.

'Oh, I told her she could stay.' Mitzi is entirely blasé. She wafts a spiral of sweet-smelling vape smoke into the air as I tackle her about it in heated whispers outside.

'Why?'

'Because we were working late, she looked tired, the taxis cost a fortune and are unreliable, and we have arranged to do a bit of planning early on to get ready for the next cohort of practitioners.'

I suddenly feel ridiculous, over-reacting and wrong-footed on every front – so why am I still so uncomfortable about this?

'That's fair enough,' I say uncertainly. 'It was a surprise, that's all, seeing her at the window.'

'Yeah, I can imagine. She's a strong character, Echo. Even for me, she's plenty.'

'Right.'

'Well, I need to get on,' my sister declares.

'Of course. Me too. Hopefully Carl's nearly finished now. He's wonderful, isn't he?'

Mitzi says proudly, 'Yes. The shower's in, which is brilliant. We'll soon be sorted.'

'And I'll be able to get the cottage back, for guests.' I need to remind her about that.

'Yes, I know. It's such a shame, though. It's a great space for us.'

'True, it's just I need every penny at the moment and it pays three or four times what you're able to give me, although I'm grateful.'

'I know, I'm working on it. It's my number one priority to find a new venue.'

Mitzi heads off towards the cottage which is un-locked and opened for her as she approaches, as if Echo has been standing behind the door the whole time straining to hear our conversation. The cottage door closes immediately behind her and the door is re-locked. I make a mental note to myself. I do not know why, I can't explain why, but *I want Echo out.*

For the next two days I watch as the parade of people come and go; irrespective of the time they leave, I note that Echo is not amongst them. Then one crazy early morning, I'm up having a wee when I hear the door of Lavander Cottage door open. I dart downstairs and tuck myself behind the curtains in the front room to watch as Echo, with a huge collection of jute bags, jumps in a battered old Citroen and drives away. It's 5 a.m. Why is she leaving at this time? I don't hesitate, I don't get changed, I dig out the old key and I am straight into the cottage.

Downstairs is set up for lots of guests; there are chairs in circles, cups in the sink, a lot of extra bits and pieces but it's stuff they might need for their events. It's what I'm expecting. I go upstairs, where things are much more interesting. The bathroom has a toothbrush and toothpaste – nothing unusual in that, she is staying over. A washing line above the shower has some clothes and towels hanging from it. Could be shaman stuff. Then I peek under the bed. There I find bags and bags of clothes, a laptop, a load of toiletries, a number of holdalls, all full of her stuff. It's not shaman equipment, I'm sure of it, it's pyjamas and underwear and lots of big hessian dresses, and in the drawers are multiple pairs of sandals and weird socks. How long has she been stashing this stuff? We're not a storage service. She must have been busy these last couple of weeks, off-loading all this lot in here, I'm sure of it.

Thank goodness the building work is coming to an end. I can insist on a big clear-out and push Mitzi into finding somewhere else to hold her events, and Echo to store her stuff! I'm out of the cottage and loitering in the living room at home when I hear the clatter of the Citroen pulling up at the top of the drive, on the street. Why not on the drive outside Lavander Cottage?

It feels ridiculous. I am behaving like an amateur Agatha Christie heroine, trying to get a view on Echo and what she's up to without her being aware that I am on her trail. The sense that I'm doing something wrong is offset by my instinct that something is going on that is even more wrong, and the sensation grows as I watch Echo tiptoe along the drive holding increasingly large holdalls.

I'm on my second cup of tea and wrapped in the kitchen curtain watching her when a voice says, 'Morning, Janet.'

I jump sky-high, but it's only Carl, half-asleep and wandering into the kitchen in his boxers and a T-shirt. He scratches himself, stretches, turns the key and is outside the patio door taking in a big breath.

'Morning,' I hear him say.

It's Echo, with what must be a dozen bags dangling from each finger. She scuttles past him into the cottage without replying and with no eye contact. She slams the cottage door and we can hear it being locked and both blinds being pulled down.

'Not very friendly, is she?' Carl comments.

It's the green light I've needed to share. 'She's not, is she? I've been watching her for the last forty-five minutes unload her car and tiptoe down the drive into the cottage.'

'Have you not asked her what she's doing?'

'I didn't want to appear nosy. It's probably shaman stuff.' But I don't believe that.

'At this time of the morning?'

'Hmm, yes, exactly. Carl, I think something's not right. I'm trying to find out what she's up to, so I've been keeping an eye on her.'

'What does Mitzi say?'

'She just says that Echo is doing the odd stopover because the hours are long and taxis are expensive.'

'She's got a car,' he points out.

I hadn't thought of that. 'Has she brought a car before, do you know?'

'Ask Mitz, she'll know.'

'Will do, in a couple of hours when she's woken up.'

'Oh, she's getting up now, Janet. I'm finishing up there today, last fix, snag list, bit of filling, put a couple of switches on, rubber feet on the metal staircase, sand down the banister and we are there, Janet. We are there. Halle-bloody-lujah. And no more disasters, I can promise you.'

He raises a hand in a high five that I go to slap when my hand drops. Hallelujah indeed. Then something clicks in my mind like a lightbulb.

'Does Mitzi know this is the last day?'

'Yeah, of course. She's going to look at some other spaces for her hipster stuff today.'

'Right . . . OK. So Echo must know this is the last day, too?'

'I suppose so.'

I don't overthink it, I pull my belt extra tight around my dressing gown, grab my cuppa and go and knock on the cottage door. I knock for an age, no answer. I rap on the windows, then get a bit more agitated and rap a bit louder. Finally a face peeks around the blind and I can see it's Echo.

'Can I have a word please, Echo? Can you open the door please, *ECHO*.'

The blind twitches again and she's ignoring me, I know. I'm feeling increasingly annoyed, so that's it. I start thumping on the door.

Nothing. No response. My agitation hits the roof.

'ECHO, OPEN THE BLOODY DOOR!'

'What's going on?'

I whirl round. It's Mitzi. She's wrapped in what looks like a US confederate flag, her hair is in bendy rollers and she is barefoot on the drive looking confused.

'You tell me,' I say furiously. 'I've watched her bring a load of stuff into the cottage since five o'clock this bloody morning in her car. What is she up to? And now she won't answer the door.'

'She doesn't drive.'

'She does today.'

'Oh. Right.' More confusion. 'Well, that's OK. She's probably preparing for the final session this afternoon with our Lavander group.'

I feel myself calming down. I try to be relaxed, be logical, be sensible. It's a strange turn of affairs when Mitzi is the one doing the reasonable.

'So why won't she open the door?'

'She will open the door, she's probably in a spiritual safe place and needs some time to step down through celestial planes.'

Mitzi taps quietly on the door and shoos me away. I take a few steps back. Carl is watching from the patio door with a huge cuppa in his hand.

He winks and whispers, 'Let's check out what plane she's on."

Mitzi continues to tap away, she turns and smiles at us both, then her tapping gets a bit louder, a bit more varied. She taps on the window, then walks around the side of the cottage, shrugs her shoulders and then properly bashes at the door.

'Echo, it's Mitzi, love, I need to talk to you about this circle time this aft.' She turns to us and shrugs. 'What's she playing at?'

Suddenly, a hand appears from behind the blind. Two hands. We watch in wonder as a flap of paper is attached to the window. I'm taking this in as a spray paint can appears around the other blind, and onto the window in bright green spray paint is blasted a huge A in a circle. My eyes nearly pop out of my head. I stumble towards the cottage having dropped my cup on the ground and register with horror exactly what the poster image says.

SQUAT THE AIRBNBS

Mitzi and I look at each other, both open-mouthed, and for the first time ever that I can recall, my sister is completely speechless.

Across the rest of the day, other posters are put on the remaining windows outlining in detail the existing legislation and rights of squatters. I am on my tenth cup of tea of the day and baking another lemon sponge, having eaten through one lemon drizzle cake that I shared with Carl – even Mitzi nibbled at a slice. She is really furious.

'What a duplicitous bitch. *Never* trust a hippy, *never*. I always say it, so why oh why haven't I listened to myself?'

Carl looks confused. 'Are you not a—'

'Absolutely not, *how dare you?* I'm a bohemian, which is quite different. I can't bear hippies. Look, we've got to get her out.'

I'm in. 'We've got a spare key, of course, but how do we do that if she's locked herself in?'

Carl pushes his shoulders back and cracks his knuckles. 'Do you want me to break the door down and carry her out?'

'No, no, no,' Mitzi objects, 'we can't have you doing that. You'll end up getting done for trespass and assault.'

'*Trespass*?' I bellow. 'She's in my bloody cottage.'

'Yes, Janet, of course that's true, but we need to play this carefully. You see, Echo knows her rights. She lived in the London squats for years throughout the nineteen-eighties.'

'Doesn't she have a house of her own? Where does she live normally?'

'No, she hasn't got a house. She was chucked out of her rented flat when the owners wanted to sell, and since then she's been living with her son and his missus. Only the wife is a very uptight bank-manager type, and I think it's been getting tense. Echo probably just needs a break.'

'And I need the income from that cottage in order to survive.'

'Never mind that – *I* need somewhere to hold a healing circle in three hours' time. What's the weather like?' She checks out the app on her phone. 'It's looking dry. Janet, I'm going to have to take over the garden. Can you pull together some blankets and some cushions and knock up some peppermint tea with some spinach vegan pasty things? Poppy seed cake, caraway flapjack – you know the sort of thing, dry, brown, plenty of seeds.'

My plans to try decorating one of the coffee cakes

and attempt the chocolate tempering go floating off into the distance. I'm now a shaman handmaiden. I double curse bloody Echo and dig out an old 1970s veggie cookbook I know does a lot about flapjacks.

Time flies when you're really annoyed. The anarchist take-over of the cottage now stands at thirteen days. Echo has not emerged once, as far as we know. The car has gone, we don't know how or where, but it was spiritually uplifted in the middle of the night which was probably a good thing. I was reaching the point of planning late at night the very rude messages I was going to spray paint onto it.

The house is overrun with shaman practitioners. Chloe, Carl and I are now largely confined to the kitchen. The attic, now fully functioning again, is the sacred space and the living room has become the home of the gong bath, after Mitzi picked up three huge gongs at a knockdown rate on Shoptree. The noise is driving us all loopy and Chloe has enrolled at college alongside her bar work so she can be out of the home as much as is functionally possible. Carl is away most of the time working on the brand-new barn extension up Elland. Which leaves me, mooching around home going out of my mind with frustration. Mitzi invited me to a gong bath for free after I explained to her that I was getting really stressed.

'No, thank you,' I replied. 'I don't think a free gong bath is going to impact on the stress I feel about having my cottage and now my house taken over with the sound and smell of bloody shamans.'

'Temporary, Janet, it's all temporary.'

'It doesn't feel very temporary from here. I'm going

mad! How the heck are we going to get her out?'

'She has to leave voluntarily and then we jump in and re-take the space.'

'You make it sound easy. The problem is, it looks like she's hibernating for winter.'

My sister perks up. 'You've given me an idea.'

'Have I?'

'Prepare for tonight, find all your keys. I'm going to ring Carl.'

Later, over tea, Mitzi explains that Carl has been prowling around the cottage at all hours trying to establish possible ways in. He's found nothing except for two air-bricks. One of which is loose.

'This air-brick – it is a brick presumably?'

'That's right.'

'So we can't sneak in that way.'

'No. Let me explain the plan, Janet . . .'

So at 2 a.m. the next morning, all four of us are dressed in baggy black leggings and sweatshirts, courtesy of Chloe when she was going through her Goth phase.

Chloe is positioned at one side of the front door, I am at the other, both of us with huge shopping bags. Mitzi is incanting something towards the moon in a silent way and Carl is delicately using a trowel to remove a brick from the side of the wall. Mitzi disappears into our house then re-emerges with a huge shisha-type smoking thing. It is enormous and she is struggling down the drive with it when the brass top falls off and the racket of it hitting the drive reverberates around the house. A light pops on upstairs in the cottage and we all cringe and stop what we are doing. The tension of being so still, with Chloe and me with our bags, Carl levering out a brick and Mitzi with her gigantic shisha thing starts to get to me and I begin to giggle.

'*Ssshhh!*' I have to hold myself in and the sudden need for a pee increases tenfold.

After a few moments the light goes off again. I'm now bursting but restrain myself. Meanwhile Mitzi starts messing about with potions and rags and matches, and before you know it she has a red-hot furnace of glowing sticks on the top of the shisha thing and she pulls out some tiny bellows and *poooph!* – a cloud of grey smoke emerges from the pipe. It's only a second or two before the intense aroma of woodsmoke and musk and really strong mushrooms is blowing around on the drive. Mitzi nods at Carl and with one confident gesture he pushes the pipe of the shisha instrument in through the brick cavity and Mitzi gets to work with the bellows. I dread to think about my curtains and soft furnishings, I'll never get that smell out.

It takes a little while, during which I cross my legs and clench everything. When a light goes on, we all crouch below the windowsill as the blinds suddenly shoot up. I can see Chloe's eyes pinned onto me with the excitement, then we hear it – the cough. Then another, then another. The sound of the key. We are rigid with attention. Mitzi and Carl nod at us both and we acknowledge them. The door opens and out staggers Echo, emerging from a cloud of smoke. We don't waste a second. Chloe is up and in behind her, and I follow in quick succession. I pull the door to behind me, and when I find the key is usefully still in the door, I quickly lock it. We hear Echo scream in rage. I open the little window at the side of the building, and I can't resist it.

'Sorry, Echo love,' I say, 'I was desperate for a pee.'

It doesn't take Chloe and me long. We rush around the cottage spotting random odd objects and what is clearly a wardrobe of strange linen dresses. One after the other we stuff them into bags and fill them. I fling open the Velux windows so we can disperse the smoke, and from outside I can hear the sound of Echo arguing with Mitzi about the rights and wrongs of squatter's legislation. Luckily for us, Anarchy philosophy is pretty much Mitzi's specialist subject, so whilst we carefully gather up everything we can and stick it into the bags, the two of them hiss at each other like rattlesnakes.

Eventually we have collected together as much as we can assume is hers, and as per the plan we knock on the window and carefully open the door. Carl acts as a barrier as we hurry out, locking the door again, and I drop the key very visibly into my cleavage. It's the first time I've ever done that, and it's probably the only time I ever will. Chloe, Mitzi and Carl all cheer as I do it. One thing's for sure: Echo is not going *there* for the key.

She looks defeated and as Carl takes the bags from us and heads down the drive he indicates to Echo to, 'Come on, love. It's over. I'll drop you home in the van.'

She turns on me bitterly and spits out, 'I wouldn't even give this dump one star.'

I laugh. 'I wouldn't let you in, love.'

Mitzi joins in the laughter. 'Off you go, Bloody Brenda.'

Her real name has struck a chord. Echo's head drops as Carl chucks her bags into his van. I could almost feel sorry for her – until she wheels around and starts gesticulating wildly with her hands, murmuring and chanting and acting as if she is throwing something towards us. Mitzi is on it like wildfire and erupts with a sort of Kate Bush-style blocking arms dance movement.

'That was a big mistake, Brenda. You know that any curse will come back to you three-fold. And it will serve you right for what you've put us through.'

The woman ignores Mitzi, picks up her bag and grumps off down the drive to climb into Carl's van.

Chloe is shocked. 'What the hocus pocus was she doing?'

'It was a curse, but I repelled it.'

'A curse?' I start to feel a bit uneasy. 'What do you mean, Mitzi? On you, me?'

'On Lavander Cottage.'

Oh no. The last thing I need right now and after all the recent disasters, is a bloomin' curse.

'Don't worry, Mum, Auntie Mitz witched her right back.' Chloe pats her on the back. 'Well impressed.'

Mitzi shrugs her shoulders. 'I did my best to repel it. Shamans should do no harm, but she's gone dark side. I should have seen it coming.'

I'm left regretting not trusting my instincts and putting my foot down. Boundaries. I struggle to enforce them. When will I learn? Carl explains over a bacon sarnie that her son lives up Cragg and wasn't best pleased apparently to be knocked up at three in the morning about his mother. But he took one look at Carl and was convinced it was the right thing to do. He helped him in with her bags of belongings, and bad witch Brenda was welcomed back into the family.

I try to go back to bed for an hour, but it's no good – I'm tossing and turning before I finally drop off, only to wake up worrying about the smell of the pipe smoke on the soft furnishings in Lavander Cottage. The place will need fumigating. I get up, go inside, walk around and start the rearrangement of all the furniture and accessories. I manage to change the bedding and open the Velux window, then feeling exhausted I sit on the bed for a moment before I take my shoes off, lie down and close my eyes. I fall asleep and dream about a Wicker Woman giant figure walking down the drive with a huge cake in her hands; the candle on top of the cake is a flame and as she blows it out, the Wicker Woman too bursts into flames.

I wake with a start, sweaty, disorientated and filled with dread. Oh God. My cottage has been cursed!

REVIEW

Don't go there.

TIPS FOR RUNNING A B&B

When you have a really suitable space, everyone wants to use it for their thing. It's a nightmare fending them off. Try to keep it booked up all the time, or make out that it's booked up all the time. If you're like me, as soft as anything, it's so hard to create and preserve boundaries. Put simply: *Keep the bloody door locked.*

Oh, and verse yourself in squatter's law. You know – just in case.

TIP ON LIFE

It's an oldie but a goodie. Trust your bloomin' instincts!

CHAPTER 13

The Foggs

I'm *so* chuffed, the cottage is up and running again with a BOOKING for this weekend from a family of Foggs. There's the parents, the two kids and a grandad, and they're coming to celebrate an anniversary. There's just enough room for them all if the kids go in the upstairs with two single beds, sharing the room with their parents in the double, and Grandad sleeps in the comfy sofabed downstairs. I'm so happy. Back on the mission for Superhost! Plus £30 per person per night, there's 5 of them, so £300 heading to the J. Jackson bank account. *Hallelujah.* I'll set aside £50 in my savings account for tax and must be super-disciplined not to touch it.

I've aired and cleaned that cottage with so much lavender polish and subtle scent sprays that it's borderline whether it smells of floral bouquet or gone-off sherbet fountain. Anyway, I can't plump, scrub or vacuum any more. I don't know what B&Bs that evil witch Brenda was used to staying at, but no stars Lavander Cottage definitely ain't!

I'm also contemplating whether I should reintroduce breakfast options? Chloe suggested it.

'You could offer it at £8.50 per person between

eight and nine in the morning. You're in control then and it's a bit of extra cash, isn't it?'

I decide she's right, at the moment I've got to maximise every penny. So I create a simple menu, laminate it and put it on the kitchen table in full view. Full English, Full Veggie, Eggs any way you like, or fruit, yoghurt and granola. The rule is you must order before 6 p.m. the day before (allows me to run to the shops if I need to). I have the hassle of carrying it over and think, Hey ho, let's see if the Foggs take me up on it.

Meanwhile, Carl has put the word out and Mitzi is going to view an empty barn up Dryclough with a bit of parking, a loo, a sink and a plug socket. We are all hoping and praying that it might become her new shaman home. The Echo debacle seems to have had an impact.

My sister is resigned to renting somewhere. She says, 'I am going to have to enter the corrupting capitalist system and set up a really successful shamanic business. It would kill me if Echo set something up now, because everything she's learned has come from *me*. The spirits are willing me on, I know it.'

After this pronouncement, Mitzi spent three days working on a logo. The only issue is, she hasn't yet got a name, so we are all drained dry with the trauma of trying to help her come up with one. I thought Carl's 'Desperately Seeking Shaman' was inspired but it was too light-hearted for Mitzi. Every meal and every conversation is hijacked by a search for the elusive right branding.

'It's less a business, more a way of life,' she tells us for the hundredth time. 'How does one encapsulate communion with the spiritual self?'

'Call it "Spirit-self"?' Chloe is packing her lunch-box for another shift. Carl and I both lean optimistically into that one, desperately hoping we might be able to bring the search to an end.

'That's very good, really good,' we say. 'Definitely the best. That's brilliant, Chloe. How about you go with that one, Mitzi?'

She ponders, sitting cross-legged on a chair, in tie-dyed cerise leggings, electric-blue legwarmers and a neon lime-green string vest hanging off her shoulders. To me, it looks like she's channelling a cross between Leroy from *Fame* and a 90s' rave T-shirt that changes colour when you sweat.

Mitzi doesn't seem energised by Chloe's suggestion. 'Yes, it's good, but is it selling Hebden as our spiritual universe – the shaman headquarters, so to speak? Our universal centre?'

Chloe pulls her rucksack over her shoulders and heads to the patio door, where she stops to leave a parting shot. 'So, like the Americans say, "Keep it simple, stupid". Why not just call it "Hebden Shamans"?'

She's out of there with a door slam and Carl and I turn to see if the most obvious and powerful of suggestions has reached Planet Mitz. She is wrapped in a cuddle, with her knees pulled up, arms draped around her legs, rocking gently to and fro. Her thought processes seem to take an age, then she suddenly unravels herself and comes to a decision.

'I love it. I think that is it. Then I own and am the Hebden Shaman. Bloody Nora, I'm setting up my own bloody business! Hebden Shamans, that's what it is, *that is it*!'

Carl lifts her up from the chair in a giant twirly hug and I clink her glass of orange juice. Thank goodness.

As it is with most of Mitzi's plans, I end up paying out for something. This time it's printer ink, as she prints pile after pile of *Hebden Shaman* flyers in multiple colour ways until she reaches one she's happy with. Then it's the website. Two hundred quid, courtesy of her good mate Techy Red, with hosting, all in, for a year. She pays for it by not paying me for the cottage for the last two weeks. As she explains this to me, rather than feel frustrated or angry, I simply smile and nod and repeat to myself in a calm and soothing way, 'Zen, Zen, Zen.' After all, this is paving the way to a job for Mitzi – an actual job, with actual money.

She shows me the rough pages for the site. It's very simple but effective, with a list of treatments and costs, dates and timings for all her different shaman sessions. There's a nice photo of Mitzi looking all windblown and barely dressed on a moor top. Frankly she's wearing so little, I worry she'd catch her death, never mind a spirit. The menu has things like *Soul Retrieval £250*, *Gong Bath Session £15* and *Ayurvedic Moon Bathing Rituals £30*. It's all done in a nice Art Nouveau-style lettering and a hand-drawn logo for Hebden Shamans.

I'm happy for her, though the biggest joy of all is that she's got a new address up Dryclough. The flood of relief this morning, as Mitzi wheels the last gong out of the living room and loads it up into Carl's van, is immense. It's been interesting being a home for shamans and hippies and builders and rituals and general weirdos, but finally, for the first time in months, to be in my own house, alone, no noise, no plaster dust, no voices, no random strangers . . . well, it sends me a bit crazy. It's as if I've been storing up the angst and simply waiting for the cork to pop off the bottle.

In celebration, I cast off my dressing gown and then

I set off running, waving a tea-towel in the air like a lunatic. I run around the house, up the stairs, down the stairs, around the living room, then, still dressed only in my nightie, I head for Lavander Cottage. The Foggs aren't due for another two hours, so I run round the cottage, tiring now but still over the moon, still gambolling like a spring lamb as I launch out of the cottage into the garden to do a final circuit around the lawn . . . which is when I notice, in my whirligig state, a blur of a figure. So I slow down, come to a halt and there, toolbox in hand, staring at me as if I've completely lost the plot, which of course I have, is Mitch.

I'm not sure what to do. So I whirl the tea-towel around my head and throw it at him, desperately trying to cultivate an air of nonchalance.

'Hi, Mitch.'

'How do,' he says, as my tea-towel hits him full in the face.

It turns out that Mitch is here to go up into the attic and take a look at the shower, which has been playing up a bit. I get dressed very speedily and try to explain my antics by popping my head round the ensuite door, distracting him from his work as he gropes around pipes on his knees. I can't help but notice that he has very strong thighs!

'It's been non-bloody-stop for months now, Mitch, and I've not had a single minute to myself. I don't normally feel the urge to run around in my nightie, it's just that it's been enough to turn anyone a bit nuts.'

'Clearly,' he says, turning his head to me, one ear to the pipe, smiling.

I'm just thinking that he does sort of understand when there's a loud buzz on the doorbell followed by excitable knocking.

'Visitors,' Mitch says encouragingly, with a wry curled-up smile playing on his lips. He then disappears into the shower, and I could swear he's laughing as he goes.

I really feel like throwing something at him now. Instead, I rush downstairs and turn all my attention to the Foggs, who are standing at the door. They appear to be a lovely happy bunch, except maybe for Grandad, who is hovering by the looks of it on the precipice of keeling over, *permanently*.

I'm chatting to Adele Fogg – she and her husband Lee are the ones celebrating their wedding anniversary – whilst Lee plays pool with the kids. I can't stop myself from glancing across at her dad as we chat. 'Jacko, I'm Jacko Marshall,' he whispers, as he drags a chair out from the kitchen and positions it outside the cottage door staring up at the treeline you can observe beyond the perimeter of the house. His complexion is a tomblike grey and he smokes like a pro; a cigarette is currently clamped between his fingers and with every laboured drag and every tap of ash a wheezing breath escapes him.

'Would you like a cup of tea, Mr Marshall?' I offer and he refuses.

'Oh, call me Jacko, love. No, ta – tea doesn't agree with me any more,' he grunts.

'Oh, that's a real shame.'

'Yes, it is, but you know, that's cancer for you.' Jacko nods gloomily.

'Is it?' I flail around for something to say. 'Are you er . . . having treatment?'

'No. No point. Stage Four, you see.'

'I'm so sorry.'

He shrugs, and I hear Adele give a big sigh.

'I've had a good innings – a really good innings. I've got to hug my grandkids. Buried my missus after a long and happy marriage, and we had this lovely daughter here. My Adele. I've had a grand life.'

Adele squeezes her dad's hand then goes back inside. I notice that where he is sitting is slowly going into shade.

'Would you like a bit of lemon drizzle cake, Jacko? I'm going to bring you over here into the sun.'

I carry a little table out from the shed and set it up outside the patio door, where the sun is still pouring into the garden. I find the comfiest garden armchair I can, prop it with a few cushions, and Jacko comes and sits in it. He's so frail and slim he's lost amongst the upholstery. After he's enjoyed his piece of lemon drizzle cake he tells me he feels sleepy. He closes his eyes and soaks up the rays.

Grandad has been there for half an hour when Adele comes past with some jute bags and explains that she and Lee are just popping out to buy some food, leaving her father babysitting. I'm immediately a bit nervous.

'Is he – y'know – well enough?'

'Oh, don't worry, they're playing pool and we've set a console up so they'll be gaming or colouring, and they're sensible kids.' She turns to the old chap. 'You OK, Dad?'

When Dad doesn't respond, I look away. I honestly think he might be dead, when he wakes with a splutter.

'Rhinos?'

'Dad, we're going shopping. The kids are inside gaming. Are you all right if we leave you here for a short while?'

'Go on with you, I'll be right as ninepence.'

'What you doing, going on about rhinos, Dad?'

'I don't know, love.'

'You must've been dreaming.'

'I never dream.' He's indignant.

Adele and I share a smile. She gives him a peck on the cheek then sets off arm-in-arm with Lee.

I'm over in the house, putting a Genoa recipe to the test. I've bashed it together and thrown it in the oven to see if I can bake it fast enough for Mitch to try before he leaves. I know it's his favourite, and yes, I'm blatantly courting him – what else is a girl to do?

I'm hand-washing up the last bowl when there's voices in the drive. I go outside and there are two walkers, a couple, I assume, all trussed up in the gear, in their late sixties I should say. They are looking a bit ragged round the edges and bickering between them-selves, but they do that thing couples do of perking up and putting on a united front when they see me.

'Could we order a pot of tea, please?'

I'm a bit taken aback, but they are staring at Jacko and I realise that he's sat at a table, with a small tea pot, cup and plate, and for all intents and purposes he could be at a café.

'I er . . . I'm not a café.' Although I passed my hy-giene exam ages ago.

'Oh. Are you not?' The wife looks so weary. Her voice sharpens. 'I *said* this was the wrong route, didn't I, Gerard? It's not a café.'

Her poor husband looks fit to drop. 'That's a real shame,' he says. 'Are you sure?'

'We're gasping for a cuppa,' the wife informs me. 'We've walked from Halifax and come up thinking this was the road through to the Pennine Way but it stopped.'

'Er . . . yes, it's a cul de sac,' I say apologetically.

The wife hoists the rucksack off her shoulders. 'We've been at it for hours, and my feet are howling. I might not make it any further, Gerard. I've had it.' She looks to be on the verge of tears.

Gerard is quite testy in the circumstances. 'Margot, why do you always have to be so dramatic about these things,' he hisses. 'We're two miles out of our way, that's all.'

'TWO BLOODY MILES!'

The bickering continues and clearly the couple have overdone the walking. I suspect a strong case of low blood sugar and take a view.

'I am just about to take a Genoa cake out of the oven, and can easily knock up some more tea for you both. Please, it's not a problem at all. Come, take a seat. Get comfortable.'

I bring a couple of chairs out of the kitchen.

'Are you sure?' Gerard looks anxious. 'We don't want to impose.'

Margot has no such reservations and is bottom down and untying her shoelaces within seconds.

'No problem. Now, I can offer Earl Grey, English Breakfast tea or Peppermint? And is a slice of lemon drizzle cake acceptable? I'll have a fresh Genoa ready in ten minutes, still warm from the oven.'

I carry another little metal table out of the shed, set it up next to them and throw a tablecloth over it. I then nip into my kitchen and fetch a couple of chairs. I'm worried about waking up Grandad, but he's fast asleep in the sun.

'Wonderful, that's wonderful,' Margot says gratefully. 'Thank you so much. What a darling you are! What's your name?'

'Janet.'

'You're a wonder, Janet, isn't she?' To nowhere and no one in particular.

Gerard is obviously used to taking the decisions and pipes up, 'Right, Janet, we'll have two English Breakfast teas, milk, no sugar, and a slice each of the lemon cake, please. I reckon I'll need it if I'm going to carry Margot the last couple of miles.'

'Cheeky git.' Margot giggles and the waves of angst drift off into the gentle sounds of the afternoon.

Gerard seems equally delighted to dump his gear and have the chance to sit down. His wife already has her socks off and is rubbing her sore feet.

'Beautiful garden you've got there, Janet,' she comments.

I take a moment to see the space afresh through her eyes, and it is lovely, I suppose, if I ignore what needs doing and instead just enjoy it. The clematis are in full glory, weaving themselves around the wicker arches, and the sweet peas a trifle of colour against the fence. Geraniums in various pots sing out in gorgeous cerise pink, and the last of the anemones in rich purple are still hanging about in the beds, a rigorous de-heading routine having kept them flowering for months now. It *is* pretty and I'm ridiculously proud and really enjoy the feeling of others seeing it and taking pleasure in it.

'Thanks,' I say bashfully. 'It's my pride and joy.'

At that point, Margot turns to Grandad, still snoozing, and asks him, 'Hello there, are you visiting Janet's Secret Garden Café too?'

My heart lights up when she says those words. I can hear Jacko chatting away with our new guests and I've soon got them sorted with tea and a generous slice of lemon drizzle. The granddaughter appears looking for her grandad; seeing that he's happy and well looked after, she gives him a hug, is given some cake for herself and her brother, and disappears back into the cottage.

It's a glorious afternoon. The sun is shining and little peals of laughter and small chatter drift into the kitchen as I pull the Genoa out of the oven. I'm feeling slightly giddy by the turn of the events. *My own little café. My Secret Garden Café.* Love it! The cake is absolutely spot on. It's a great colour, with a split across the top revealing the odd glistening cherry.

I'm in heaven cutting up slices of the warm Genoa for everyone when Mitch comes into the kitchen. He really is a hunk of a man, broad-shouldered and hefty without any extra padding, and arms that could carry you up the stairs. Oh Mitch. I give him a big dreamy smile. This really is turning out to be a special afternoon.

'What's that?' he asks. 'Smells amazing.'

'That will be me, Mitch.'

He laughs. 'May I wash my hands, please?'

I let him through to the sink, enjoying the wriggle past him as I move away. What a perve I am! I take a couple of slices of the Genoa out to our two walkers sitting in the garden, who are ready for another slice of cake, and when I come back in to make them a fresh pot of tea, Mitch has his nose close to the cake and is breathing it in, his eyes closed.

'What is it, Janet?' he asks without opening them.

'It's a Genoa.'

'Yes, I thought it was . . .' And he heaves a sigh of pure delight.

'I was going to give it to you as a thank you for doing the shower,' I explain. 'I know you said you liked it. It's just . . . it's just it seems I've opened a tea shop whilst you were upstairs, so it's nearly all gone. I'm really sorry.'

He opens his eyes and says, 'Get me a bloody slice sharpish then, Janet – no, better make it two, before anyone else gets a look-in and scoffs the lot.'

We laugh, and he takes a seat in the kitchen on the last of the chairs. I make him a strong tea with only a little milk, the way he likes it, and put two thick slices of the lightly fruited, moist and still-warm Genoa on a plate for him. He goes quiet as he reverently demolishes both slices and drains the cup.

'I was thinking, Janet,' he says, brushing a few crumbs off his lap.

My lit-up heart does a little leap, which is ridiculous. *Calm down, Janet.* I'm jumping to assumptions that I might be included in his thinking. I try to look as relaxed and carefree as I can, leaning on the worktop whilst surreptitiously propping up my boobs. As luck would have it, I'm wearing one of my saggy old bras and my boobs could do with some extra underarm support.

'Oh, right, yeah?' I wait.

He's paused – how do I encourage him to come out with more words? I shuffle my boobs, for all the impact that has.

After a pause: 'Yes, you see, Janet, I was thinking—'

'Any chance of a pee?'

It's Gerard. He steps into the kitchen, oblivious to the moment he's currently ruining. I try not to shout out: 'Bugger off, Gerard, Mitch is *thinking*.' Instead, I say politely, 'Yes, of course. Go down through that door, the loo is at the end.'

Once Gerard has gone off, whistling, to relieve himself, Mitch takes a deep breath, as if he's preparing himself for something important. He looks into his cup, puts it back down, gathers himself. I am going to have to encourage him on.

'What were you saying, Mitch?' *Please, please, please, tell me what you're thinking, I'm all ears, all body, all soul, ready to listen and so much more.*

'The thing is . . .' he clears his throat, 'well, I was wondering, Janet, if you—'

'*Help! Help!* I think this gentleman is—*HELP!*'

My eyes still locked on Mitch, I pivot reluctantly to Margot, who is looking panicky and is calling from outside. Old Mr Marshall has slumped and slid halfway off his chair and is now being propped up by a distraught Margot.

Mitch and I rush outside. I check, and the old guy is still breathing – but only just. 'Oh God,' someone says. 'Call an ambulance.'

I run inside for my phone and ring 999. Gerard arrives back from the loo and goes into First Aid mode; he's an ex-first aider apparently, so he has the poor man on the ground with a pillow propping up his head, as I'm explaining Mr Marshall's symptoms to the kind woman on the end of the line. Once I hear the ambulance is on its way, I rifle through my correspondence until I find the contact number for Adele Fogg.

The ambulance arrives in record time; luckily they were already in the area. As the paramedics take over, Mitch mouths, 'Goodbye,' to me. I can't really concentrate but I know he has said something like, 'I hope all's OK and sorry, I've got to go now.' What can I do but give him a thumbs-up and a wave. Meanwhile Jacko is being uploaded into the ambulance and Adele, thank God, is back in time to jump in with her father and hold his hand.

As the ambulance door slams shut, Mitzi is approaching along the drive, dragging a huge tree branch.

'What's happened?' she asks, looking worried.

'Mr Fogg's father-in-law has collapsed. He's not a well man.'

Mitzi doesn't miss a beat. She drops the branch in the middle of the drive, runs inside the house and returns moments later, both hands clasped around large sheafs of various barley-type stalks. She sets one sheaf alight and begins what I can only describe as a Native American kind of prairie dance, chanting gobbledygook and liberally wafting the stinky sticks whilst she parades around the garden and the outside of Lavander Cottage.

Lee and the two kids emerge from the cottage into a drift of smoke, all looking stressed about poor Grandad and prepped for a walk. They are visibly bewildered by what Mitzi is doing, and set off down the drive with the two kids walking backwards so they can continue to keep watching. I try to minimise the impact with a cheery, 'See you later!' It makes no difference: my sister in full flow is a sight to be seen. Why wouldn't you look?

Gerard and Margot are also watching, also startled, at their table.

I whisper loudly, whilst vainly pretending to be doing a bit of dead heading, 'Maureen – *Mitzi* – what the heck are you doing?'

She reaches both arms into some sort of upright yoga position and drops her head to her chest. 'I'm blocking the Curse.'

'*Curse?*' Ears obviously primed over decades for any high-class gossip, Margot is on it like a pincer. 'There's a curse?' She sounds excited, whereas a cold dread floods through me.

In a wave of spaghetti limbs and spiral smoke trails, Mitzi makes a dramatic spin then drops to her knees and splays both arms out wide, letting the still-smoking barley sheafs fall on to the ground.

'It is done. All is gone.'

I have to give it to her, it's first-class showmanship.

Gerard, elbowed by Margot, joins in with his wife to give my sister a round of applause. Trying to normalise a far from normal situation, I clap too.

Margot is hugely enthusiastic. 'Oooh, I loved that! Wasn't that good, Gerry?'

Meanwhile, I'm hissing to my sister: 'Don't be bloody stupid. That's no curse, the poor chap has Stage Four cancer.'

Mitzi is resolute. 'You're wrong. It's a curse.'

It's time for the walkers, now greatly restored, to get back on the trail. The couple zip up, refasten layers and pull on gloves.

'Well, that was very entertaining,' Margot says happily. 'What do we owe you, Janet dear?'

Mitzi gives me a meaningful look as she lifts up the huge tree branch and starts to drag it along the drive again.

I get her message: if the ritual is to work, this must be a gift.

'Nothing,' I tell the woman. 'Thank goodness you were here. I wouldn't have known what to do if you hadn't turned up.'

'Poor guy. We were only too happy to help, and I reckon we were obviously meant to come along. I always follow my instincts, they're never wrong, and they led us here today.' Like another Mitzi, Margot is absolutely convinced of what she says. 'You, Gerard, were brought here today to save his life, I know it.'

Very cheerful after his sit-down, with a happy tummy and empty bladder, her husband nods and says, 'You're rarely wrong, Margot love, rarely wrong. Now Janet, let us give you something for the delicious tea and cake.'

But I stick to my guns. 'No, really, it's my pleasure. And thank you again for saving our elderly guest.'

Gerard smiles, shrugs humbly and grabs his sticks. Margot gives him a peck on the cheek.

'You see, Gerry?' she tells him. 'We were meant to come and get a performance, a cup of tea, cake and a pee – and all for free.'

She giggles and with that cheery pronouncement the couple are on their way, and I wave them off before beginning to clear up the crockery. Mitzi parks her branch by the patio door and follows me into the kitchen.

'Who were they and what were they doing here?' she quite naturally wants to know.

'They saw Mrs Fogg's dad sitting outside and thought it was a tea room.'

'Nice,' she comments. 'No wonder you wanted rid of me. I'm getting in the way of another of Janet's money-making schemes.'

My older sister has a knack for making me feel really bad at times, when I've done absolutely nothing wrong. I feel a burst of annoyance.

'It was a one-off – plus what if I am doing some money-making schemes? Someone round here has to!'

'*Oooh*, thousands of pounds' worth of interior upgrades not enough for you, Mrs Snotty Jackson? I'll tell Carl he needs to cancel his extension and move on to doing your kitchen.'

'You'll do no such thing. I've just nearly caused a death with my lemon drizzle, that's all – it was obviously too rich for that poor chap. Look, I'm in need of a calm moment, not more bloody drama, that's all.'

'Well, don't hold your breath because I've just seen Echo flyer-ing in town. She's setting up Calder Coven in Midgeley.'

Weirdly, I'm not surprised by the news. I knew we hadn't seen the last of that horrible woman.

'Yes, well, that confirms everything I have ever thought about her – she is a ruddy witch. She'll be sending bad vibes down here via Midgeley Ginnel if we're not careful.'

'Don't you worry about that. I'll set up a counter curse at the kissing gate.' Mitzi means the gate in a meadow near Redacre Wood. She wanders around the kitchen for a while picking things up and putting them down before coming to a halt and announcing: 'You know what? Your new café has given me an idea.'

My tummy does a lurch. It's like muscle memory, the inevitable fallout from when Mitzi hatches anything.

'You can stop right there,' I say forcefully. 'There *is* no café.'

'Shush, just hear me out. I want to introduce the shaman experience to those people who, y'know, like a scone with their spirits.'

'Eh? What are you on about? You've lost me.'

'Janet, I'm riffing aloud here, go with me, open your imagination to the possible. If Hebden Shamans is going to be the incredible success I'm anticipating, I need to reach out to customers from all walks of life, ideally ones with some actual income. You saw that woman today, she loved it – she gave a round of applause. This is the perfect space – a large, beautifully kept country garden, high quality cakes and delicacies, wonderful, charming service – it would attract the upmarket curious, and they, my friend, are who I'm after.'

My mind is boggling. I can't resist saying, 'Beautifully kept garden, amazing food, charming service – what the heck are *you* doing in this dream scenario, Mitz?'

She's too excited to take offence. 'The show, of course, a shaman show! Let's set a date. Three weeks on Saturday? We'll call it *Scones and Spirits*. I'm going to make it my first Hebden Shamans Insta post.'

And with that she drags the branch in through the patio door, leaving a trail of twigs and leaves everywhere. 'Why a tree?' I shout after her.

'Nature vibes for the bedroom, Janet, nature vibes.'

I go outside and slump into one of the seats vacated by Margot and Gerard, taking the last slice of the Genoa cake with me. I sweep the lemony crumbs off the tablecloth into my hand and scatter them on the ground for the birds, then stare out at the garden in a daze. What an afternoon. One thing after another. Setting up a café? In my garden? People coming in and buying my cakes and me working at home, from my own kitchen, doing the thing I love most of all. Cooking and making people happy for a living. Visitors enjoying my lovely garden and my best cakes.

An electric thrill races through me, and I take a bite of the Genoa. Mmm, that *is* good. Mitch will be back for another slice of this, surely?

All my emotions are stirred up: hope for the Foggs' beloved grandad, dread about that awful woman Echo, my heart racing when Mitch is close by . . . The series of dramas of the afternoon wash over me, and I almost feel weepy. I'm all mixed up and wondering what on earth I have agreed to now. I don't really know. But guess what? I am excited.

REVIEW

**** Four Stars from the Foggs

Pleasant stay at Lavandar Cottage. Good breakfast. Interesting hosts. Life-savers.

TIPS FOR RUNNING A B&B

Learn First Aid. You never know when it might come in handy.

Keep spare crockery and linen for things that happen. Unexpectedly. Like Secret Garden Cafés!

TIP ON LIFE

Dare to dream.

CHAPTER 14

Scones, Spirits & Rik Feathers

Mitzi has organised for a celebrity to come and open the very first Shaman Fest! We agreed it needed a couple of weeks more to sort out, which happened to coincide with an appearance at the local theatre of a once quite well-known comedy actor, Rik Feathers. Apparently, my sister stalked him over social media, until his people reached out and messaged her privately, asking her to stop. At which point she pulled out the offer of free accommodation in exchange for a brief appearance at our event. One phone-call later, to establish she's not a psychopath – how you can tell from a phone-call I'll never know – and hey presto, his people have agreed for him to open the first Scones & Spirits Shaman Fest.

They are all coming to stay in the cottage, hence *two doubles required,* in separate rooms. We can offer this. There's the double bed upstairs and the sofabed downstairs. That should be fine. Rik Feathers was famous for playing the bartender in popular sitcom *Troy of the Rovers.* He had the catch phrase 'Everything's better on ice'. Anyhow, he's agreed to cut the ribbon, or smash the bottle or whatever Mitzi has in mind, and we'll get somebody to take some photos and then she'll try to get it into the paper. It's all very exciting.

The cottage is immaculate. I've put some candles out, bought a couple of new bedside rugs because the others were looking a bit tatty even after a vax. I splashed out on two new starry duvet sets, made up the sofabed ready, put an aromatic sleep spray next to the pillows and a wrapped-up posh soap in the bathroom. Is that enough? What else do famous celebrities expect of their B&B?

Mitzi is vague and told me not to worry. She herself is too busy drumming up customers. She's on publicity hyperdrive and between her spoken-word network and her social media thingies and flyers all over the Valley, she's sold more than forty tickets at ten pounds apiece. She's already persuaded the local paper to run an article on her. Chloe helped her with her make-up for the shoot and she looks super-glamorous with her hair cascading in waves down one shoulder and her top falling off the other.

Meet Shaman Mistress Mitzi,
in her Scones & Spirits
Introduction to Shamanism event.

'Mistress?' We're all in the kitchen and Carl is reading and eating at the same time. I've done a trial run on wholemeal apple scones and he's gamely agreed to try them. He chokes and I can't decide if it's the scones or the headline.

'Too dry?' I enquire.

'Too bloody sexy, if you ask me.' He turns to my sister. 'You'll be attracting some wrong 'uns with that picture and that headline, Mistress Mitzi!' Then he chokes on a crumb.

Mitzi jumps off the kitchen island to thump him on

the back.

'Don't be silly, Carl, it's a misprint. I never said anything about *mistress*, they've misunderstood. I said "Shaman *Mystery*". Anyway, all publicity is excellent and it's going perfectly to plan. I've had another twenty ticket requests since the article went out.'

'I bet you have,' he grins, taking a swig of tea.

'Another twenty?' I don't know whether to be pleased or worried. That's a lot of tea and scones. 'How many people are we expecting, do you think?'

My sister says airily, 'Oh, I don't know exactly. Fifty, maybe a hundred?'

What? Fifty! A hundred!

'Where will they all sit?' I am wringing my hands. 'I don't have a hundred chairs, or cups, or scones.'

'Don't worry, people will come and go during the day.' She nips a bit off an apple scone and tastes it tentatively. 'Not bad, not as good as the plum and date one, though. How are you getting on with the cheese variation?'

'Who put you in charge of catering, Mistress Mitzi? I'm the taste-tester round here.'

Carl chases her around the kitchen island. These two are so loved up at the moment, it might make me sick, only I'm so pleased for her. It's taken my sister a long time to find anything approaching this kind of happiness. She's especially in her element when she's bossing me about. At least I put my foot down about the costs. We've agreed to split the proceeds 50/50. I insisted, what with all the gas and electric I'm using to wash all the linen for tablecloths, cook all the bloody scone variations you've ever heard of, and supplying the teas, coffees, milks, etc. Plus, we have all agreed to pay Chloe, who's taking a day off work to help out.

As Chloe, Carl, Mitzi and I go through the final details, the day before the Scones & Spirits spectacular,

Mitzi drags into the kitchen a huge zipped-up holdall.

'Now, people, *final touches*, I need us all and everything we do tomorrow to amalgamate into a cohesive spiritual Hebden Shamans philosophical vibe – yeah?' She delivers this as she pulls out of the bag and hands to Chloe a tie-dyed bunch of feathers and silky scrap of material with a German Bierkeller gold-tie corset detail.

'What is *that*?'

'It's your outfit, darling.'

Chloe looks horrified. 'I'm not wearing that.'

'You haven't seen the headdress yet.'

Mitzi produces the article with a flourish. It's an elaborate flower and feather thing and it makes me think of Pocahontas, *on drugs*.

'No, *no way*.'

My sister says patiently, 'It's about evoking the nature spirits. As I said, everything must amalgamate into a cohesive vibe.'

'And as I said, no.'

I am struggling with the giggles, when Mitzi hands to me a bright purple medieval princess dress, similar to the ones in those children's books where the fairy godmothers appear at the christening.

'OK, that's quite nice.'

But that's before she pulls out a huge matching, pointed hat.

'Eh? How the heck am I meant to keep that on my head whilst making a hundred cups of tea, and getting scones out of the oven?'

Now Chloe and Carl are laughing at me, then she hands Carl his outfit.

'Friar fucking Tuck, Mitzi? Are you having a laugh?'

That's it, we are on the floor howling; even Mitzi can't help herself and begins to shoulder shake with a fit of giggles.

'Please don't ask me to shave my head like a ring doughnut,' Carl splutters. 'I'm hanging onto the last few hairs on my head for all I'm worth.'

It's hysteria for at least five minutes. Once we've calmed down, Mitzi runs through the schedule. It feels well organised. There's a plan to the day and we all know what we're doing. I'm chef and on kitchen duty, producing hot drinks and scones, Chloe is waitress for the day and Carl is ticket-handler and security. Mitzi has refused to bring anyone in to help her.

'Once burnt, twice shy. After that business with Echo I've decided I'll manage this alone. I'm not showing anyone else what I do just so they can run off and open a coven and steal my ideas.'

I feel for her. What a shame she can't trust anyone to get involved. 'It's a lot on your own.'

'I'm not on my own, you're all here.'

A warm feeling runs through me. I register that it could be panic, or heartburn, but it could also be actual love and camaraderie. *We do feel like a team*. I'm excited about seeing my garden come to life. People eating and enjoying my food, like my very own café.

I don't have long to ponder though, because the doorbell rings and Chloe, who is entirely oblivious, announces, 'There's that bloke Rik Feathers at the door.'

Mitzi and I share an excited look and rush to meet him. He's very laid back, has a lovely smile and very dark quiffy hair that looks too big for his head. There's a definite hint of teddy boy about him. I wonder how old he is? He looks very tanned, not the fake stuff, too leather satchel to be anything other than a lot of long holidays.

Rik is accompanied by two people, one either side of him, a man and a woman. They are both middle-aged, both dowdy and both look drawn with worry.

When they introduce themselves as Titch and Tina, I'm guessing they're a couple. They seem oddly preoccupied with Rik. They never take their eyes off him, as if he's a wayward toddler they're desperately trying to manage. I don't know what they're so worried for, he's perfectly charming and stringing coherent sentences together. He's also very jolly and agrees to have a couple of photos with Mitzi, which she's absolutely delighted about.

Carl introduces himself and offers to carry any bags, but they refuse. I can't help but notice the chink of bottles as our guests pass by the patio door. Oh well, at least it's only for one night, they can't do too much damage. I have a million things to do, to spend precious energy stressing about the cottage.

The trio soon get settled in Lavander Cottage which, thankfully, they seem delighted with. I leave everyone to it and get to work on baking another 120 fruit scones. Mitzi wanders around the garden planting tent pegs with silvery ribbons into the ground, *to attract the good spirits*. Chloe appears dressed to the max in a tight black pencil dress that accentuates every curve; with her hair on top of her head and wearing a pair of teetering platform wedge sandals, she must be nearly six foot.

'Off out somewhere, love?'

'Yeah, I've not been out for ages 'cos of work, so I'm meeting Charlotte and the gang in town for a quick sesh and then we're going out for a few in Fax.'

I try to keep a friendly smile on my face, though inwardly I'm seething with frustration. Really? A big night out *tonight*? The night before the big Fest thing? For the first time, in the garden, when we're paying you to be here?

But what comes out of my mouth is: 'Great, have a good night, love. Don't forget we're going to be very busy tomorrow.'

'Bye, love you.'

As she slams the patio door behind her, I know it. I'm on my own. My eyes drift around the kitchen, seeing it for the first time. It's a total bombsite, like a bad *Celebrity Bake Off* episode – flour everywhere, trays of scones waiting to be put into containers. Jam to dollop into pots, butter to be curled into ramekins, cream to be whipped, tea pots to be cleaned, all the boxes of old china to be washed and dried. I'm contemplating a mini-breakdown and wondering if I could get away with it when Mitzi waltzes into the kitchen with a clipboard and two bottles of unopened prosecco.

'How are you doing?' she asks breezily.

'I'm struggling, Mitz.' I feel like crying. 'I've bitten off more than I can chew and I don't think I'm going to get done. I've got to get all that crockery unpacked and put in the dishwasher, I've got to pack up all the scones, prepare a load of mixture for tomorrow, iron the tablecloths, dig out the napkins and maybe iron some of them, wipe down all the chairs—'

'Stop right there,' she commands me. '*No ironing*. I don't believe in it. It's an offence against women. If people are fretting about a creased tablecloth then they're in the wrong place. Chairs, that's Carl's domain. Scones, cups – you've got it. Are you forgetting, you are Janet Jackson, *Superhost*?'

Never have I felt so hoist by my own petard. I could kick myself. When did I mention Superhost to Mitzi?

'Open one of these.' She hands me a bottle of prosecco. 'I was taking this round to Rik on request of his helpers, they're a very thirsty bunch. Anyway, it will be the third he's had, so you enjoy this one and I'll be in to help you in a bit, to stir or dry or whatever you need.' She hands me a bottle, and then grabs me in a hug. 'You know what, Janet, I think this just might work tomorrow.'

I hug her back then take her by the shoulders and look her in the eye. 'Yes, and it will be down to you, you bloody lunatic. I'm so proud of you.'

Mitzi wells up and shakes me off.

'Oh stop, don't get me all emosh. I've got to stay cool until this time tomorrow night, when I can collapse. Thank you, darling sis, for all your support.' She stands up straight. 'Right. Focus, *charm the celebrity*, here we go . . .'

She lets herself out through the patio door and I give in, break open the prosecco and slam on the 80s' tunes. I can do this. *Of course I can do this*. If I was running a café I'd be doing this every day.

I'm well on the way with an almost empty bottle of prosecco, piles of clean old china washed and dried on the side, the scones in Tupperware containers, the cake stands I've dug out of retirement, all hand-washed and dried. It's then that a text pops up on my phone that I ignore, as I'm expecting yet another instruction from Mitzi. However, when I eventually get round to reading it, it's from Mitch. I leap and drop the phone down the sink. *Mitch*. In touch!

See you tomorrow, hope there's a genoa scone ☺

What? Why is he coming to a Scones & Spirits thing? Oh God, Oh God, Oh God. The pressure is on, to make this thing go well *and* somehow now also to look half-decent. I check the time. Oh no, it's midnight! Where did the time go? I've still got hours of cleaning up to go, and I'm knackered. I need to go to bed and get some sleep and then I won't look half-dead, even if I am. I must go up to bed, right now! I can get up really early to do everything else. Is midnight too late to text back? Bugger it.

There's a whole stack with your name on it ☺

Hardly sexy talk, is it. I've no idea how to flirt in a text. Genoa scone, there isn't even such a thing. I'll put some extra cherries in a couple and call them Genoa. What if he actually turns up? I'm too tired to fret.

I'm just turning off the kitchen lights when Carl and Mitzi pile in through the patio door, both staggering. I turn the lights back on.

'He's hilarious,' Mitzi giggles.

'Boy, he can put it away.' That's Carl, looking very much the worse for wear.

'Have we anything else booze-wise? He's asking—'

I cut Mitzi off. 'At midnight?' I can't help but give a reproving shake of my head. I'm so bloody puritanical, and let's face it, stressed and tired.

'There's that bottle of Southern Comfort,' Carl remembers, slurring slightly.

'How old is it?' It's been around for ages as none of us really likes it.

Carl reaches into the back of the top cupboard to retrieve it, while Mitzi does a melodramatic yawn.

'You take it round, Carl. I need to get some rest for tomorrow.'

'Do I have to?' Carl slumps. 'I'm exhausted, I can't smile any more.' Looking at me, he explains, 'He's really funny, Janet, but he just never stops.'

Mitzi wipes the dusty bottle and hands it back to Carl.

'Carl's right, Rik's never off. He isn't paying those people to look after him, he's paying them to be an audience. They were overjoyed to have us in there and now I understand why. No wonder they sloped off for a chat as soon as we arrived. You should pop round, Janet,' my sister says craftily.

Yeah, right. I'm not falling for that one. It wouldn't matter how funny he is, he's not better company than my electric blanket and my magazine.

'Night night,' I say firmly.

Carl groans. 'I want my bed too.'

Mitzi takes charge. 'Look, just nip over there, Carl, drop the bottle off and come straight back. Big day tomorrow and all that. Use me as an excuse if you like. We've got to get up at six.'

I'm convinced I've misheard. Never, ever, have I heard those words come out of Mitzi's lips.

'Six? Did you say *up at six*?'

'Er . . . yes, Janet, this is a big day for me. Anyway, I'm often up with the dawn.'

'Are you?'

'Yes, then I go back to bed and sleep in till later.'

'Right . . .' I had never considered that Mitzi's lie-ins were a consequence of an up-with-the-dawn habit, and now, I wisely decide, is not the time to challenge her.

Carl reluctantly heads to the door with the Southern Comfort.

'Send me a text in half an hour, so I can use it as an excuse to come back. Please.'

After a lightning-quick shower, I pile into bed exhausted, set my alarm for 5.45 a.m. and collapse.

What's all the noise? It's 2 a.m. and I'm now wide awake. Down in the kitchen, sniggering and holding half-eaten scones, are Rik Feathers and Carl. Carl attempts to speak but spits scone crumbs all over the kitchen and erupts into a coughing fit that has Rik in hysterics.

'Janet, Janet, I can exshplain,' he manages finally, tears in his eyes. 'I wa' jusht bringing Rik in to show him what we're planning for tomorrow.'

I can't produce even the faintest hint of a smile. My sense of humour is locked away in a deep dark chamber never to be recovered.

'BED NOW,' I bellow. 'And you,' pointing at Rik, 'OUT.'

I literally push the booze-drenched Rik out of the door and quickly lock it. Carl has fled upstairs – I can hear him dash to the attic at gallop speed. I take a look at the mess. It's not too bad, a few scones short and a pile of crumbs, it's retrievable. *The bloody idiots.* I shuffle back up to bed, yawn deeply, fling my head on the pillow and it's lights out.

It's 3.30 a.m. I wake up, almost unconscious, and switch on the light. *There's yet more noise.* If it's Rik bloody Feathers he's going to get an earful. Downstairs, the kitchen light is on, and there is Chloe, standing at the cooker, happily tossing a pancake beside a very tall young man who is holding a plate to catch it.

She sees me. Says, 'Hi, Mum. This is Spencer.'

Spencer immediately flushes hot red and struggles to know what to do with the plate. In the end, he sheepishly hides it behind his back.

'All right, Ma Chloe?'

He makes his way over, hand outstretched for a formal shake, but I bat it away.

'No handshakes before eight a.m., love. Keep the noise *down*. Do *not* touch the scones.' I reverse out of there, turn the light off, turn the light back on, on account of the shocked squeals, and back upstairs I collapse into bed after adjusting the alarm to seven. No way is this going to be a 6 a.m. day.

The first Scones & Spirits Introduction to Shamanism Event is agogo. From the moment I open my eyes it's full throttle. I throw some clothes on, aware I'll need to change into my princess frock later.

Outside, I spot a grey-faced Carl, obviously nursing a chronic hangover, gamely lugging tables and chairs all around the garden, whilst Mitzi points at spaces. She follows up with a sponge and bucket of water wiping everything down, including him across the face, when he moans for the umpteenth time about having a headache. I chase after them with un-ironed tablecloths of every shape and size, and deliver a large glass of water and headache tablets to a grateful Carl.

The sun beams positive rays around the garden that are so hot they burn my neck. It's going to be a gorgeous day! I stack up the mismatch of china cups, saucers and tea pots onto the tables. Mitzi gives the order at 10.45 that we are all to get changed. I put the dress on that she gave me and it fits, *just*! The cleavage on this thing is outrageous and the hat is ridiculous. Carl looks impressive, more strongman than monk, whilst Mitzi herself is a wow of rainbow butterfly, with long flowing see-through wings and an astonishing flower crown that seems to defy gravity by balancing above her head.

I attempt to knock up Chloe, to no response, and it's too late to bother as people are already arriving. Mitzi gets into full performance mode immediately, spinning, dancing, guiding, reciting poetry and demonstrating yoga poses, along with some scarf-waving, some spirit animal manifestations, a gong bath, some Tarot cards . . . you name it, she does it.

When the time is right, Carl carries Rik Feathers

out of Lavander Cottage in a fire-man's lift, to hit the gong to start the day's proceedings.

Rik manages a garbled, 'Like scones and spirits, everything's better with ice,' followed by a bang on the gong, after which he collapses into a drunken coma over a terrified pensioner.

Chloe appears about eleven-thirty in costume with Spencer who, it turns out, has had a stint at silver service when a bit younger. Between them they make fast work of collecting crockery and redistributing scones, jam, butter, cream and fresh tea as required.

Midway through the day, Mitzi's mate Techy Red appears with a clip-on microphone for her to use, as her voice is going hoarse from bellowing. The rush doesn't seem to stop, and mid-afternoon, another wave of people arrive. Carl has his work cut out fielding traffic; the street is rammed nose-to-tail with people reversing and attempting to park, as well as collecting tickets as they enter. I take one look at the queues and bake up another batch of classic fruit scones, thinking, Thank goodness I bought a load of extra ingredients just in case.

I'm bent over the oven testing the top of the next batch, just about balancing my hat, when I get a tap on the shoulder and a gentle cough close to my ear. I turn around and there's Mitch. Gorgeous, stocky Mitch with his gentle eyes and wide generous mouth turned up in a smile.

'Janet, or is it Princess Janet? Are you ever allowed out of this kitchen?'

Well, I don't need a second invitation. I take the scones out from the oven, whisk off my apron and hand over responsibilities to Chloe and Spencer who are canoodling in the pantry.

'Mitch, fair sir, have I ever shown you around my lady garden?'

Well, that has us both laughing. I take Mitch's hand and lead him away from the gong bath that is in full session on the lawn. There must be thirty people laid or slumped at all sorts of angles, their eyes closed, as we pick our way amongst them. There are some snores, some heavy breathing, and a polite acknowledgement from a couple of old guys who are definitely not joining in and are busy pouring tea and building cream scones to enjoy.

Mysteriously emboldened by exhaustion, excitement and the need for some pleasure in a life that can quite often feel like a list of chores, I lead Mitch around the back of the house away from any noise or interference. There, I lean him against the side of the house and kiss him. No asking permission, no nerves, no questions. It was the moment for it. *I needed to know.* He kissed me back. Oh yes, gentle reader, again and again, he kissed me back.

REVIEW

** 38 x Five Stars for Lavandar Cottage It's all got mixed up with the Scones & Spirits Event, courtesy of Mitzi's bad IT. I'm over the moon!

TIP FOR RUNNING A SCONES & SPIRITS EVENT

Book Security. Rival Shamans don't send bad vibes, they send ringers. When Mitzi spotted Echo recording the event on her iPhone, Carl and Mitch were good at encouraging a fast exit on her broomstick.

TIP FOR RUNNING A B&B

Buy extra rugs. I found my new one curled up into a ball with a turd wrapped inside it. A celebrity turd, no less. Very much the same as an ordinary one. *Grrr.* Honestly, where's the respect?

TIPS ON LIFE

Celebrities are very much like real people. Real, *needy* people. The neediest people you've ever met. Same goes for Celebrity Alcoholics. They are very much like the alcoholics you meet in real life. With better jokes, perhaps.

Be brave when it comes to would-be lovers. The worst that can happen is you get a fabulous snog.

CHAPTER 15

The Desmonds & the Foyles

I don't know about you, but I'm the sort of person who gets suspicious when things are going too well. It puts me on my guard. With so many positive reviews, I've got to be on the cusp of Superhost. I'll be higher in the listings, so everyone will notice – and at a good price and with great reviews, that should translate into more bookings. What's more, there might even be enough cash coming in from the sales of my cakes that will replace my receptionist income. So why am I not delighted?

I think I'm a bit anxious about our next guests. Understandably so, given recent experiences. What will I be dealing with, I wonder anxiously? It feels so personal when guests leave Lavander Cottage in a mess, when they tramp through my garden and crush the flowers. I don't get those feelings with the garden café. I love every minute. The people come, they eat and drink and enjoy themselves – and then, best of all – *they go*! It's so much easier.

I've decided to do a trial run every Saturday and Sunday, see if the café takes off. Chloe has offered to put some adverts out on socials and we've made a free-standing sign for the bottom of the street. If Laura bloody Watson kicks up a fuss about it, I'll get Mitzi to put a hex on her. Anyway, she's been very quiet lately. No doubt, if her guests are like mine, only richer, she's finding the B&B business far more taxing than she'd anticipated. Serves her right.

The café – I'm only just keeping my excitement under control. More baking cakes – more time in the garden? It's all too much to hope for. Who *is* this lucky woman?

Mitch and I shared a kiss. Will that turn into something? He is so gorgeous, but *so* shy. At the end of Mitzi's event, he sloped off without a proper goodbye, and I was so busy I didn't even notice. Ah well, I'm sure he'll understand that it was a crazy day.

Mitzi is flying since the Scones & Spirits do. She is inundated with requests from people wanting to join her classes or book in for one of the experiences she advertises; also, she's been invited to do a couple of corporate away days, presenting meditation practice and yoga for health. You get very well paid for those. She's been splashing the cash on some very annoying drums, bells and a fire pit. The first time she experimented with it, the amount of smoke and stink it gave off caused one of the neighbours to phone and ask if they needed to call the fire brigade. Carl and Mitzi were in hysterics. When they weren't looking, I threw my peppermint tea on it: *that soon put it out*.

That same night, I was fast asleep when Chloe returned home late from a shift, came into my bedroom and woke me to tell me she's been promoted to manager in the restaurant where she works.

'I'm proud of you, love. That's brilliant.'

'Oh Mum, I reckon I'll be good at anything I put my mind to. It just takes hard work. I've decided I'm going to apply to Uni – I don't know where yet. I might stay at home to save the cash, or I might think, Fuck it, and go. I could study Event Management. Run gigs. See stuff for free. Yes. I've decided, I'm doing it.'

I didn't know my daughter had enough qualifications to go to Uni? But apparently, she has enough points from the studying she squeezed into this year.

'Don't you remember me doing the Access course at Halifax Academy every Tuesday and Wednesday?'

I'm a terrible mum, because I remember nothing about it. Anyway, all she has to do is have a look round and get the application in to whichever universities that offer the subjects she's after, get accepted, find accommodation, find finance and open a student account – all within the next four weeks before autumn term begins in October. I am struggling to breathe thinking about it all. She, on the other hand, is completely relaxed.

I never went to university. Only Big Brains Maureen, as we called her at the time, went to Uni, in her twenties – to Manchester, or maybe Bolton? I don't even know if she finished her degree. She studied Drama, I recall, and possibly Spanish – and Environmental Studies came into it too, somewhere along the line. Anyway, it was one or all of them. It's a blur of postcards.

My sister never went back to the family farm once she left. I reckon she only saw Mum and Dad three or four times after that, before they died a decade or two later. The 'Goodbye, I'm going to Uni,' turned out to be a permanent farewell.

I'm sure Chloe has collapsed into bed and is enjoying a lovely restful night, but for me now any chance of sleep has gone. The doubts and fears draw in. Will Chloe come back and visit *me*? I'm going to miss her so, everything about her, the mess after she cooks, my phone charger going missing, the tuna pasta leftovers going mouldy in the fridge, the hair blocking the shower, even her stinky pile of washing like a carpet on the floor of her bedroom. I'm ready to go into premature mourning. But Chloe is still very much at home and I think we get on a lot better these days than I did with my parents. In fact, I'm certain of it. We talk, we laugh, we share plans and the plans include one another. If my daughter can go to Uni and thrive, I've done a really good job. So why do I feel like I've been punched in the tummy and my heart is hurting already?

I distract myself from the thought of her going. I thank the Universe for my family, the garden, the cakes, the cottage, the sleep I desperately need – and even, of course, *the guests*.

The Desmonds and the Foyles are lovely, I can tell. They send polite messages – even if there are too many of them. How far to the local canal? Is it true there's a small cinema? Is it correct there's a local artisan food market every Saturday? What do we do about towels? Soap? Milk? Is there a fridge? Dishwasher? *Stove?* That does it, they're so posh. *Who has a stove?* There's a four-ring electric hob, love, and a microwave that you can pronounce mi-cro-wa-vee, if it makes you feel better. They are an upmarket brand of guest, I decide. I have prepared the two double beds, the feather pillows, the best bedding, oat milk as well as the dairy, and a sourdough loaf from the artisan market. All that should, I hope, do the trick. I can't be losing my Superhost chances now.

It's been a hectic morning prepping for their arrival. I'm up ridiculously early baking, cleaning the cottage top to bottom, third lot of laundry in and out, dishwasher filled and emptied twice. I could do with a supermarket shop but I wait to welcome them as they wanted an earlier than normal arrival. They're forty-five minutes later than they said, which is irritating as I need to get to the post office. When they do arrive, they are pretty much exactly as I imagined. Both couples turn up purring in their own up-to-the-minute four-by-four electric cars. I had already pulled out the long extension for charging them up. I'll have to mention an extra charge for the electricity. It's so expensive these days, and they look like they can afford it.

The men are good-looking blokes with glasses, and their wives are yoga-type yummy mummies, both blonde, skinny and taller than average. They are super-relaxed, in their Fair Isle jumpers and designer shearling gilets, with expensive sloppy socks and immaculate walking boots that have never seen a cowpat or dog poo. I'm glad once they're in the cottage, where they seem happy enough. I give them the welcome book to read and point out the wifi code, thinking, *Please let that be it*. I'm feeling low on interaction, wanting to chill and sit with my 'Chloe might be leaving' emotions.

I make it to the post office to send a couple of birthday cards, pick up the papers whilst I'm there and promise myself a rest. Back home, I run a deep luxurious bubble bath and have a pamper session with face-pack, hair mask and moisturiser. I then put on comfy loungewear – a fluffy pink velour two-set. I assemble a big cup of tea, a cheese savoury mix sandwich on brown, today's *Daily Mail* and, like a gift, the sun runs through the garden and onto the double seat in front of the patio door. Grabbing a cushion and a throw, I take everything outside and set myself up. I lay the throw onto the seat, place the cushion in corner position, take a couple of bites of the sandwich, a good slurp of tea, wriggle out of my crocs and put my feet up, breathing a big sigh of pleasure.

The sun hits my face and it's as if the weekend has finally, *finally* arrived. I open up the paper to the centre where there's a 'lottery-winner disaster relationship' special. I know it's mean, but it's interesting to contemplate, should I ever win the lottery, exactly what I'd be dealing with. This, of course, is on the under-standing that I might be in a relationship again. I'm not exactly being bowled over by attention from Mitch since the kiss. In fact, he's not been in touch at all. Oh well. He's shy, he's just biding his time, it's only been a few days. *Yeah, keep telling yourself that, Janet. Once Chloe goes, you're going to be a hermit, a lonely singleton with only your cakes for comfort.*

I stop and tell myself to *relax* . . . The sun is re-charging my tired bones, the lottery stories are satisfyingly scandalous, the tea is delicious, the sandwich perfection.

'Excuse me.'

I almost blank it out. Almost. Then I reluctantly close the paper and fix a polite smile to my face.

'Hello? Everything OK?'

'Well, actually, so sorry to disturb you,' says one of the men from the cottage, 'but there seems to be some sort of leak coming from under the kitchen sink. It's quite a pool.'

'Oh dear.' I leap up and go into Lavander Cottage where, no question, the lino is awash with a thin layer of water. Oh Gawd.

'We only turned on the tap to make a pot of tea,' whines one of the blondes.

'It's nothing *we've* done,' whines the other. 'It must have already been faulty.'

'Ever so sorry to bother you,' the other man puts in.

'I see.' I'm baffled. 'I cleaned the cottage this morn-ing and there was no leak then. I'm really sorry to have this happen. Let me fetch some towels to mop it up and

I'll try to get hold of someone who should be able to help. Excuse me, I'll be back as soon as I can.'

I rush into the house and dig out the scratchy old towels from the back of the airing cupboard. It turns out I've got more scratchy old towels than actually any nice towels. It's quite a pile. I haven't time to overthink this. I know it's pushing things, but what choice do I have? I call Mitch. He doesn't answer. I'm now mortified. *He's so not into you.* He sends a text. Thank God, this day couldn't get any worse.

On a job.

Sorry. People stopping in cottage kitchen and floor flooding. What do I do?

He calls me. Asks, 'What colour is the water?'

'I just think it's normal water.'

'Right, go in, pull off the kickboard and videocall me.'

I throw every towel I own onto the kitchen floor, then with enormous effort lever off the kickboard from below the sink unit. I now lie full length in a pile of damp towels, my lovely newly washed hair resting in slimy water, whilst I videocall Mitch.

'Show me the floor, right, run your hands up the pipes, that's it . . . Now, can you feel water on any of them?'

My pink velour top is now black from the accumulated dust under the sink, and my lovely clean hands, all freshly moisturised, are scraping along an old slimy pipe.

'Yes, I think so, I'm not sure . . . yes, I think so, on this one – can you see it?' I vainly attempt to show him the pipes on my phone, giving him I'm sure an up-the-nostril worst view possible of me ever, when it's obvious it's really too dark for him to see anything.

'Not really,' he replies. 'I'm up to my elbows in crap here or I'd come over. Put some more towels down,

Janet, and just check it's not coming out of the pipe when you turn the tap on?'

He sounds irritable and up against it in the way you get when you're struggling to manage things. I turn the tap on, check again, but it doesn't seem to make any difference to the water that's accumulated.

'It's not making any difference.'

'Double check.'

I'm back on the floor, feeling around the pipes, rolling around on the ground to really reach under the sink in the dust and slime.

'I don't think so.'

'OK, that's good. Stick some towels down, and leave the kicker-board off. I'll get over there tomorrow. Got to go.'

'Thanks.' And he's rung off. I can't say it was the friendliest call.

As I'm lying there, all crumpled, damp and defeated, my hopes for Mitch collapse. I could weep. Why does my life have zero romance in it? I roll over and realise that the Desmonds and the Foyles, the quartet of immaculate lovelies, are all standing there looking at me prostrate on the floor. With a complete lack of any kind of dignity, I wobble my way back up to a standing position. I'm damp everywhere, dripping wet in some places, with dirty hands, filthy pink velour loungewear, grubby matted hair. I suddenly hate having people in Lavander Cottage, observing me on a down day, putting pressure on me that I don't need and can barely cope with. I give in, I can't find the energy to pretend this is all fine.

'I'm so sorry that this has happened, and I don't know what is going on. I think it might be better to cancel your stay and find somewhere else, because I can't solve this today. I'm unable to get anyone out to see to this until tomorrow.'

The foursome look at each other stunned and disbelieving. I reckon it might be the first time something like this has ever happened to them. Their luck, charm, inheritance and good looks have no doubt smoothed a glorious life, only for them to be washed up on the shores of a Janet Jackson crisis. Their expectations of a perfect existence where nothing bad ever happens has just gone banjo.

'Oh, we don't want to cancel,' says one of the chaps. 'It's only a bit of water, and the towels have soaked it up. We're fine, aren't we, everyone?'

'Yes, yes, of course – it's only a bit of water.'

They're lovely. They're kind, they're the nicest people imaginable. I hate them at this moment. *Please just go away and let me collapse somewhere in a small heap of anger, humiliation and frustration.*

'Only if you're sure?' I say weakly.

'Of course, and we're so sorry to put you to all this trouble. *You poor thing.*'

Poor thing? *Aaarrrggghhh!*

'We're going out now anyway, aren't we?'

They collect their immaculate rucksacks and their empty water bottles, which they clearly daren't now fill up with water, and head towards the door.

One of the blokes turns to me with a sympathetic expression and says, 'Don't worry, Ms Jackson, we won't be booking any breakfast.'

I force a smile, go ahead out of the door and let them close up. I wave them off and then go into the house through the patio door and lock myself in the bathroom. I look at myself in the mirror and flinch. What a state I am in. Right now, I cannot acknowledge what I'm feeling: I'm too scared of the implications. Then I berate myself. It's time to own up. To come clean with myself and work out what to do.

The fact is, deep in my heart, *I don't want people*

staying in the cottage any more. Gulp. I've put it out there. *It's too stressful*. From dodgy drunken carers who trash the place, eco witchy squatters who have to be smoked out, grumpy walkers, crazy kids that smash you in the head with a pool ball. It's problem after problem after problem. There are too many people, it's so difficult to manage. They're either on their deathbed or they're your boss who overstays his welcome and you lose your job that you had for years which was easy and which you enjoyed, all because of *the bloody cottage*. Or it's your shitbag neighbour who gives you a One Star review, or the bastard celebrity getting a free stopover who repays your generosity by popping out a poo on your brand-new rug. There have to be easier ways of earning a living.

I give myself a moment or two to calm down before asking myself: Am I out of my mind? Superhost is tantalisingly close to happening. It would be madness to give it all up now. I'm tired, I know, and a bit emotional. But the fact remains: *I really don't want to do this any more*. The feeling of relief in owning up to the truth is overwhelming. I've no idea how I'm going to do it, but I don't care. I just know that the Desmonds and the Foyles are the last paying guests at Lavander Cottage.

Right now, in my grimy dishevelled state, I need to start the day all over again, and turn the shower to hot max. Out of nowhere, once I'm under the water, I feel a swell of emotion, and a few tears plop unceremoniously on to the shower tray. I suck it up for a few seconds, and then my shoulders drop, and in a wave of surrender I finally and completely give in and cry myself a waterfall of my own. Oh God. What a day. All the leaks.

REVIEW

*** Three Stars

Pleasant enough. Close to canal.

TIP FOR RUNNING A B&B

Prepare yourself. Sometimes you don't want to have to face people, and guests are always in your face.

TIP FOR NOT RUNNING A B&B

I'll soon find out.

TIP ON LIFE

Worth repeating; befriend the Trades. Or spend hours on those videos teaching yourself.

CHAPTER 16

The Honeymooners

Some days later . . .

It has to be one of the most surreal moments of my life when I wake up to a rough licking on my face and the sensation of what I can only call 'slaver'. I blink and struggle to focus on the scruffy spaniel who is enthusiastically washing my face with his dog spit.

'What the chuff?'

'I've found him, can we keep him? *Isn't he adorable?*'

It's Chloe. Dressed in a Panda onesie, she's jumping up and down in excitement at my bedroom door making daft doggie noises, while a collarless spaniel is racing around my bedroom barking. I'm extremely groggy from a ferocious late night celebrating Carl and Mitzi's surprise wedding. The bed erupts next to me and Mitch emerges from under the duvet, naked, red-eyed and looking horribly confused. Chloe takes one look at him and staggers backwards.

'Oh God. Sorry. Dog? *Come on, dog,* OUT!'

I'm almost as surprised as Chloe. Except, of course, I remember last night – lovely things that happened last night. But ugh, my head is pounding. Mitch gives me a sneaky sideways glance, a shy grin and then at lightning speed he leaps out of bed and throws on his clothes. He picks up his shoes and begins a creep round the bed as if he doesn't want to wake me up.

'Er . . . you off then?' I ask.

'Yes. Got to, y'know . . . go.'

'Right. Bye then.'

I plant an 'everything is fine' expression on my face as he rushes out of the door, but as soon as he's gone I collapse back into the pillow with a huge groan. Not only do I no doubt look crap, I feel crap, hungover and now emotionally on the floor. What is it with this guy? Hot to trot one moment, freezer geezer the next. I suppose that's a bloody plumber for you.

I try to go back to sleep for all of two minutes, but it's impossible. I'm a wreck. What a weekend this is turning out to be. It began as it always does with Mitzi, *dramatically*. An unexpected phone-call Friday morning.

'Where are you?' she demands.

'Egypt, edge of the Nile, sipping cocktails with Robert De Niro. Why?'

'Hurry. Get dressed UP, you and Chloe, and get to Halifax registry office for eleven, please. And like I said, *hurry*.'

'What's the rush?' I'm baffled. But the phone goes down.

I've got a two-tin chocolate cake ready to come out of the oven and I'm whipping some double cream for a ganache. Sunday is my first proper Secret Garden Café day. Chloe has advertised it on the socials and she's had thirty likes. Given what I'm feeling about the cottage, and its days being numbered, those likes had better turn into real people buying some of this delicious chocolate cake or I'm really kyboshed. I'm torn between pretending I've not had the conversation with Mitzi and continuing my day exactly as I planned, but if this is what I think it is – and since it's a registry office, *it is* – and with just ninety minutes to go, I need to get the cake out of the oven and get ready pronto!

'CHLOEEE!!!'

I park in a rush using the stupid app, then totter in my best navy courts across the back-street cobbles of Halifax to reach the registry office. I'm wearing a navy wrap dress I turn to in emergencies, since it's got Lycra in it, which means it's good on cleavage without poking anyone's eyes out and pulls everything else in. Chloe strides ahead, teetering in silver stilettos and a strapless turquoise blue sheath dress. I am her lumpy maidservant next to her lamé wrap, chainmail bag and random bouquet of Honesty. Oblivious to traffic, she is glued to her phone, her thumbs going at speed.

'Hurry up, Mum, they're going in!'

We pile in the door of the office, are pointed right, barge through another set of double doors and run headlong into Mitzi, Carl and Mitch loitering in a grand tiled quadrangle. Mitzi is wearing a V-necked bohemian dress of cream lace and sequins with minuscule straps holding it all together beautifully. Her hair has been whipped into long curls threaded with ribbons, topped with a 1920s-style headpiece. She is stunning. The groom is in a cream shirt and matching beige tweed waistcoat and trousers with a satin cream cravat. Mitch looks as shell-shocked as I do, in a thrown-together smart suit, trying to wrestle a knot into his tie.

'We weren't going to tell anyone and then last minute I knew I wanted you both here. Carl asked Mitch and here we are, *we're doing it*!' My sister wraps her arms around us both and takes the tiny bunch of Honesty Chloe has brought that matches her outfit perfectly. 'Thank you, darling Chlo, I love you both *sooo* much.'

Cuddles over, we're ushered into the room and settle quietly when the registrar calmly explains the seriousness of the occasion. Carl and Mitzi are dewy-eyed and so in love that it's wonderful to watch. I resist going back in my head to my wedding day; it's such a long time ago anyway. Instead, as one of the two witnesses, it's a strange and faintly embarrassing affair being so intimately close to Mitch. Forced to stand together, as the couple run through their wedding vows and blessings, I make a conscious effort not to touch him at all. As soon as they are pronounced man and wife and they get stuck in with a suitably inappropriate snog, Chloe produces some rice out of somewhere and flings a handful at them, which provokes a bollocking from the registrar.

'Not in here! Jaz, get the hoover!'

We step outside and are instantly whipped by a squall, ripping down the street at speed. Mitzi hangs on to her hem and her headdress.

'Jesus, get me a drink quick, somewhere warm.'

Which is how the reception begins. Over the day it evolves into a gathering of what feels like everyone they've ever known. A rabble of friends, colleagues and relatives. Carl, it seems, has lots of relatives, who all appear ready to celebrate and buy drinks at an hour's notice. Thank goodness some people bring cake, because I am steepled by lunchtime and gulp down two pints of lime and soda water and three packets of differently flavoured crisps, to try to keep me upright. The jukebox is turned on, the dancefloor is filling up and the booze flows to celebrate the deliriously happy couple. I'm praying someone has plans for food, when a load of pizzas arrive at teatime, thank goodness. Whilst everyone is tearing apart the Italian spread, Mitzi steps up, takes the karaoke mic and does a raucous poem that brings the house down.

'So, ladies,' she says loudly, 'I know you'll understand. This poem is called "Hitting the Spot". Here goes:

'I never thought I'd do it,
No man could hit the spot.
Until this big man swooped and dived,
and ladies, I was got.
He's got the biggest heart,
he's got the biggest . . . part
to play in my life.

' 'Cos together, forever, whatever the weather,
this man, he hit the spot!
My man, my joy, my love, toyboy.
God help us –
we've only gone and done it!'

The crowd goes bananas and the tempo gets wilder; there's more booze, more dancing and it's impossible to keep up. I spot at least one of Mitzi's exes out of the corner of my eye. Uh oh. I watch her consoling one of them at the bar, then she runs and jumps onto Carl's back, and he races her around the place as if she's a featherweight. The music gets louder and everyone's doing some sort of variation on jigging about. Someone shouts out, 'A pair of knickers have been found on the dancefloor,' which has everyone howling with laughter.

Carl gets on the mic and insists that all his female cousins, of which there are many, show off their various types of underwear to prove the random pants are not theirs! It's all a bit wild for me. In the midst of the noise and the good-natured chaos, Mitch and I really get chatting and we are increasingly friendly and a bit more touchy-feely, and before I know it, he's asking me outside.

'Do you fancy some fresh air?'

We are soon gripped in a passionate snog, and with little persuasion on either side, we decide to escape everyone, jump in a taxi and fall noisily and passionately into my bed. Which brings us spinning and shaking to this morning and the hangover from Hull, Hell and Halifax. *Argh,* why do I do this to myself? I can barely make it downstairs. Three slices of toast, two glasses of water, two giant cups of tea and two paracetamol later I am texting Mitch in a sulk.

No need to run off. Why not stay for breakfast?

Job on.

OK. Well, have a good day.

Thumbs-up emoji.

I feel like throttling him. Is it me or is it all a bit too casual? I'm too old to be pushed and pulled around like an emotional yoyo. We are something, aren't we? It started with a kiss. *Doesn't it always, Janet?* Was it just a drunken shag thing? That's what he's making me feel like. I'd be really disappointed in myself if I've misjudged things so badly. Come on, we've had lots of conversations now.

I gloom around for an hour and decide I'm in no fit state to think about anything sensibly. All I'm good for is eating and sleeping until this hangover wears off. There's a note on the kitchen table from Mitzi.

We're honeymooning in the cottage. Hope that's OK?

My inner Good Sister wants to cook them breakfast and take a tray in with flowers and a fresh pot of English Breakfast and china cups to enjoy their first day of married life. In reality, I'm glued to the chair, my elbow propping my head up, barely able to keep my eyes open. Just then, Chloe piles in through the patio door with the dog, which immediately starts barking and jumping around my legs.

'Chloe,' I say feebly, 'please tell it to stop.'

She picks the spaniel up and puts it on my lap where, warm lump that it is, it collapses. Its head rests on my leg and I can't help but stroke its soft coat. The spaniel turns to my face and its eyes pour such affection and tenderness into mine, I almost well up.

Chloe sees and understands. 'I told you.' Her voice is gentle. 'He's adorable.'

'Where's he from? Why have you got him?'

'We found him when I was out walking with Spencer. He was asleep by the bins at the Community Centre. We went looking around but no one seemed to be searching for a lost dog so we went inside the Centre and asked, but no one knew anything about him. I put a picture up on local socials and no one recognises him. I think he's been dumped by someone passing through. So, Mum, I've been to the vet's with him and it turns out he's not chipped. He's only a few months old, so they reckon he's been abandoned. Apparently, it's really common at the moment as people can't afford to feed their dogs. He's gorgeous, isn't he?'

'Yes, he's lovely.' I know it's ridiculous, but the

weight on my lap and the soothing process of stroking this dog into what is now a blissful oblivion of tiny snores, is so comforting, like those long-ago days with baby Chloe. My emotions all kick-fire in.

'But you're going to Uni, aren't you?' I say. 'You can't take a dog with you there.'

'Yes, no – you're right, Mum. I probably won't be able to take him to Uni. But there's no way I could have left him by the bins.'

The dog gives a plaintive little sigh, and settles on my lap as if he's found his all-time favourite bed.

'Of course not. Right, put the kettle on, Chloe. I can't move, I've been adopted.' And then I too give a plaintive sigh and a groan. 'I need greasy carbs and lots of tea, if I'm to manage this hangover.'

It's at this point that Harvey strolls past. He stops at my chair, looks at the sleeping dog and with an air of disdain leaps up onto the windowsill and stares at me without a blink for the next half-hour.

'Open a tin of tuna for the cat, keep him sweet.'

Chloe rushes to oblige us all and I have the calmest, sweetest half-hour being a dog-sitter for the gorgeous little thing, with a double egg butty on the side. I tell Chloe that Mitzi and Carl are honeymooning in the cottage and it might be nice, if I didn't have a dreadful hangover, to take them breakfast in bed. Not that Mitzi will ever eat much, but Carl can demolish two break-fasts, no problem. Chloe gets on it, and whilst she does that, I put the sleeping spaniel in a plastic washing basket with a blanket, then go upstairs and have a reviving shower. Afterwards, I pull on my comfiest clothes and decide that what I probably need is some fresh air – and maybe this dog could do with another little walk?

It's a bright cold day and good to be out, even if I am haphazardly retracing my steps and getting caught up in the lead, as the spaniel bounces excitedly from one tree trunk here to a clump of grass there. The collar is the wrong size for his neck, it's too big, so it's up near his ears all the time; I'm a bit anxious that he will slip out of it and run off. I'll have to get him another. The canal is glorious, sparkling with light, and the tiny spaniel is ecstatic to be chasing ducks and geese, getting as close to the edge of the water as he dares. He's such a joyful little thing, and his happiness is contagious. He makes me feel buoyant again and strong and capable, so I pluck up courage and call Mitch. Will he answer? Will he? He does.

'Yo.'

'Hi. I um . . . I hope you're OK, Mitch.'

'Yes, I'm sound, are *you* OK?'

'Well, er . . . I suppose I'm looking for a bit of reassurance, Mitch. I felt a bit weird, you running off this morning without saying goodbye.' There, it's said.

'Oh. Right. Sorry about that. I thought I did say goodbye?'

'A very fast goodbye then.'

I can hear him thinking.

'Right. It's just – you know I've got a job on?'

'Yes, you told me that, by text, after I asked why you'd run off.'

There's a pause, it feels like an age. I'm quietly seething and feeling unsettled. I need to ask these questions. I also need to hear a response that reassures me more than he has so far. If this is just shag-land, then it isn't happening, it's not worth it. I need to know where I stand.

'Er . . . Janet. I don't want any drama.'

'You're not *getting* any drama.' But that sends my pulse racing and out of nowhere arrives my temper. 'I'm simply suggesting it's not really a nice thing to leap out of bed and do a disappearing act, the first time we've slept together, Mitch.'

A couple walk past me on the canal; eyebrows are raised, I couldn't care less.

'You see?' Mitch says. 'This is what I'm scared of – *this*. This is why I don't want to start anything with anyone.'

'I'm not anyone. Start what?'

'It's too hard, relationships are too hard – they fall apart and I'm left broken. I can't do it again. I'm sorry, Janet. I can't.' And the phone goes down, leaving me winded.

Scared. What does he mean, scared? That's it then. Great. Over before it even got started. I'm taking this in, when the dog picks the middle of the towpath to squat down and poo. Thank God I've some tissue in my pocket. I bend down to pick it up, mindful of being a very good dog-owner and making sure I catch every scrap when, just as I'd feared, the dog escapes his collar and races off down the canal path and beyond the next bridge.

Could things get any worse? I'm holding a dog poo tissue and a dog lead but no dog – and how do I even call him back as this puppy has no name? I hurry along the towpath, shouting, 'Dog, come here, doggie, come here!' What I see as I race under and around the bridge is such a surprise it takes my breath away. Miles wobbling on a bike, with the dog haphazardly skittering around his wheels. There's a scream and an almighty splash and when I look again the dog is swimming enthusiastically in the water next to a shocked, purple-faced Miles! He is shoulder-high in the water, his bike wheels momentarily visible before they slowly sink. Looking panicked on the towpath is a twenty-something Lycra-clad young woman, perched on her bike staring at him in horror. I can barely keep the smile from my face.

'Hello Miles,' I say, and I can't help it, I laugh. 'Nice to see you.'

'Janet, right. Yes, er . . . hello.'

I kneel down, reach in and grab hold of the tiny spaniel by the scruff of the neck and yank him onto the towpath where he shakes himself and showers the Lycra beauty with freezing cold, dirty canal water. In spite of my amusement at the situation, I hope he hasn't caught any germs from the water.

I pick him up, wrap my woolly scarf around him and tuck his shivering body inside my jacket so he can get some of my body warmth, then stride off. However, I can't help but turn back to watch Miles. He is shouting something to the woman, who gets off her bike and reluctantly approaches him. He struggles to elbow himself out of the water and on to the bank, while she attempts in vain to grab some of his skintight Lycra cycling outfit.

'I can't do it, I can't – *ow*,' she squeals, 'I've broken a nail!'

Hilarious.

'Forget me, grab the bike,' Miles bellows. 'There's six thousand pounds' worth of bike there.'

'I can't reach.'

There are howls of frustration from Miles as he finally climbs out of the canal and attempts to pull his precious bike out of the water, against the repeated sound of metallic crunches and scrapes. Now I may be nursing a tender heart, but some things are a solace to the soul. Miles and his bike in the canal is definitely one of those things. God, I laugh. I laugh out loud! I can't help but love this dog even more than I thought possible. I'm giggling to myself every step of the way home.

As we reach our street, I'm just contemplating putting him down with his lead on and letting him go, when Laura Watson jogs out in full matching camou-flage wear and an angora sweatband. I try to veer past but she sidesteps me and blocks my way, so there's definitely no escape. But I need to get this puppy home and dry and in the warm, so she'd better be quick.

'Janet, I've been meaning to have a word.'

Here we go. Groan.

'I'm sorry, Laura, I've got to get back, the dog's wet through.' I make to set off but she calls me back.

'Scones and Spirits, the festival thing you did at yours. Am I right in thinking you had public liability insurance?'

The hackles go up. 'Why are you asking?'

'Because we had someone reverse into the Japonica. The parking was atrocious that day, you must have been aware of this. It was a shame we didn't get any advance notice either, because we might have been able to avoid any accidents, had there been *proper signage*. As it is, the Japonica – it's thirty years old, Janet, and now fatally damaged we believe by one of *your* cars on leaving the event. And you know how keen a gardener Oliver is.'

Since when?

'He wants to replace it and of course there are some costs to employ an arborist, plus we'd have to import it, you see, because of the size. And the costs can add up, as I'm sure you understand. So it's better, I think, if you have insurance, that you pass on the details. And in the future, if there is a plan for any more outdoor events involving the public, can you assure me that we will be informed well in advance, so we can approve it? I assume the council were aware you were running a festival? There *are* implications attached to these things, Janet. As well you know, such events have an impact on the neighbourhood and how it's perceived. We need to protect what we have here. The exclusivity of where we live, *the standards*.'

'LAURA? *LAURA!*'

It's Oliver. He's sounding agitated, and thankfully it's enough to drag her back down her drive before I'm obliged to respond. However, as she steps away she calls back: 'Make sure you let me have those details.'

Gloom sets in. She's always the fly in the ointment, is Laura. I'm going to have to cancel tomorrow's Secret Garden Café trial. She's on a mission and I can't have my little café venture being a controversy before it's even had a chance to get going. I cuddle the shivering puppy closer to me, thinking about all the baking I've done. There are thirty scones in the freezer, two chocolate cakes, a red velvet, a lemon drizzle and a carrot cake all in Tupperware waiting to be split and iced – what will I do with them? What a shame. *What a pickle*. I daren't open up tomorrow now, she'll be on to the council pronto.

In one short walk it seems I've lost a business *and* a boyfriend. Laura bloody Watson! Bloody Mitch! Honestly, don't I, Janet Jackson, would-be Superhost, deserve a bloody break? I suppose Miles in the canal is as good as it gets. I'm going to have to make do with that sweet little revenge.

Then I spot Chloe at the foot of the drive, obviously waiting for us. She's waving and signalling for us to hurry up. The puppy sees her, gets excited and wriggles his way out of my arms. I put him on the ground and he bounces towards her. As he reaches her, he whirls around and is off again, racing back to me so I have to corral him towards the house as if I'm Shep the bloody sheepdog.

When we get indoors, I find Mitzi and Carl are there, crowded around Chloe on her tablet. Before I check what's going on, I pick up a warm towel, rub the little dog dry and put him all cosy in his makeshift bed, at which he goes fast asleep.

Mitzi is ecstatic. She tells me: 'It's the best thing I've ever heard *in my entire life*!'

'What is?' I'm intrigued by the size of her smile.

'You will never guess, Mum,' Chloe says, 'not in a million years. It turns out that Laura's B and B is a sex club!'

'*What*?'

'Get this: Rowntree, the local councillor, has just posted on to village socials that they have evidence Laura's B and B is being used as a brothel.'

My eyes pop out of my head and roll on the ground. Mitzi joins in, reading avidly from the tablet.

'"It's letting down the tone of the whole neighbourhood. Bringing the whole village into disrepute". Oh, this is too good. Look, Oliver has just responded: "It's a load of absolute rubbish. Where's your proof?"'

'He never thinks, does Oliver,' Carl says, shaking his head. 'Would Rowntree really put something like that up unless he had the proof?'

Chloe says breathlessly, 'Hold your horses, everyone: here's the proof – look!'

We all stare at the screen, as what looks like a film that's been recorded off the telly stutters and then plays. Everyone involved in the cast is very er . . . under-dressed, and the sign 'Lake Villas' is clearly in evidence in the background of one of the um . . . *action shots*. Even though things have been blurred out, what's going on doesn't require a lot of imagination.

'Wow,' is all I can say. 'You know she's just been having a go at me about the visitor parking during the Scones and Spirits event?'

Carl looks annoyed. 'Has she now?'

'I wouldn't worry about that, Mum.' Chloe is very matter of fact. 'After this she can object to absolutely nothing. There may be criminal charges to come yet!

Her fancy extension is the home of a sex tape.'

Mitzi is still gazing at the tablet, fascinated.

'Sex tapes, people tapes, plural,' she corrects Chloe. 'It's a montage. There's more than one film there. I reckon it's a sex porno factory. Oliver and Laura are running the Soho Streams of Calderdale.'

Within minutes the item gathers hundreds of likes, laughs and comments to suggest this has gone all over the village and beyond.

Sometimes life really does turn around. I check on the pup and find him blissfully asleep and twitching in his dreams. I leave a bowl of water and some shredded chicken breast beside it for when he wakes up, and so he doesn't feel too left out, I pamper Harvey with a few risky pats and strokes and a boiled egg. I hope he leaves that chicken breast alone. If we are going to keep this puppy, he will need a name and proper food suitable for his age and breed. Harvey will also have to learn to accept him. The poor little spaniel: I want him to thrive after his terrible start in life.

After all the excitement, I put the kettle on and as I'm reaching for the tea bags I spot a brown envelope waiting for me on the kitchen table. I open it up, having no idea what it is – and to my astonishment, inside I find a shiny certificate. On it are the words I have longed for these past many months and through all the dramas we've shared.

Superhost Status Awarded to Lavander Cottage and Janet Jackson!

Blimey. I dig out an old frame, fit the certificate inside and rest it against the kitchen window. After all that angst and stress and cleaning and hosting, I've got it. Now I'm not even sure I want it any more. Isn't life always like that?

Anyway, there's one thing I *am* sure about. My café will be opening tomorrow for everyone who is in need of a sit-down, a warm welcome, and my baking and hospitality.

I take the sign up to the street myself and tie it against the lamppost there, where passers-by and motorists can see it.

The Secret Garden Café – This Way

I catch sight of Laura in the garden of Larkspur House, plucking and dead-heading with a fury. She spots me and ducks down. I'm tempted to wave, to strike up conversation and have a go at her snooty, judgmental, awful, mean-spirited, destructive ways and how she can't fool anyone now. But I don't. I don't need to torture her. I know she'll be in bits. I'm not a Laura, I'm a Janet, and I try very hard to be a good neighbour. A neighbour with dreams which, without hurting anyone else, she very much intends to follow.

REVIEW

***** Five Stars

A wonderful honeymoon location. Staff, location, breakfast, all Five Stars. We'll be back.

TIP FOR RUNNING A B&B

Sometimes it is helpful if you can get a couple of 'friendly' reviews, to help boost things a bit.

TIPS ON LIFE

Bloody men. I wish I could do without them. Maybe I will.

Karma is definitely a thing.

CHAPTER 17

The Dogs

The next day, I wake up at 5 a.m., log on to all the apps and suspend all bookings for the cottage going forward. It's a gigantic feeling of relief. My heart's not in it any more. I'm way more excited about being a café Superhost from now on. Chloe and Spencer have taken the puppy's bed upstairs with them as he's so young and needs a lot of care and attention, plus of course house training, for which Spencer has brought a big pack of puppy pads – who knew there was such a thing? We'll keep him out of the way of all the visitors for as long as possible.

By ten o'clock, the garden is busy with customers. The weather forecast is a bit dodgy for this afternoon, but the sun is out this morning and people are making the most of it. It's the novelty, I reckon, a café in a garden. The customers consist of a mixture of local couples and families, walkers, some Scones & Spirits followers looking for a gong bath, and a couple of random passers-by in search of a loo. I also reckon there's a fair few have wandered down to take a peek at Vale Villa. Laura has inadvertently been great advertising for us.

As I move around, serving, chatting and taking

away dirty plates, I receive lots of compliments for my cakes, along with plenty of gossip about the Watsons' sex scandal. I get very welcome help from Chloe, and even Mitzi jumps in and does a bit of waitressing, though it's not long before I notice she's giving someone a Tarot reading. Never one to miss a business opportunity, my sister.

I know this is outrageous, but I've even knocked up a few dog cakes! I love the idea of being able to treat my customers' dogs too, so I found a recipe online last night and I've stuck it on the bottom of the menu for £1 a time. The cakes are going like Hot Dogs!

After a couple of hours, Chloe wants to go off with Spencer and I agree immediately. Why not – they deserve it. I think they're off for a quiet snog. I ask if they can take the puppy with them, for another little walk. They brought him down to the garden, where he is being very well-behaved, but gets over-excited when a couple of customers arrive with their own small terriers.

But it's a no go. Chloe explains, 'We can't take him, Mum, because we're going to this thing where dogs aren't allowed. I promise we won't be long. We'll look after him when we get back.'

Meanwhile, the poor pup – we're going to have to give him a name soon – is under my feet in the kitchen as I fill a couple of tea pots and pull everything together on the trays. I find the customers outside and, although I could swear I shut the door properly behind me, the spaniel follows me out, wrapped around my ankles like a Slinky.

I pick him up and cuddle him while I stop to have a chat with Judy from Valley Dental. It's great to see her: she's turned up to give me some moral support.

'Miles is in such a mess,' she tells me. 'Can you believe it? He's on the third girlfriend this month.

What's more, without you there, the place is a mess. The booking system's gone to pot, and did I tell you the fish died?'

It's ever so mean, but very gratifying to hear that your presence is missed. I knew I was the only one who looked after those poor bloomin' fish! Just then, the puppy wants to go and sniff a guest who is keen to stroke him, so I put him down, still holding the lead, and I'm busy telling Judy about the canal incident and she's hooting with laughter, when there's an impressive roar of engine as a motorbike pulls into the drive.

Could it be Malky? The old flame that never quite burned out?

I'm so busy focusing on who's going to emerge from the helmet that I loosen my grip on the lead, and the spaniel, terrified out of his wits by the growl of the bike, races through the tables and bravely starts defending us all by barking at the rider. I hurry over and catch up his lead, and I try to calm him down, but once more he wriggles out of the collar and flies off at speed, pelting down the drive. At any moment, he's going to get run over.

Oh God! NO! *'DOG!!'* I scream, and run after him, but it's too late, he's up at the end of the drive and is turning right onto the road.

'I need to go and get him,' I cry desperately.

At that moment, the visor on the helmet is pulled up and there are the sparkly blue eyes and the grizzled chin I remember. *Malky*.

'You need a lift somewhere, gorgeous?'

'Yes, please. I need to follow that dog!' I run to Judy and Mitzi, panting, 'Watch the café for me. I'm going for the dog.'

Malky hands me a helmet and I climb aboard. He confidently turns the bike round and pumps it into action. I wrap my arms around him and as soon as we reach the bottom of the road, I freeze.

'Stop, Malky. STOP!'

'Eh?' he shouts back at me. 'Already?'

'Yes, I want to get off.'

He reluctantly slows and pulls into the kerb. I take the helmet off and hand it over.

'Second thoughts,' I say breathlessly. 'Sorry. Bye, Malky.'

He looks confused, but I don't try to explain. Instead I cross the road and step in behind Mitch who is carrying the pup in the direction of my home.

'Excuse me, are you kidnapping my dog?'

Mitch turns, sees me and laughs. 'I was coming up to visit you when I saw him racing towards me. I thought, I know who you belong to, young fellow-me-lad.'

I am so relieved. 'Yes, I don't know how it happened,' I reply shakily, 'but he's definitely mine. And first thing tomorrow, he's going to get a new collar and lead.'

Mitch tucks the dog under his arm and in the most natural and comforting way, he takes my hand. I hear the roar of a motorbike engine behind me but I don't turn around. Instead I look at Mitch and give him a peck on the cheek.

'What's that for, Janet?'

'Rescuing my dog.'

'Fair enough. I'll have a piece of cake too, if there's one going? I hear there's a really good new café opened up in t'village.'

'Yes, it's brilliant. And you can have as much cake as you can eat.'

'What an offer.' He grins.

I feel a spot of rain, and then with all the energy of a summer monsoon, it tips it down. We race hand-in-hand up to the house, both laughing and absolutely drenched, the pup warm and dry beneath Mitch's jacket. Once in the garden there are customers everywhere, sheltering vainly underneath half-open umbrellas and overhanging trees. Mitzi and Chloe have their hands full, rushing back inside the kitchen with plates of cake.

I take a decision and don't think twice.

'Follow me,' I call out to all our guests, then throw open the door to Lavander Cottage, upon which everyone gratefully scrambles inside. I drag in a chair, and then a table, give them a wipe with a towel. After putting the puppy back in his bed upstairs, Mitch comes back and wrestles multiple chairs and tables in at a time. In just a few moments, there's nothing left outside. The tables and chairs are all wiped down and rearranged comfortably into the downstairs area. A couple of old boys have already picked up the pool cues and are setting up for a game.

It doesn't take long for everyone to get settled again. Chloe winks at me as she comes in with Spencer. She's carrying a big Brown Betty tea pot and delivers hot tea to any available tea cup. With the rain pouring down outside, I flick on some lights left over from her birthday, which gives the room a party glow. Mitch, I see, is chatting to one of the customers. He registers my stare, looks up and gives me a broad smile that could melt an iceberg. Oh wow, this is so nice.

The cottage door creeps open and Carl edges in with a dripping folded umbrella and an overloaded tray of scones and cakes. Like a good husband should, he traipses after Mitzi as, clipboard in hand, she walks around the tables demanding names and delivering their orders. Chloe and Spencer get to work collecting up any used crockery. Everyone's relaxed and happy, and as gentle chatter fills the room, I take a moment. This feels so good. It looks like a café . . . and I realise that *this could possibly work*.

I'm pulling tight a window-catch as the rain dashes against the panes when the door crashes open and a crowd of older women all pile in. In a whirl of jazzy raincoats, laughter and loud voices, they shake off their hoods and umbrellas.

'This it then? The new café?'

'Better be, Joyce, I'm bloody soaked.'

'Hello love, we've done the gym so it's cake time now. Have you room?'

'Of course, let me organise you a table.'

Mitch helps me push together a couple of tables and put some spare chairs around them. The ladies gratefully unwrap themselves and the steam of their wet things hits the warmth of the room. Without taking a breath, they launch into a full-throttle natter, one voice on top of the other as they get comfy and peruse the damp laminate menu. I reach over and give it a wipe with a dry tea-towel.

'This is lovely,' one of them says to me. 'Is it your place? What's it called?'

I'm stumped. I look at Chloe and shrug. What *is* it called? It can't be the Secret Garden Café any more – for one thing, the weather up here in Hebden Bridge is too unreliable. We'll have to think again.

I watch out of the cottage window as Chloe dodges the rain while carrying a tray of dirty crockery back home to wash. As she opens the front door, the naughty pup appears and tries to get round her feet to escape outdoors. Quick as lightning, my daughter dumps the tray and runs to pick him up, ignoring his whines of frustration. Carrying him over to Lavander Cottage, she pops her head back in, as the dog, defeated, does a shake of his fur, sending droplets everywhere.

Chloe shouts over to me, 'I know – let's call it The Rainy-Day Dog Café!'

I take it in, for all of a second. *It's perfect.*

'Yes, that's it! "The Rainy-Day Dog Café. Open every weekend".'

'Lovely name, but what about during the week?' one of the ladies calls over. 'We do Over-Sixties Keep Fit every Tuesday and Friday, so you'll be open then?'

I smile. It's less of a question and more of a demand.

'Yes, of course I'll be open then.'

Another voice pipes up: 'We do swimming Wednesday, we always need something after swimming.'

'Right – so Wednesdays too, you reckon?'

Mitch, overhearing the conversation, starts to laugh, as do I.

'Thursday morning it's Pilates, more of a soup day,' another one of the ladies advises sagely.

'Well, that's no problem,' I reply. 'It can be Thursday Soup Day.'

Mitch, Mitzi and Carl are laughing and I join in too, as I get strong-armed by this gang of fabulous ladies. I give them all a full-beam smile.

I'm excited, I'm grateful, I'm lucky.

Here we go.

Another Janet Jackson adventure is about to begin.

REVIEWS

Chocolate cake – worth the calories. Genoa scones – a revelation.

We look forward to Soup Day.

TIP FOR RUNNING A CAFÉ

Upgrade your dishwasher. Consider making Dog Cakes.

TIP ON LIFE

Do what you love.

ACKNOWLEDGEMENTS

A huge thank you to:

Joan Deitch for her patient, skilful editing.

Sara Simpson for her wonderful cover design.

Nicola May for her continuous generosity, expertise and fabulous quote!

Family and friends who will me on and soak up the speculation about Mitzi.

Particular thanks to Graeme and Lizzie for support services and endless encouragement.

To all the readers, reviewers and well-wishers, may your lives be full of warmth, laughter – and good gravy.